TIMOTHY'S TAKE-OUT

PAUL J. BARKER

PublishAmerica
Baltimore

First printing

ISBN: 1-4137-3164-3
PUBLISHED BY PUBLISHAMERICA, LLLP
www.publishamerica.com
Baltimore

Printed in the United States of America

For Joy, Mom, and bedeviled restaurateurs the world over

Dear Ursula,
Thank-you so much
for supporting this
struggling author. What
can I say - the second
novel will be better! ☺
Happy Reading! &
Best wishes!
Paul Brand

CHAPTER ONE

What happens when you take a relatively normal twenty-year-old Canadian male, oust him from that utter complacency he's known since birth, and thrust him suddenly into an atmosphere of chaos, negativity, and abject fear? This is the question I will try my utmost to answer as I recount my wacky, two-and-a-half year tenure as manager of "Timothy's Take-Out," a fast food joint at Robinson's Pt.

Robinson's Pt. is one of several tiny resort towns bunched together on the eastern coast of Lake Huron. It is situated in central Ontario – that is, in the center of the inhabited part – and tends to get hammered each summer by sun worshippers from the "Golden Horseshoe" business district to the south.

But more about that later. At this time I would like to briefly summarize my life up until Timothy's.

My name is Carl Fellows. I was born and raised in Toronto, and my childhood was, at worst, idyllic. I had numerous friends, a beautiful home, doting parents, and even a childhood sweetheart. Yeah, you heard me, a bona fide childhood sweetheart! (Don't scoff; it was the most stable relationship I've ever known.)

But more about that later. I was soon immersed in "athletic competition," a term which in 1960s Canada pretty much meant *hockey*. Indeed, when I do look back to this period of my life, I envision nothing so much as a long, uninterrupted road hockey game. And my transition to adolescence? Ripple-free. I could have cared less about the more conventional preoccupations of teen-dom (sex, drugs, acne, etc.), wrapped up as I was in a plethora of infantile pursuits.

Unfortunately, nothing lasts forever – particularly this extent of naiveté. The real world was stealthily pervading my cocoon, on several fronts. It threatened to topple the happy world I had built and send it crashing down about my feet.

For one thing, I was an indifferent student. I did enough schoolwork to pass, but that was about it. Even upon completion of Grade Thirteen I had no idea what I was going to do with my life. I was also very shy, and not good-looking, which made it difficult to initiate contact with the opposite sex. What's more, at age eighteen I learned of my parents' desire to move out of downtown Toronto and into its most insipid suburb: Forest Hill. Now I loved the quick pulse of the city, and absolutely adored life in the country (having spent many a golden summer alternately assisting and exasperating my farmer uncle), but for me "the burbs" had always seemed an unholy union between the two lifestyles. I made my peace with the impending move, however, and when finally we did settle into our new neighborhood, did my best to cope with the insufferable rich kids I seemed to run into at every turn.

The biggest threat to my tenuous sense of security was, of course, my advancing age. With age comes responsibility, although I was doing my utmost to disprove this aphorism. Eventually, after attending more colleges within a shorter time period than just about anyone in history, I was ready to snub my nose at academic training and step boldly into the real world.

I wasn't as wet behind the ears as you might think. I was armed with some pretty formidable weapons. Despite my relative youth, I had already considerable experience in the workforce – although few of my vocations were what you might term "highly skilled."

By no stretch of the imagination was I afraid of hard work.

Another attribute I had come to believe in was my innate toughness. Physically and mentally, I was tough. I may only have stood a sawed-off 5'6", but I had a genetic predisposition to strength and large muscles. And my attitude toward life was similarly robust. We all have our share of obstacles in life; my admittedly unsophisticated way of dealing with them was to wade right in and hack 'em to pieces. I wanted absolutely nothing to stand in the way of my own personal happiness and well-being.

My ultimate goal was to become rich and famous. Every hour upon the hour, it seemed, I would encounter at least one poor bastard entirely caught up in his struggle to make ends meet. People of this sort lived and died like cattle in my view, achieving little of significance other than the rearing of their young (who themselves existed solely to perpetuate the cycle.) I, on the other hand, ached for fame, and desperately wanted to become great at something.

Egotist that I was, I felt I had reason to view my blank slate of a future with optimism. Little did I know just how sorely tested my aforementioned "formidable weapons" were to be over the next couple of years.

Now I invite you to sit back, relax, and have a real good laugh at my expense, as I relate to you the saga of Timothy's Take-Out. The restaurant of the damned.

CHAPTER TWO

"Carl! Phone!"

My mother's singsong voice, wafting up from the kitchen, roused me from yet another night of lousy, fitful, semi-sleep. I proceeded to stagger downstairs, but found our ridiculously steep staircase as treacherous as ever. I flipped out on the fourth step and crashed down the remaining twelve, smacking my head on the wooden stereo cabinet that lay in wait on the landing below.

"Son of a...!"

Willing my voice to trail off (I knew what was good for me), I hobbled into the kitchen, my head afire with stinging pain. I took the phone from my mother, who, oblivious to my suffering, gave me her warmest smile. I saw it as an annoying smirk and thought to erase it by puking down the front of her dress; instead I addressed the speaker on the other end of the phone.

"Hello?"

"Hey, dude," came the laconic response. "Got any plans for the summer?"

It was my best friend, Harvey.

Although it wasn't officially spring yet, I answered him without hesitation.

"Not a bloody thing."

As I listened further to Harvey my sour mood evaporated, and I felt adrenaline course through my veins. I slammed down the receiver without so much as a farewell, and grabbed my mother in a bear hug.

"A job prospect, and a great one!" I shrieked into her ear before she could speak. I tore upstairs and jumped into some street clothes.

I could hardly contain my excitement as I attacked my hearty, five-course breakfast. As it was later in the day than I'd originally suspected, I dined alone; welcoming the solitude, I soon found myself deep in thought.

For two weeks I'd been feeling guilty and uncomfortable, as though I were an unwelcome guest in my own home. I had recently walked out on my fifth and final opportunity for a college education (more correctly, I'd failed to show up after the Christmas holidays), and had done little since. I was sleeping in, watching inordinate amounts of afternoon television, and otherwise driving my family to distraction. I resembled nothing so much as a lethargic hippopotamus, hopelessly mired in what had seemed, initially, an attractive wallow.

That is, until Harvey's liberating phone call. In lieu of his customary prattle he'd actually presented me with a honest-to-goodness job opportunity.

It seemed his folks (in a blinding fit of insanity?) had recently sold their gorgeous, outrageously expensive summer home at Robinson's Pt. Whilst on a mission to haul back furniture, Harv happened to notice a rather shoddy homemade sign hanging in the window of a local restaurant. "Manager Position Available – Apply Within," it proclaimed. Aware of my previous experience as a short order cook (and apparently thinking it an impressive credential), my friend was good enough to speak to the proprietor about my desire for work. Even more unbelievably, he managed to coerce said proprietor into arranging an interview for me, despite the guy's having no idea who I was or where I came from.

Those of us who knew Harvey knew also of his persuasive powers, but he usually reserved them for women he wanted to seduce. I took it as proof of our friendship that he was willing to expend a bit of his mysterious charisma for my sake.

The fact that he had tried for the job first did not bother me in the least. I was just thankful for the opportunity, and vowed not to let it slip through my hands. I saw it as a chance to escape the mind numbing drudgery of life in endless suburbia, if only for the summer.

"Aren't you going to finish your breakfast, Carl?" my mother asked, returning to the kitchen from God knows where.

I snapped out of my daze and glanced down at my plate. My distracted fork twirling had created a nauseating potpourri out of what remained there. I managed to push away from the delectable concoction, opting instead to take our Staffordshire Bull puppy, Shindig, for a brief stroll around the neighborhood. I recall being so happy, so full of anticipation at that point in time. The remainder of the day was spent in earnest preparation for the job interview, which beckoned – to my thinking – like blue sky beyond a squall line.

CHAPTER THREE

I got the job. Suffice it to say I made a good impression with my three-piece suit, glib tongue, and clean-cut looks. The owner seemed genuinely impressed with my overblown elegance, even saying to me at one point, "You'd be surprised at some of the hippies and scumbuckets I've had apply so far. Jesus H. Christ!"

Scumbuckets? Well, it only goes to prove what I've always maintained. Cultivate a respectable appearance, cut your hair once in a while, and the doors of the seemingly impenetrable job market will swing open. To those punk rockers and displaced flower children out there who refuse to sacrifice their "individuality" when seeking employment, I can say only this: Quit trying to cite discrimination when you are refused work, take it upon yourselves to learn some humility, and do what is in your power to alter your bizarre appearance. Is not true individuality within you?

The restaurant owner, a Mr. Tobias Renwald, announced just five minutes into the interview that the coveted position was mine. Understandably euphoric, I did not think to more closely examine the building in which I would be spending much of the subsequent two-and-a-half years of my life. In fact, as my services would not be required until that April, there seemed little else to do but head back to the bus station.

* * *

I had quite adapted to lying around the house all day, to the extent that I was reluctant, come April, to give the lifestyle up. Despite the prospect of spending summer at the beach, I believe I was fearful of the move. I was, after all, a person who loved security and disliked change – and this was change with a capital "C".

All things considered, April Fools' was a fitting day to leave for Robinson's Pt. and the madhouse that was Timothy's. There was one lucky break in that Harvey was tagging along. He and I would be sharing the ground floor of an old beachfront estate. It would be nice having someone I knew up there with me, but, more importantly, Harvey's daddy had money coming out of his ass (and was not averse to loaning it to people he liked).

How vividly I recall glancing out our bay window the morning of April 1, hoping beyond hope that Harvey's old jalopy would make it the two blocks to my house. The two blocks to my house? That heap was supposed to take us the hundred miles plus to Robinson's Pt.! We were relying on a car that seldom went two weeks without having a crippling seizure of some kind.

At length I detected the telltale squeal of the old Lincoln's brakes, and estimated Harvey's distance at about a block from the house. Grabbing my two suitcases in slimy paws, I silently bid my room adieu, and, of course, fell down the stairs again, nearly decapitating myself in the process. The suitcases spewed forth their underwear and socks, which proceeded to float down upon my now motionless carcass. Looking back, I wonder if the silly incident wasn't a harbinger of things to come.

I was resuscitated by the dog, and after some difficulty was able to respond to the persistent ringing of the doorbell. Harvey stood before me, wearing a grimace I could entirely relate to.

Harvey was a small fellow, delicately featured, with fine blond hair. Although the essence of respectability in polite company, he was boisterous around friends – and the quintessential "wolf in sheep's clothing" around chicks.

So there he stood on my doorstep with this uncharacteristically sullen look on his face. Right off the bat I sensed something was amiss.

"What's up your ass, bud?" I asked uncomfortably. "We've got a long road ahead of us, and the sooner we get started, the better."

Harvey was shifting nervously, avoiding my gaze. "Carl, before we leave, I got somethin' I gotta tell you. I –I 've been holding it back a long time, but I guess you got a right to know."

My suspicions were certainly aroused. I prayed the revelation would do nothing to alter our plans concerning Robinson's Pt. I was dependent on the undependable Harvey for too many things, or so it was beginning to appear.

"I'm bisexual, Carl," he blurted out. "I thought I'd better tell you before we actually move in together. You think it'll be a problem?"

I didn't know what to say. I could not believe what I was hearing. I mean, all this guy ever talked about was women, twenty-four hours a day.

"You, Harv? You, of all people, GAY?!"

"Bi," he corrected.

"I – I can't live with ya then," I stammered. "I'm straight. Straight as an arrow."

"April fool, man!!" Harvey screeched, ducking nimbly past me before collapsing to the living room floor in gales of laughter.

I was too relieved to be angry. I had always wondered how I'd react in a situation like that, and what I felt was *drained*. Harvey had an uncanny ability to make me forget my problems – usually by supplanting them with others.

I repacked my suitcases, and hauled them into the "Grey Ghost" (my pet name for Harvey's battered old hulk of a car). Having mumbled the majority of my goodbyes the previous evening, I gave Shindig a farewell pat on the head, urged him to be a good dog while I was gone, and looked around for Harvey, who had disappeared into another section of the house.

I found him in the basement, flipping through one of several dirty magazines I had stashed amid some weathered sticks of furniture.

"How the hell did you find those?" I asked, bewildered. When it came to sex, Harvey had the instincts of a bloodhound.

He was reluctant to part with his newfound treasure, and so I suggested he take some of the magazines along. It seemed the only way to get him to the car.

"I can understand," I said to Harvey as we set about locking the place up, "a sex starved misfortunate like myself perusing those filthy rags. But you get so much of the real thing, it seems redundant that you drool over pictures like a horny teenager." (He was, in fact, twenty-two, a couple of years my senior.)

"My friend," Harvey said, with a roguish twinkle in his eye, "by the time the summer's over, we'll both be doin' the backstroke in steamy, wet –"

"I get the point, Harv, and I marvel at your optimism."

CHAPTER FOUR

And so it began. The day was bleak and unseasonably cold as we tore up the northbound highway, Van Halen screaming out of the car's twin speakers. The car itself was cooperative, and the trip to Robinson's Pt. surprisingly uneventful. Perhaps I should tell you what I remember of it.

After about an hour or so of travel we'd stopped at one of the many nondescript little diners along the way. Much to my embarrassment, Harvey shamelessly hit upon the poor waitress there, addressing her as "gorgeous" and "sex bomb" at every opportunity (despite her being slovenly, overweight, and every bit of forty years old.) As I watched the poor woman do her damndest to simultaneously serve everyone, I couldn't help but draw speculative comparisons to Timothy's Take-Out. I reminded myself that Timothy's was basically a take-out joint where the customers ordered their stuff at the counter.

However, as I continued to watch the woman juggle complaints, advances, and heaping platefuls of food, I began to get a sickly feeling in the pit of my stomach. What the hell was I getting myself into? As confident as I was trying to appear on the surface, I knew damn well I had never been able to effectively interact with people, and here I had just gone and accepted a job as a personnel manager! That moment was probably the closest I came during the journey to turning around and hightailing it back home.

At approximately four p.m. we rolled up to the intersection of the north and eastbound routes that comprised one boundary of tiny Robinson's Pt. As we turned left onto the main drag, I opened the car window a touch, and drank in the sea air. It tasted great.

The little town appeared deserted. The gaudy shops and arcades seemed to belong to a different era in time, the early fifties perhaps, and all were closed. Their windows were still boarded up for winter; according to Harvey they would remain so till May.

"There's Timothy's," Harvey said, pointing across my face. I caught a brief glimpse of the restaurant as we continued toward the lake. It was about a hundred feet down a dirt road, and was clearly open for business.

All thoughts of Timothy's vanished temporarily as we came upon what had really put Robinson's Pt. on the map. Harvey "parked" the car on the extreme westernmost tip of Main St., and we continued ahead on foot.

In no time at all we were standing upon the outermost reaches of a truly magnificent sandy beach, which stretched back in convex fashion on either side of us. The only sizable objects in view were a few buildings that dotted the seascape in an erratic, haphazard manner. They seemed to have sprung right out of the sand. I counted three little snack shacks, a deserted band shell, and, in the distance, what looked like a derelict pavilion.

Harvey, of course, had seen all this before, and was eager to press on. So we hopped back into the Grey Ghost, and commenced driving south along the narrow lakeside road, toward our beachfront lodgings. Glancing out to sea, I noticed traces of ice bobbing in the water, and what appeared to be a minute island, almost out of sight on the horizon's edge.

"That's 'Isolation Isle,'" remarked Harvey. "I almost killed myself paddling out to the damn thing in my dinghy once, and there was nothin' there."

As I'd told my mother only months before, I would've happily dwelt in a lean-to if it meant spending summer at the beach. It was obvious, as my buddy and I approached our new home, that a glorified lean-to was precisely what we were getting. The sprawling three-story structure suggested that it had once been some rich old businessman's summer mansion – in 1920. It was now a crumbling ruin, the rotting black timber giving it a dark and foreboding appearance even in the day's last gasp of sunlight. There was no driveway as such, which was probably just as well. (Harvey's Lincoln would only have defaced it!)

As we unloaded the Grey Ghost and lugged our suitcases onto the dilapidated front porch, I wondered why Harv had selected this dismal place. I could certainly have afforded a little better. I voiced these thoughts to my friend, taking care not to hurt his feelings.

"Well, the place looked a lot better in the paper," was his only response.

"You mean you arranged the whole deal without even seeing the joint?!" I asked, aghast. "You haven't even been through the house yet?"

"Relax, Carl. The realtor assured me it was in tip top shape."

Harvey's naiveté when it came to business matters was astounding. But I suppose I was equally to blame, as apathetic as I had been toward house hunting.

"Cheer up," Harv chirped. "The house is a steal, and we've got it for as long as we want it. Besides, we haven't seen the insides yet."

True. We hadn't.

"Well, open 'er up, Harv, and let's take a look inside this palace of yours."

"Oh, no. Oh, shit...You ain't gonna believe this, pardner..."

"Please," I groaned, "I've had all the April Fool's jokes I can stand today."

"No joke, Carl. I forgot the freakin' key!" It's at home on my coffee table."

It was all too much for me. I collapsed on the spot and just lay there on the porch, flat on my back. Harvey tried the front door, and, sure enough, it would not budge. Its locking mechanism was apparently the one thing about the place in good working order.

"Now what?" I asked him. "Can you get another key from the landlord?"

"He lives seventy-five miles away."

"Of course. Well, if there's one thing I don't feel like doing, it's spending another hour-and-a-half in your car. It's a miracle she got us up here as it is."

With no other alternative in sight we combed the exterior of the old house, searching for any opening large enough for us to crawl through, particularly the diminutive Harvey.

At length, having burrowed beneath an exceedingly low-stationed deck at the back of the house, Harvey discovered one cellar window slightly ajar. I scampered up onto the deck and peered through a crack in the floor planks, in time to watch my indefatigable pal attempt to force the thing open.

"It's probably been this way for fifty years," Harv grunted. "The bloody window's petrified."

Of course I had to try, and I can't describe vividly enough the ordeal of having to wedge myself under that ramshackle old poop, convinced all the while I'd either become hopelessly stuck, or else would get picked up by unfriendly police (as it was rapidly becoming dusk and the two of us must have looked mighty suspicious skulking about like desperate fugitives). I fought off the mounting sensation of claustrophobia long enough to heave open the window, but found I was quite unable to squeeze through. Chagrined, I went instantly into retreat mode, backpedaling clumsily through the dirt as though I were an expectant sea turtle. (I could certainly have done with a shell on my back, for when finally able to stand upright again I found I was a mass of scratches and ugly bruises.)

Harvey scuttled under the porch again with relative ease. The window, now agape, no longer impeded him, and he passed right through. Unfortunately, he misjudged the size of the room he was plunging into, and all I heard from my position overhead was an agonized shriek and the collapsing of furniture.

"Are you okay, buddy?" I asked anxiously.

Harvey's voice, weak, trickled out of the inky black hole.

"My balls…"

I stifled a chuckle. "What's it like down there?"

"The walls are damp, and made of stone."

The way his voice was bouncing off those walls gave me some indication of the cellar's hugeness.

"Find the staircase leading up to the ground floor."

"Hey, Carl!" he called out excitedly. "I found an old wooden chest!"

"Harv, we're not the Hardy Boys. Just find the goddamned staircase and climb the hell up!"

"Yeah, yeah…. jeez, I'm soaked! It's wet down here!"

I wasn't surprised. It seemed madness to build such a gargantuan cellar so close to the water. Of course, at the time of its construction the water may have been miles away.

"The chest is padlocked."

"Just ignore the chest and climb out of there, jerk!" I shouted down at him. "If you recall, we rented the ground floor, not the cellar!"

He finally managed to locate the steps, but, predictably, the entrance to the ground floor was boarded up. Whoever had rented us the place did not want us down in that cellar. I clapped my forehead in exasperation.

"Smash it open," I instructed my friend, "and we'll nail it up later."

At length Harvey made his way upstairs, and opened the front door for me. The inside of the house proved every bit as attractive as the outside.

"This place sucks," I stated irritably.

"Are you kidding? It's beautiful! It's like a castle! Imagine the parties we could throw in here!" Harvey danced about excitedly, and plunked himself down upon an aged, pre-Victorian chesterfield.

In fact, all the furniture seemed pre-Victorian. The wallpaper looked like something out of the fifteenth century, and the beds actually had curtains around them. Cobwebs clung subtly to just about everything. The entire scenario would have made for a fine establishing shot in most any horror film, and one fully expected some ghastly apparition to leap out from behind every sizable object.

"Here's a letter from the landlord!"

Harvey's voice, erupting out of the silence, startled me. I joined him in the kitchen, snatched from his hand what resembled, at first glance, a grocery list, and began skimming over it.

Aside from various rules and regulations (several of which we had already broken), the letter conveyed little.

Upon further investigation of our prospective living quarters, we were amused to discover that the top stories were also sealed off. Evidently, the landlord was not mincing words when he said "ground floor for rent."

But for all its Gothic cheerlessness, the house was beginning to grow on me. The primitive appliances, ancient furniture, and peculiar odor contributed in equal measure to an otherwise indefinable sense of tranquility. I was especially fond of its isolated locale. We were perhaps three miles from Robinson's Pt. proper, and still had a chunk of beach to call our own. There were no buildings to our immediate left or right, although a few cottages were visible through the rear kitchen window. I imagined strolling down the beach on my way to work, sidestepping the numerous strewn, bikini-clad sun worshipers, the cool water lapping at my bare feet. A pleasant walk, indeed!

Work? Ye Gods, I had almost forgotten. The following day, Saturday, I was to convene with the entire staff of Timothy's for the first time. The part-time summer crew had already been selected, and all of 'em – even the young school kids – were making the journey up to Robinson's Pt. for a powwow of sorts. I was excited at the prospect of meeting everybody, although how much of this excitement was just my standard nervousness and queasiness I'm not entirely certain. As the meeting was scheduled for the ungodly hour of seven-thirty a.m., I knew it would be in my best interest to get a decent night's sleep beforehand. This line of thinking, of course, was at odds with Harvey's plans for the evening.

"Okay, there's this hot little nightclub on Seventh Street we'll hit first, then Robinson's Rodeo out on the highway. Between the two of 'em, we're bound to pick up somethin'! This is gonna be one superlative summer, Carl – I can sense it!!"

Easy for him to say. He had no real plans for the foreseeable future, certainly none involving gainful employment. Harvey was the quintessential hedonist, and had the money to make it a full-time pursuit.

"Listen, Harv," I pleaded. "Let's finish unloading your car and get settled a bit, then I'll see how I feel, okay?"

We spent the next hour doing precisely that. Harvey had brought along his terrific stereo system, which we quickly (and shoddily) set up in the front room. His parents had generously donated a small color television, which we hooked up in the front room as well, to find that its range of channels was one. We even had silverware and a bit of fine china, courtesy of my folks. Harv insisted on carrying his most precious possession in himself: the stack of girlie magazines. The only casualty during this phase of the move was a small hand mirror, which shattered to pieces as I accidentally stumbled over an uneven floor plank on the front porch. Seven years of bad luck.

Harv claimed the larger bedroom as his. The bed in it was gargantuan, certainly bigger and more comfortable than the glorified cot allotted to me. I voiced no objection, taking for granted that my friend would have more need of the additional bed space! Besides, I was fascinated by the bed curtains around mine, which were velvety and jet-black.

Another order of business was to wash up and change into fresh clothes, as the two of us were truly in pathetic shape.

While not a pressing concern just yet, the boards Harvey destroyed in order to gain access to the ground floor would have to be replaced, and in such exacting fashion that the true owner would suspect nothing.

Taking absolute precedence, however, was an urge on both our parts to sweep, scrub, and dust. The place had obviously stood unoccupied for the longest time (who else would have paid to live in it?), and so we set to work, doing our best to thoroughly decontaminate the entire ground floor. Our excitement about just being there – at the beach, in our own pad – all but obliterated the drudgery component, and clean up was a relative breeze. In no time at all we had finished, with Harvey chomping at the bit to go out and hit all the local nightclubs.

"But we don't have a key to the house. We can't leave it unlocked," I protested lamely.

"We'll lock up the house, alright. We'll get in like we did earlier, through the cellar window!"

Yeah, of course. Why hadn't I thought of that? And so, against my better judgment, we left to sample the diverse array of nightlife known to exist within the mighty metropolis that was Robinson's Pt.

At about 8:30 p.m., we pulled into "Happy's," a small tavern on a little dirt road. (Of course, this ain't telling you a hell of a lot; ninety per cent of the roads in the area are primarily dirt.) The joint appeared busy, more so than I expected, but then, it was a Friday night. As we walked toward the entrance, I tried to envision the customers inside. Would Harv and I fit in, with our short hair and preppy-ish appearance? We were hit with a blast of warm, fetid air as we opened the big red doors, and I immediately found myself face-to-face

17

with a grotesque, life-sized cardboard cutout of a clown.

"That's Happy," remarked Harvey.

I couldn't wait to see the rest of the place.

Happy's proved to be no different than any cheap dive you could find in the sleazier sections of any scummy borough, anyplace. Well, maybe a *little* different. The bar was tastefully appointed with shriekingly loud red and white stripes. The majority of the clientele were Indian, with hard, coarse features, although the atmosphere in general was blithe and jovial.

We sat down at a vacant table in the middle of the room. (Harv preferred to be centrally located, to attract the attention of the young ladies in the establishment.) The most comical moment of the evening occurred as our waitress approached to take our order. It was all Harvey and I could do to keep from sliding out of our seats with laughter, when first she came into view.

The woman was dressed conventionally enough – her dumpy figure concealed somewhat by a loose fitting blouse – though someone must have shoehorned her into her Levis. The real shocker was her face.

It was a clown's face, complete with pancake makeup, painted-on smile, and bulbous red nose. She wore a black derby on her head, and from it hung fringes of red, straw-like hair.

What made her so amusing was not so much the outrageous get-up, but the fact that – underneath it all – it was obvious that the last thing in the world she wanted to be doing at that moment was to be serving drinks looking like a clown. The ultimate in degradation. What we won't do for a buck!

She curtly asked Harvey for identification; it was an embarrassing ritual my pal had to undergo each time he visited a place like this. Although older than I, he looked barely fourteen.

Hours passed. Booze flowed freely; girls and guys intermingled. The disc jockey spun contemporary hits nonstop for those who wanted to dance, alternating fast music and slow, tossing in the occasional crude joke between records. As the evening progressed, the air became further saturated with smoke and alcohol.

Harvey had long since abandoned me in the center of the room, and was chatting up a vivacious brunette in the corner. An older man who had clearly overdone things a bit was propped up against the wall beside them in a drunken stupor, doing his best to remain conscious. I sat alone in my original seat, sucking back my eighth brew of the night.

I've never liked bars much, nor crowds of people. And I absolutely despise making small talk, although, truth be told, I'm pretty good at it. I'm really most comfortable on my own (or in small groups), and tend not to remain sober for long upon extended subjection to a tavern full of strangers.

I would have been completely satisfied with just one of Harvey's numerous girlfriends; that night at Happy's, it looked as though he was working on number two-hundred-eighty-nine, or two-hundred-ninety-seven, or whatever outrageous number he was up to. I'd once asked Harvey to reveal his secret.

"Carl," he said to me, "you work your butt off lifting heavy weights. You think girls are attracted to big muscles, but you're way off base. They're attracted to that elusive something I call, 'The Look.' And you, my friend, do not have it."

I asked him if he would kindly elaborate on "The Look."

"For starters, I got large, luminous, baby blue eyes. Yours are small and bloodshot, like a pig's. You're afraid to look chicks in the eye, but I'm not. It's very important. And you look so intense all the time. Smile more, asshole!"

He assumed a mocking, effeminate pose, and pinched me on the cheek.

"You've got thuch a cute smile!"

"Screw you, Harv."

So there I sat in "Happy's," all alone and miserable, and getting progressively drunker as time went on. I practically wept with relief when Harvey returned to the table and suggested we leave.

"What happened to your girlfriend?" I asked him.

"I'm...uh...afraid I admit defeat this time, pal."

"Wow! Casanova II has met his match? I can hardly believe it! You struck out?"

"Not exactly. See that big bastard over there?" He motioned across the room to where a titanic figure in construction boots and a baseball cap was making his way towards us, looking as though he had something very important to discuss with my friend.

"Let me guess," I laughed, as we quickly slipped into our jackets. "A jealous boyfriend?"

"Close. A jealous husband. Let us depart!"

Back on the road, I realized something was wrong. For starters, it was not the right road.

"Harvey, I think you took a wrong turn. We're heading out onto the highway."

"Can't fool you for a minute, can I?" he grinned.

Before my liquor-soaked brain could make sense of what was happening, we were stumbling up the walkway of a much larger tavern than Happy's, by name of "Robinson's Rodeo." I tried to dissuade Harvey, to get him to turn around and head back to the house, but my slurred words were apparently falling on deaf ears. Once inside the building, however, I was easily convinced into sticking around for a while.

There must have been ten girls for every guy in there, and, believe you me, nothing looks as delicious to an intoxicated man than a roomful of equally intoxicated women. Several enticing sets of eyes followed us as we stumbled through the crowd to one of the few empty tables. I was grinning stupidly from ear to ear, and Harvey, needless to say, was glancing around like a fox in a chicken coop.

Compared to Happy's, this place was a ballroom in the Waldorf-Astoria. Clearly, it was *the* in spot of Robinson's Pt. if you wanted to party serious. Everyone was talking excitedly, and the tavern seemed to hum with the sound of their collective voices.

I was scanning the room for a waitress when all of a sudden the house lights fell.

"Ladies, please welcome this week's feature attraction at the Rodeo – Ramrod Randy Rapscallion!!"

Say what? No! Aaarrgghh! Harv had taken me to a male strip joint! I glared at him accusingly.

"Did you know about this?"

"Sorry, I, ah…must have hit the wrong night," he answered sheepishly.

"Gee, REALLY? You asshole! Let's get out of here! These broads must think we're a couple of fags!"

"Not so fast," Harvey whispered. "Think of all the horny chicks in this building, man!"

"Forget it, Harv." Even I wasn't desperate enough to take to hanging around male strippers in the hopes of picking up a girl. "Let's go home."

Miraculously, he concurred, and we scurried out to the car with our tails between our legs. I would have preferred bags over our heads.

We drove back to the house without further incident (no mean feat in Harvey's car), and once there Harv headed directly for the back of it, presumably to squeeze through the cellar window again. What he was doing when I caught up with him was urinating on the back lawn. It was a ludicrous sight to be certain – a full moon, the sinister old house, and Harvey taking a piss.

"You slob! Can't that wait?"

"Hey. I got a big job ahead of me."

With that, he disappeared under the porch. I returned to the front of the house and waited expectantly at the door. It was now approximately one fifteen a.m., pitch black, and very cold. After what seemed like an eternity, the door creaked open and I popped inside, eager to warm up, just as eager to use the "facilities". (I lost track of how many beers I'd downed that night.)

"What took ya so long?" I asked Harvey. He had a curious expression on his face.

"Carl, there's something very strange about that old trunk in the cellar."

Before I could remind him that it was really none of our damned business, he dashed down the stairs. He returned after several minutes, his expression even more peculiar.

"That chest has to be a century old at the very least, but its padlock is brand spanking new. As if the contents of the chest are still being used for something."

"That's highly unlikely," I responded. "Whoever rented us the place obviously didn't want anyone prying. The trunk is probably an old heirloom, or something to store heirlooms in. It's locked up for safekeeping, bud."

"But they boarded up the freakin' cellar! Why bother to padlock the trunk?"

"To keep jerks like you away. Forget about it, Harv."

I was concerned, but not about the silly trunk. It was my friend's all-too-inquisitive nature that had me stewing, for I knew it could very well get him – and me, by association – into serious trouble over this issue. You see, I was pretty much convinced that ol' muttonhead Harvey was sooner or later going to bust the chest open, unless we resealed that cellar but quick.

Fortunately, Harv put the whole affair out of his head for the time being, and prepared for bed. But I still had one thing left to do before I retired on this, our first day at Robinson's Pt.

Once in my room, I quickly stripped down to my shorts. Then I burst forth, a-whoopin' and a-hollerin',' into the drawing room and out the front door. I sprinted over our front lawn (such as it was), picking up speed. I dashed recklessly across the road and onto the cool wet sand, the spongy consistency of the latter barely decelerating my flight.

I was waist deep in the frigid water quite before I knew it, bellowing as my nerve endings transmitted the distasteful sensation. My voice must have carried for miles that night. I glanced at the silhouette of Harvey doubled over in laughter on the front porch, and then dove into the surf.

* * *

My jackhammer of an alarm clock jolted me into consciousness, and for a moment I did not know who or where I was. I sat bolt upright in my bed where I'd lain all night like a corpse, and panicked as I strove to get my bearings. Either I had died and gone to hell, or was a fetus suspended eerily within a womb.

It dawned on me that my pernicious enclosure was comprised chiefly of bed curtains, and that I was in my new room at Robinson's Pt. I got up, much relieved – until I attempted to walk across the room. Yikes! While perhaps not the worst hangover I'd ever had, it was enough of one that each routine movement one associates with getting up in the morning had to be performed in slo-mo. The pain in my head was excruciating, and I teetered on the brink of nausea. Hangovers are much easier to weather if you are able to look back on the great time you had the night before, but there was no such recollection for me that morning. Damn Harvey and his infernal night clubbing!

And, of course, I vowed never to drink again.

As I entered the washroom to begin the ordeal of shaving with no shaving lotion, I looked briefly towards the door of the other bedroom, beyond which Harvey was undoubtedly sleeping peacefully. I was so envious of that guy, I made an additional vow: To somehow, someday, become every bit as filthy rich, so I too could routinely sleep till noon.

But now it was seven a.m., and I knew I had to hustle or I'd be late for my first day at work. I had several people to impress that day, and, frankly, was nervous as shit! I dressed quickly and stepped out into the sunshine.

It was a beautiful spring day and there was not a soul on the beach. I jogged easily along the shore, taking care to remain just out of reach of the languid waves. By the time I reached Main St. the power of the sun and the sea had combined to work a miracle upon my ravaged body, so poisoned by that drinking marathon of the previous night. I trotted smartly toward Timothy's, virtually cured of my hang over.

It wasn't long, however, before I contracted "the shakes." Today was my day to be introduced to a group of total strangers as their new manager, and from what I understood many of them had been employed there for several years. How would they receive me? I longed to be anywhere but pattering up that last stretch of dirt road, in the manner of a condemned prisoner walking his last mile!

I had expected a fairly sizable contingent to be milling about the restaurant, but there appeared, at first glance, to be less than ten employees and prospective employees. Most were perched on picnic tables in front of the building, watching my every move.

Timothy's Take-Out seemed innocuous enough from the outside, a small, rectangular-shaped structure comprised of just one story, made to seem even smaller by the vast, gravel parking lot surrounding it. Behind the store was a densely wooded area, home to several white pine trees, which towered over stands of denuded poplars and maples. Across the road, oddly enough, was a large and creepy-looking cemetery. I remember thinking that it's relative proximity could hardly be conducive to brisk food sales! The mammoth dimensions of the restaurant's parking area, however, did suggest otherwise.

No one really knew why the establishment was called "Timothy's." The store was very old, but to present owner Tobias Renwald's knowledge there had never been a proprietor by that name. *Unless,* I thought with a wry smile, *it was merely for alliteration's sake.* ("**T**imothy's Take-Out" beckoned one and all from high atop an antiquated signpost.)

As I weaved through a veritable forest of picnic tables, searching for the aforementioned Mr. Renwald, I was struck by the overwhelming silence of the group. They just sat there – some staring down at their shoes, others gazing intently in my direction – but absolutely no one spoke. Feeling terribly self-conscious I continued on toward the building itself, trying hard to ignore the gauntlet of expressionless faces. At last I found Renwald, sitting some distance from the others at a table of his own.

There he was, cradling his head in one hand, leafing through an old workbook with the other. He was preoccupied with his notes, and oblivious to my approach.

"Hello, sir," I croaked, propping my foot on the bench of the picnic table and clasping my hands together in an attempt to appear suave.

Renwald closed his notebook and glanced up at me. He was a very stern-looking man, almost to the point of being frightening, and, while not tall, his bearing was such that he seemed larger than life. His hair was white, a trifle darker over the ears, and had receded greatly. His deadpan visage betrayed surprisingly few wrinkles, and I estimated his age at fifty-five years.

"Ah, our new manager has arrived!" he yelped with that big voice of his, and I smiled uneasily. He rose slowly, grasping the table in front of him for support.

"May I have everyone's attention?" he intoned thunderously, though it was hardly necessary for him to do so. "This is Carl Fellows! He'll be managing Timothy's as of tomorrow, and I hope you will all give him your support and co-operation throughout the summer. Carl, tell us a little bit about yourself."

I felt my cheeks flush a deep crimson hue.

"Hi, folks. How's it goin'?

"Well, let's see…I was born and bred in Toronto, and I have plenty of experience in the fast food business, since my father owned at one time a successful burger joint – er, restaurant…"

Hearing no hecklers or disclaimers among my captive audience, I continued, a little more confidently.

"And so, I grew to love the business, and it was my overwhelming goal throughout high school to someday manage – and ultimately, own – a fast food franchise. I heartily thank Mr. Renwald for offering me the chance to realize part of my dream, and I sincerely hope we can all become good friends over the summer, and make 1981 a particularly good year financially for our boss here. Thank you."

Now only I was aware of just how much pure bullshit my little speech contained (pretty close to 100%), but it seemed to satisfy Renwald, who took it upon himself to further acquaint me with those present.

He gestured toward the figure sitting closest to him and introduced him simply as "Rupert," a fellow who had been working at Timothy's for pretty close to sixteen years. I gaped incredulously at the guy, who had to have been eighty years old if he was a day. He sat very stiffly, with fists clenched, a tiny, tiny, wisp of a man, whose head nodded back and forth ever so imperceptibly (as though lending its assent to some major deal set back in his formative years). He appeared to be chewing tobacco, and chewing it with ferocity. My voice instinctively raised a few decibels as I greeted Rupert, and I hoped it was not too obvious.

"Hello, sir," I said respectfully.

Rupert neither responded audibly nor looked my way. He just continued to stare blankly ahead, chewing furiously, and I suspected that senility was beckoning this unfortunate individual from not far off. I swear his form-fitting white turtleneck had to have been a boy's small, and what little hair the man had left complimented his shirt color perfectly.

"Now this young man is my son, Toby."

Renwald pointed to a chubby teenager with long, bushy hair and a pockmarked face out of a dermatologist's worst nightmare.

24

"Hey, Toby," I addressed him amiably.

The little oaf didn't even look up, immersed as he was, I suppose, in fondling his belly button through a tear in his ratty, "Black Death On Tour" t-shirt. (Ratty – Black Death – ouch!) Never in a million years would I have suspected a kid like that of possessing so distinguished sounding a moniker as "Tobias Renwald II." Not the least of his strange attributes was his facial hair, which sprouted from his cheeks and chin in absurd little tufts.

The next person I met, Allison, or "Allie," was without question the largest girl I have run into outside a circus sideshow. Though she was seated, it was overwhelmingly obvious that she was close to six feet in height. Her enormous girth and hatchet face made her seem middle-aged; she was, in fact, only fifteen, and this was her first day at Timothy's. Her hair was inexplicably close-cropped, further accentuating her elephantine proportions, and there was no doubt in my mind she weighed in excess of three hundred pounds.

The introductions continued mercilessly, without respite.

"Carl, this is Glenda…"

This little chickadee was rather soft and flabby looking, with shoulder-length dark hair drowning in all the excessive waves and curls a torturous session of artificial perming can produce. You know the look. If there's a single outstanding memory I have of Glenda it is her remarkable 360-degree pie face, with eyes perpetually on the verge of tears, irrespective of her demeanor.

The next couple of staffers were the only ones of the bunch who could have been labeled average – or even normal – in appearance.

The first, Margaret Humes, was supervisor of Timothy's. An exceedingly well-groomed young woman, I might even have considered her attractive had it not been for her haughty, scowling face. The face had potential, don't get me wrong, but it was unnaturally contorted and positively riddled with deep worry lines, particularly about the eyes and mouth. It seemed as if the very act of meeting me disgusted Margaret. I quite understandably wanted no part of this bitch, who, as luck would have it, was third in command after Renwald and myself.

"One more new face for you," Renwald wheezed, obviously ill at ease with appearing before so many people over so extended a period. He could not have been more uncomfortable than I was.

"This is David Gardner."

"Superhero," someone cried, and I heard the sound of chuckling amongst the staff members for the first time.

David was a handsome, broad shouldered man with thick black hair. He looked at me and smiled, and although I half-expected him to come across as vain and snobbish, I could detect no trace of condescension in his gaze.

What a cast of characters! They were truly the most morose bunch one could have encountered outside a Dickens novel. Rude, mean looking, ugly; whatever the negative attribute, they had it covered. I hated every one of them, and was certain the feeling was reciprocated.

But wait! Had Renwald forgotten someone? For, a few tables away from him, hidden up till now by Allie's more-than-considerable bulk, sat the loveliest girl I had ever seen!

"Hey, we forgot Radiance!" Allie barked in her husky voice, as if on cue.

"Oh, yes," Renwald acknowledged. "This is Radiance."

Radiance? I would have burst out laughing where I stood, had the name not been so very appropriate. She was indeed the glowing embodiment of everything I had ever looked for in a woman, a fairy tale princess come-to-life, who rose demurely at the mention of her name and murmured a bashful "hello," before returning to her seat and once again out of sight.

But one glimpse was enough for me to fall in love with her – madly, irrevocably, irretrievably in love.

Her face was astonishingly beautiful. Her nose was small and exquisitely shaped, her eyes: large, fathomless, and blue. I remember being particularly enthralled with her full lips and how they glistened. Her head was actually a little big for her body, but what an incredible body it was! Her plump breasts were very much in evidence beneath the flimsy yellow windbreaker she wore that April day, as was her big but magnificently shaped rear end. What a woman!

I stood on tiptoe to get a better look, completely enraptured, aware of nothing but Radiance. Blatantly, I drank in detail after gorgeous detail, every one of which I think shall remain in my heart forever. I must beg your indulgence, dear reader, as I indulge myself, in the happy memory of that first meeting, the first time I laid eyes on the wondrous Radiance. The day is actually historically significant to me.

As corny as it sounds in this day and age, her hair was the color of spun gold, fine and straight, yet cascading into curl as it fell about her lovely neck. Though her fingernails were short and a little uneven, they in no way detracted from the beauty of her hands, the incredible softness and overall perfection of which could scarcely be believed.

Whew!

Once I'd made everyone's acquaintance, it was time for a guided tour of the premises. The veterans of the group – Rupert, David, Margaret, and Toby Jr. – feeling no need for a refresher course, chose collectively to depart. There was no camaraderie amongst the four of them, I noted, even though they had to have known each other inside-out by that time. And sure enough, when they left, they left in separate directions.

The store was closed that day, to allow the newcomers to familiarize themselves with various cooking procedures and the subtleties of customer-employee relations. In the ensuing training session I made a point of sticking close to Radiance, who looked even more beautiful alongside Glenda and the gargantuan Allie.

To get some idea of the store's basic layout, try dividing the building into theoretical sections: the customer order area, which was accessible from either side of the building; the customer service area, generally referred to as, "behind the counter"; and the cooking area, accessible from the service area by means of a small doorway – actually, more of a large hole. This entrance was a torment for poor Allie, as I learned that very first day, and it was great fun watching her squeeze both her body and composure through it. (Much later, however, in the heat of some lunch or supper rush, it became positively an agonizing thing to watch, as the wasted seconds would often prove catastrophic.)

The training session concluded shortly after three o'clock. Glenda's parents arrived on the scene in a big Grand Marquis, and the family then left directly for their hometown of Kitchener, Ont., about a hundred miles southeast of Robinson's Pt. At the end of the school year, sometime in mid June, Glenda would return.

Likewise with Radiance and Allie, who were friends. They left together in a rusted-out black sedan driven by Allie's mother, and returned to their hometown of Mississauga.

Only Mr. Renwald remained in Timothy's, taking advantage of the "holiday" to complete some much-needed repair work on the old building. By his own admission he hated to renovate, preferring to spend his valuable time and money sprucing up that which already existed. As a result, Timothy's was a sparkling clean little restaurant, its admittedly outmoded equipment in pristine condition.

Having made arrangements to meet Harvey back at the house around six, I spent what was left of the afternoon searching Robinson's Pt. for two crucial institutions: the library and the gym.

The gym was easy to find, and was actually quite close to the house. It was more of a gym for boxers, but in a small room out back I found what I was looking for: a flat bench, a squat rack, and loads of barbells and dumbbells, more than enough for my workout needs. I approached the owner (funny how they all seem to resemble "Mick" from the *Rocky* films) and immediately purchased a six-month membership to the place.

I was not a serious lifter, not by any means, but it was something I did dutifully, like brushing my teeth. I have always been intrigued by power – in any form – and had made a vow years before to continue "pumping iron" until such time as I was rendered incapable. It was all part and parcel of being different, I suppose, of being somehow better than average. While the therapeutic and healthful aspects of regular exercise did not go unappreciated by yours truly, I was basically in it for the muscle. Muscles in my view were akin to heavy armor, in that they offered their fragile occupant safeguard from the slings and arrows of everyday existence.

I considered bodybuilding one of the great truths in life, heartless and demanding at times but giving back more than it took *always*.

Turner's Gym, as it was called, was about as far from being a modern health club as could be imagined. In addition to being at least forty years of age, the building was, despite its lovely backdrop of sand and surf, an eyesore of major proportions.

As I alluded to earlier, most of the space inside was devoted to the manly art of fisticuffs. Two Lilliputian boxing rings stood side-by-side, and several heavy bags hung suspended from the ceiling. Enormous, yellowing posters of legendary fighters (Rocky Marciano, Muhammad Ali, Sugar Ray Robinson, Joe Louis, etc.) dotted the cement walls, lessening their austerity a bit. To a man, these athletes had obliged their respective photographers by assuming poses of mock ferocity and bravado.

I took to this atmosphere from the start. It was unpretentious and harsh, with little in the way of distracting frills. No wall-to-wall broadloom, no pandering full-length mirrors, and, best of all, no piped-in disco music. Just iron, and perspiration. Evidence of the latter was everywhere – the locker room, the lobby, within the porous hardwood of the floor…It just permeated the place.

I had to shield my eyes upon leaving this dungeon; the contrast between it and the gorgeous spring sunshine was that great. I wandered aimlessly for a time, ostensibly in search of Item Number Two on my list. There were no libraries in Robinson's Pt. as it turned out, so I made for the neighboring town of Port Radcliff, five miles to the north. The hike was a difficult one, as tired and hung over as I was, but I used my feelings for Radiance to my advantage, allowing her angelic visage to dangle before me like a carrot before a pack animal.

How she'd gotten under my skin so easily remains something of a mystery. I mean, I didn't even believe in love, much less love at first sight. Yet it seemed a classic case of the latter.

And its intensity frightened me.

Port Radcliff was even smaller than Robinson's Pt., if that can be imagined, but damned if they didn't have a great little library right in the center of town. Although puny, it was robustly constructed and opulent, looking for all the world like a scaled-down version of the one in downtown Manhattan. I spent the next hour probing the extent of its facilities, and was pleased to find it literally crammed with books, all neatly categorized and easy to access. Incredibly, I believe I was the only person there the entire time, excluding the library staff.

Quite before I knew it, it was time to make my way back to Robinson's Pt., where Harvey was no doubt waiting impatiently, "our" plans for the evening mapped out in full. Following the highway back to town, I was struck by the scenic beauty to either side of me. Acres upon acres of luxuriant woodland were sullied only by the odd sandy lane winding languorously inward.

The sun was casting long shadows when finally I reached the house. I was on the verge of total exhaustion, but I was happy. It had been a wonderful, leisurely paced, tranquil kind of day, and I didn't expect to see its like for many moons.

In fact, the tranquility evaporated the second I opened the front door. The first thing to catch my eye was something that should not have: the cellar light bulb. It was glowing through the jagged hole Harv had hacked into the downstairs barricade. I thundered down the steps, only to have my worst fear realized; Harvey, sitting cross-legged on the cellar floor (and oblivious to the inch or so of sea water flooding it), had broken into the old trunk and was studying its contents intently. I was about to yell something at him, when I too caught a glimpse of the objects in the chest.

I could not believe my eyes. I don't think either of us spoke for about five minutes. We merely gaped in stupefaction at the articles to our fore.

There were but three: a jewel encrusted chalice, a hooded black robe, and the most fiendish looking dagger I had ever seen. His gnawing curiosity satiated at last, Harvey exhaled forcibly and sank back on his haunches, like a man who had just experienced an orgasm.

The frightening thing about the aforementioned items was not the fact that they so obviously belonged to a Satanist or "black witch." The unnerving thought persisted in my head that they were in such damn good condition, as was the trunk's padlock. This implied – to me, at least – that they were not simply grotesque keepsakes, a part of the house's shady past, but were *still being used.*

Up until Harv and I had moved in, anyway.

"No wonder the landlord boarded up the cellar," my friend muttered, voicing my thoughts as well.

"Shit, Harv, what are we gonna do if he decides to pay us an unexpected visit, and finds you've broken into his trunkful of goodies?" I asked, spinning the fractured padlock around on one of my fingers.

"No sweat," he replied. "Today I paid the friendly neighborhood hardware store a visit. I bought a hacksaw, and this." Out of his pocket he produced a shiny new padlock, virtually identical to the one I was playing with. "Davison (our landlord) must have done his business at the same store – wouldn't you agree?"

"Probably did, Harvey. Lock up the trunk and we'll say no more about this, alright? Let's just hope the keys are the same. And for the sake of all that's holy, put that thing down!!" He had picked up the dagger and was caressing its handle, which had been elaborately engraved with tiny skulls and serpents.

He set it down obligingly, but, before I could protest, unfolded the black robe and held it against himself.

"How do I look?" he laughed.

The garment clearly belonged to someone bigger than either of us.

Once Harvey had returned the profane items to the chest and locked it, we started up the steps. I was so close to the security and relative cheeriness of the ground floor when I heard my little pal exclaim from somewhere behind me:

"The floor! Carl, look at the floor!"

I clumped back down the stairs. Sure enough, there on the center of the cellar floor, distorted a bit by the water, was an encircled pentacle. It was vermilion in color, and I only hoped it wasn't blood.

As we once again proceeded up the stairs, I wondered how in God's name I would ever get any sleep in this dark, creaky old house, which was spooky enough without the knowledge that the landlord performed satanic rituals in the basement. To my relief, Harvey did not insist on another "night on the town," and so we remained at home, devouring the groceries my buddy had picked up at the town's lone supermarket earlier in the day. I asked him over dinner his impression of Davison the landlord, whom I had never met.

"He's a pretty big dude," Harvey admitted.

I pressed further. "Did he seem, well...evil to you?"

"He didn't strike me as the kind of guy who'd march around in a black gown, sacrificing babies and chanting prayers backwards, if that's what you mean. But I guess you never know these days."

We brought dessert out into the drawing room. The TV was a joke, relaying only one channel, and even that one was barely visible, especially at night. Regardless of what show happened to be on, the people always seemed to be rocking to and fro as if on the high seas or in the midst of a particularly violent hurricane.

And so we continued our little chat, primarily a reiteration of the day's events. As I told him of the strange assortment of weirdoes at Timothy's, I deliberately refrained from speaking too much of Radiance. *If Harv should ever decide to move in on her*, I could not help thinking, *my ass is grass.*

Harv had a story of his own to tell. It seemed that around eleven that morning, a handful of local youths had assembled on the front "lawn" of the house, peering through the windows and slouching against the car. Harvey estimated they were about our age, and eight or nine in number. Oddly enough, they didn't appear to be doing much of anything, and by noon had disappeared completely.

"I was just about to leave for my friend's place when I saw all these geeks," Harv explained. "I was afraid, so I hid in my room until they were gone."

I wasn't overly concerned. Did not every community in the civilized world – respectable or otherwise – harbor gangs of such human refuse, with every last "man" among them just itchin' to make trouble? It's been my experience that most gangs are basically harmless, that their thoughts of evildoing tend to ebb with the harkening peel of a school bell, or timely appearance of a police vehicle. Harvey's bunch had probably abandoned us in search of a more promising (i.e., derelict) facility; Lord knows there were enough of them around Robinson's Pt.

My eyelids were growing crushingly heavy. I staggered off to my room around ten-thirty, leaving Harv, barely conscious himself, in front of the TV set. I dove under the covers of my small-but-cozy antique bed, and sleep was upon me in seconds.

I awoke the next morning rejuvenated and raring to go. The sea air will do that for you. Summer might be the most popular season for beachgoers, but I'll tell ya, the seaside in spring has its own special kind of magic. Although never before a bird fancier, I delighted in their sweet strains that morning as I hastily dressed for work. The sun shone with incredible intensity, illuminating every nook and cranny of the old house, beautifying it immeasurably in the process.

I was practically out the door when I spotted Harvey, over on the drawing room chesterfield. At first glance he appeared to be engaged in some sort of advanced yoga exercise. It became apparent, as I moved closer, that he was asleep, and had been there for most of the night. During the course of his slumber, his torso had slipped off the couch in such a way that his legs were now dangling in the air behind him. The poor bugger seemed comfortable enough in this bizarre position; I made a point of closing the door gently as I left, to avoid unduly disturbing him.

I had no sooner descended the porch steps than I caught sight of the bastards, all nine of them. The troop that had scared the jeebies out of old Harvey the morning before had apparently returned. Again, they didn't speak, or make any kind of overt movement. They were loosely assembled on a fringe of the property, and neither advanced nor retreated appreciably as they saw me leave the house.

I could now understand why they'd instilled so much fear into the heart of my friend. They were hardly the schoolboys I'd envisioned. Indeed, the majority of them were brawny, threatening types, guys you'd expect to find on a varsity football squad. Even I was becoming perturbed, although anger was rapidly displacing any actual fear within my being.

I looked at them contemptuously, but said nothing. It had long been a policy of mine to keep to myself, to tend to my own affairs exclusively. I left them to their voyeuristic pursuit, and set forth on my journey into town.

I just prayed the dipshits weren't about to storm the old house. I hadn't so much as locked the front door, as we were still without keys. Christ – what chance would little Harvey have, confronted with such a mob?

I smiled, in spite of myself. *Those fellas better have their track shoes on, because Harv will most assuredly lead 'em on a wild goose chase throughout the house.*

The beach was deserted, if one chose to disregard the spectacle of two large dogs tussling over the remains of one tiny seagull. Giving the combatants a wide berth, I hurried on toward Timothy's. It was approximately five minutes to ten in the a.m. when I reached the restaurant, ten being the starting point of my eight-hour shift. No fewer than four huge signs proclaimed the store "CLOSED," but the main door was open. I crept inside, not quite knowing what to expect.

Toby Jr. and Margaret (the supervisor) were engaged in heated conversation behind the counter, something to do with the nightly clean-up. A bit taken aback by the shouting, I stood hesitantly before them, reluctant to interrupt for fear they would vent their collective hostility on me.

The argument ended abruptly when Margaret called Toby Jr. a name, and stalked off. I'm not entirely sure, but I believe the term she used was "pissant." Toby muttered something in reply, although waiting discreetly till she was beyond earshot.

At last he noticed me shifting uncomfortably from one foot to the other out in the order area.

"Hi," I said meekly.

"It lifts up," he said, referring to a part of the countertop under which it was possible to enter into the service area, and beyond.

As I followed Toby back to the storeroom – where I was to receive my prestigious "Timothy's" uniform – I practically crashed overtop of a giant dog, fast asleep in the cooking section. It was stretched out before the grill, that area naturally being several degrees warmer than the rest of the building.

Before I was so much as aware of what I'd collided into, the monster was on its feet and snarling wickedly, every muscle in its hairy body taut, poised, and ready to do me grievous harm. It obviously did not appreciate being awakened in that manner, and I counted the seconds I had to live.

"Jeremy, stay!" commanded Toby. "Stay! Good boy!" The beast froze, and I got to my feet shakily.

Jeremy was the biggest dog I had ever seen. There might have been a few taller in existence, but could any have possibly matched his outrageous girth, or the sheer size of his head and paws? He looked to be a Mastiff/Rottweiler cross, perhaps with a touch of Airedale in his ancestry. The latter would certainly have accounted for his brittle, wiry hair, which was largely "butterscotch" in color and liberally accentuated with ugly black splotches.

"Sorry, he don't take to strangers," was all Toby offered in the way of an apology, as we approached the entrance to the tiny storeroom.

"This is the staff room of Timothy's," he announced. "You'll find a boxful of pants, shirts and hats in here. Find somethin' that fits, and change into it."

Opening the door, I was greeted by the stimulating sight of Margaret, in bra and panties, about to slip into her uniform. Her back was turned to me, but she whirled around upon detecting the door's telltale creak – and screamed and screamed and screamed. Mere words could never depict the degree of embarrassment and shame I felt as she stormed past with blood in her eye. I suspect the ultra conservative Margaret has held a grudge against me ever since.

I emerged from that storeroom looking more like a Walt Disney character than the manager of a restaurant. The pants were orange, the shirt was orange, even the little triangular cap, which evoked memories of being the class dunce in grade school. There was no attractive Timothy's logo emblazoned on the short-sleeved t-shirt; only a tiny, cartoonist's rendition of a hamburger, its bun partially open.

But the bright orange flood pants were far and away the most humiliating component of my new uniform. No human being should ever have to be subjected to an indignity like that. Other, classier fast food establishments supplied their top brass with tie and vest, but, as it turned out, everyone at Timothy's – even old Renwald himself – was expected to don the orange idiot costumes. Now, I ask you: Who the hell can feel comfortable eating at a restaurant that appears to be staffed by a bunch of mental defectives?

And that's exactly how I must have appeared to my co-workers that April morning so long ago, as I flew hither and thither like a madman, trying to assist them in opening up the store. I still had virtually no idea where anything was kept, and succeeded only in running around in agitated little circles, contributing nothing.

Fortunately, my "opening day jitters" lessened considerably within the space of a few hours, and by noon I was taking orders and serving beverages like a pro. I did my best to adhere to Mr. Renwald's hallowed commandments, of which there were three: serve customers efficiently, serve good food, and, above all, keep the place clean.

Traditionally at Timothy's, it was the counter person's job to tidy up after the customers, as he or she was frequently the sole employee working out front. The others labored behind the scenes, preparing food that was delicious if not exotic: hamburgers, fish & chips, onion rings, chicken sandwiches, and what Renwald proudly referred to as the best hot dogs in the province, bar none.

Thus it was my duty that day to rid the outside picnic tables of debris, and to retrieve the (orange!) plastic trays on which the food had been served. There seemed to be hundreds of damn picnic tables; instead of being arranged in an aesthetic, orderly fashion they were scattered helter skelter about the parking lot, and the resulting spectacle bore more than a little resemblance to some mammoth, impenetrable labyrinth.

It was on one such table cleaning excursion that I first beheld a certain sign plastered on one of our windows, facing outward. It was just one of several, but its message shall linger on in my memory for all eternity:

> Disorderly customers will be
> severely chastised.
> The Management.

Now suppose an unruly bunch of bikers decided to invade Timothy's. Did Renwald really think that they would become instantly cowed the moment they saw his ludicrous sign? Would they forgo the wreaking of havoc in fear of a scathing admonishment from one of his tangerine-tinted buffoons? I think not.

Customers were inexplicably few and far between this lovely spring day, but I found plenty of work to keep me busy. Eager to impress, I allowed the seventeen-year-old Toby Jr. to order me about, and did all his tasks in addition to my own. Margaret still refused to speak to me, but I counted that as a blessing.

In fact, the only one I was able to win over that day was Jeremy. The huge animal had been allowed to remain in the cooking area, in flagrant violation of virtually every bylaw in the Health Code. Upon sensing the others' acceptance of me (such as it was), he sought constantly to reaffirm his own, most often by feverishly licking my hands whenever I ventured within range of his vacuous maw. It only occurred to me recently how vigilant I should have been about washing my hands afterward.

During my break that afternoon, I'd phoned the beach house (yeah, it did have a phone!), but there had been no response. Had the gang taken possession of our humble abode? Had they kidnapped Harvey? Perhaps they'd beaten him to a bloody pulp and he was too weakened to respond to my call.

I managed to suppress my fear. Harvey was probably out basking in the sun someplace, or visiting friends, or doing whatever it is that rich people do while their more industrious counterparts slave away relentlessly and worry about them.

Business was poor that day, but that didn't prevent Mr. Renwald from making at least six separate visits to the store, dropping off supplies and checking up on us. Unlike his sluggish son, he was a highly-strung sort of fellow, and appeared to possess boundless energy.

Before I knew it, it was six o'clock – the end of my shift – and there was Renwald again, this time prepared to work straight through to close. Hot on his heels was wizened little Rupert, who had to have been listed in the Guinness Book of Records somewhere as the oldest living short order cook on earth.

The weekly work schedule was posted out back, so I scribbled down the rest of my hours, then took my leave.

Although absorbed in thought as I headed homeward, I regarded with some interest a couple of families that lay sprawled on the sandy beach as if it were a hot July afternoon. All had swimsuits on, but none seemed willing to brave the icy cold lake. Closer to the house, of course, the beach was less accessible to the public, and remained desolate. Still, it was wildly beautiful in the ensuing twilight, as the sun smeared its reddish pastel across the dusky sky.

I was less appreciative of the pretty scene than I might have been ordinarily, for I had more important matters occupying my thoughts – my friend's safety, for one. I'd tried to contact Harvey a few times that afternoon, without success. Approaching the house, I steeled myself for whatever grim spectacle lay in wait.

What a huge relief it was to discover Harvey reclining lazily on our living room sofa, head propped up by our respective bed pillows. He was watching some insipid game show on the tube and participating in it enthusiastically, alternately praising and berating the contestants based on their responses to the host's none-too-challenging questions. I yanked a pillow from under his head, and fell to the floor in a heap.

At commercial time, I besieged him with questions of my own. Where had he been all day? Visiting old friends. Had the gang of young toughs given him any trouble? He hadn't even seen them. Did he purchase the lumber necessary to reseal the cellar yet? Nope, not yet.

"But I did pick up a forty-ouncer of rye," he said with a roguish grin, obviously believing a substantial measure of hard drink to be just the thing after my eight frantic hours on the job. But work had been anything but frantic that day, and Harvey should have known that I was not much of a drinker, under any circumstances.

Neither of us were overly surprised the next morning, however, when we awoke to find puke on the carpet, chairs overturned, and all the liquor gone – the unmistakable result of a wild, night-long binge.

Oh, but it had been glorious! What I can recall of it, that is. Even when sober Harv and I made for a pretty damned goofy pair – booze had only contributed to the zaniness that night. We ran wild. I remember Sly and The Family Stone being cranked full blast on the stereo, and echoing for miles around. We held foot races on the beach, and scampered up and down lifeguard perches. We built a couple of sandcastles there under the starry sky, and they were most impressive, with meticulously sculpted turrets and large, water-filled moats.

Conversation that evening, when coherent, had mostly to do with the gang that seemed so interested in our house. (We'd christened them "Robinson's Rowdies.") The rest of the time was spent pretty much laughing our asses off, over stuff too idiotic and nonsensical even for this lighthearted tome. We felt as though we were the only two people in existence that night, and I personally felt that everything was well and good, and finally coming together for me. If only I had known…

CHAPTER FIVE

A week passed, uneventfully. If I wasn't hard at work in the restaurant, I was at the library in Port Radcliff, or pumping heavy iron at Turner's Gym.

"Robinson's Rowdies" did continue to make sporadic, early-morning appearances in front of our house, congregating just beyond their perception of where our property line lay. As no foul deeds were being committed on their part (so far as I could tell), I responded with none of my own. I even attempted to befriend the dorks, smiling and greeting them affably one morning as I strode down the porch steps. Predictably, I was received with nothing but stony silence, which did not do a heck of a lot to ease the tension. From that point on I felt compelled to summon the local authorities whenever these guys appeared, although I struggled to resist actually doing so, reluctant to provoke our "guests" any more than was absolutely necessary.

The mysterious antics of Robinson's Rowdies were one thing, but working conditions at Timothy's were becoming increasingly difficult to tolerate – by the millisecond. Every day was busier than the day previous, yet still Renwald refused to schedule more than two or three employees at any one time. As a result, we were woefully understaffed for much of the day, ill equipped to handle the massive lunch and supper rushes that were steadily becoming the norm.

If I was slated to work the grill, I was happy. I was familiar with the position, having worked it years before at my father's "Hamburger Haven." There I had learned of the peculiar, rhythmic cadence one just sort of "fell into" while preparing fast food. You handle, in a perfunctory manner, no more than three orders at any given time. Ceasing to think, you instead rely on your instincts and reflexes, flipping hamburgers, toasting buns, rolling hot dogs, "dropping" rings, fries, chicken, etc., repeating the process for the next three orders in line.

Ad infinitem. Ad nauseam.

This harmonious groove, so fundamentally a part of Hamburger Haven, was rarely in evidence at Timothy's, where your cooking partner was usually an imbecile, and the order-taker out front likely still hadn't a grasp on the most rudimentary concepts of the English language. Your orders came back for the most part indecipherable, looking as though they'd been written in cuneiform.

The worst cooking partner one could even *conceive* of having was the excitable Mr. Renwald. For all of his experience, he really had no idea how to cook at all, and insisted on throwing everything on at once, even if there were twenty-odd orders hanging over his head. Thus it followed that everything was ready to come off "at once," and the stuff would slowly but surely burn to a crisp as it all awaited transferal onto a bun, tray, plate, etc. No "bun person," as the cooking sidemen were called, could hope to keep up with Renwald's frenzied activity behind the grill, with the possible exception of one, whom we shall discuss in more depth a little further ahead.

Good Friday, 1981. I was summoned to work two hours early by Margaret, who shrilly declared that she and Toby Jr. were "bombed out of their minds" (translation: swamped with customers).

Jogging uneasily up the main drag, I couldn't help but notice that – for the first time since I'd been in town – the street was literally crawling with people. What made this seem practically surreal was the fact that the shops were still boarded up for the duration of the off-season. (What storekeeper, after all, could possibly have anticipated the freakishly warm weather that Easter weekend?) And when I first turned onto Fourth St., the pothole-ridden dirt road leading to Timothy's, my heart dropped into my Adidas.

The little store looked as though an immense, writhing centipede was passing through it. As I closed in, however, the creature took on markedly human characteristics. It was, in fact, an enormous, pulsating, mass of customers, which had spilled out both doors.

Puzzled as to why these pinheads seemed willing to wait in excess of thirty-five minutes for a mere fast food repast, I pushed my way into the restaurant, ignoring the icy glares of those who thought I was butting into line. Once inside, I found no alternative but to leap over the counter as though I were Errol Flynn, much to the amusement of several children, who laughed at me derisively. I scrambled back to the staff room, and with all the speed I could muster changed into the loathsome Timothy's uniform.

I gazed into the hazy, full-length mirror that stood in a corner of the staff room, and had to grimace at my idiotic reflection. I then dashed out to join Toby Jr., who was somewhere out in the cooking area, buried beneath an avalanche of food orders.

"Heathen bastards," he muttered. "Don't they know it's a religious holiday?"

A fascinating comment from one who had never observed a day of worship in his life, but I let it pass, and concentrated instead on bailing him out of his Augean predicament. The harder we struggled to gain some ground, it seemed, the further behind we got. For every food order we managed to send out, Margaret would stick no less than five fresh slips through the pass-thru, unceremoniously reciting their contents in that maddening, disgustingly nasal voice of hers (as if Toby and I really cared a rat's ass anyway, with all the orders we had already to contend with). It was not unlike slowly losing ground on a fast moving treadmill.

The pass-thru was similar in construction to the cooking area/order area entrance – that is to say, little better than a rough-hewn hole in the wall. It was strategically located right over the grill, and I suppose it goes without saying that whoever received orders or passed out food through it ran the risk of severely crisping themselves.

Ordinarily it was the task of the order taker to hand out the grub, but as it was all Margaret could do that day to serve customers and prepare drinks, that most distasteful of duties was left to me. Why distasteful? Allow me to explain.

Once a customer placed an order, he or she would be issued a particular number, which we would subsequently screech out as soon as his or her order was completed. I don't know about you folks, but after receiving such a number I would make a beeline for the designated pick-up area and wait ravenously nearby, ready to snatch up my food the moment it was done.

But the moronic geeks who patronized our store (and that's the most flattering description of them you're ever gonna hear from me) often felt inclined to return outside to the picnic tables, or even back to their vehicles! And, of course, you can shriek out their numbers till you're blue in the face; they're not going to hear you.

Further humiliation would descend upon us if we had to actually scour the grounds for the bearer of the unclaimed food. We at Timothy's were already laughingstocks among the rowdier set for our faggoty uniforms, but the effect was radically compounded if we were forced to run from car to car like the subservient court jesters we so strongly resembled. Valuable service time would get flushed down the crapper while we endeavored to recover the "lost little lambs" who had strayed from our fold.

Later, and much to my satisfaction, we adopted a less tolerant decree.

We'd shout the number to the best of our capabilities, a total of three times. If there was still no response from the butt-wipes who ordered the food, we were not to be held accountable. This "tough love" approach did not completely eradicate the problem, however, and it became imperative that we resort to still greater measures to facilitate the dispensation of food, as we shall see.

There were to be many days like that Good Friday to come, and the overwhelming droves of people would have a profoundly negative effect on my inherently sensitive personality. There have always been elements of misanthropy in my make-up, I suppose, but there was also a time in which I held people and their achievements in genuine esteem. My boyhood heroes and inspirational figures tended to be glorious, mythological strongmen of yore: Siegfried, Sampson, Thor, Achilles, and, of course, Hercules.

Oh, but I'd been so impressionable and idealistic as a boy. Timothy's Take-Out was my first exposure to the populace *en masse* – in all its selfish, petty, base glory. I found the experience bitterly disillusioning, but also something of a wake-up call, an induction, of sorts, into the "real world."

Admittedly, I had encountered my share of cretinous customers at my father's restaurant in Toronto, but things had somehow been different there. For one thing, my dad had had the foresight to hire only the best looking girls he could find (believing, correctly, that the sizable male faction of his clientele would be more forgiving of their poor work habits). And should some pompous, overstuffed old patron have accosted me from across the counter in those days, demanding to know precisely how I'd managed to dredge up the unmitigated gall to have garnished his or her quadruple burger with – sin of sins – dark relish instead of the lighter variety, well…I was able to dismiss people like that with nary a care. I only had eyes for my co-workers!

The lone female on staff at Timothy's those first few months was Margaret, and she was a shrew. A hideous, nagging bitch who resented the fact that I as manager had "undue" authority over her. Her resentment would manifest itself in the most bizarre forms.

Enough of my extraneous ramblings, there was a little drama destined to unfold before that particular Good Friday became history. I closed with the old man, Rupert, and David Gardner, alias "Superhero." The latter's nickname was apparently well deserved. He was an extraordinarily capable and congenial young buck, who would dive jubilantly into the most intimidating throngs of customers, taking all the orders clearly and concisely in a matter of seconds. Unlike almost everyone else at Timothy's he was not content to sit on his ass, and if working the till on any given shift would even hasten back into the cooking area to assist those preparing the food. I was most grateful to have David around that Friday evening, since Rupert was more of an annoyance than a productive coworker.

It was partially as a result of David's heroics that I was able to close the store without incident that evening, and immediately we set upon the long, arduous "Clean Up" session – a nightly chore few looked forward to. (I happened to adore it, as it meant a respite from the bickering, insipid public.)

Only after several exhausting rounds of cleaning counters, mopping floors, and washing dishes did we consider ourselves *finito*. It had not been an easy Clean Up by any means, since the premises could have in all seriousness been labeled a disaster area after the landslide of food we'd sent out. Indeed, it looked as though a massive food fight had taken place out back. Streaks of dried mustard adorned the walls, the floor was littered with every imaginable type of debris, and globules of relish clung to everything. (Relish is a bitch to wipe up, since it tends to smear nauseatingly upon contact.)

The mighty Superhero and I did the bulk of the work. I was reluctant to push old Rupert too hard, as he resembled nothing so much as an aged gnome, washing the dishes there in his grimy Timothy's get-up, oblivious to the fact that he was soaking himself with more efficiency than he was the pots and pans. But one thing I'd learned about Rupert: not only was he more cognizant than he appeared much of the time, he was also quite a spry and limber old codger, who could move deceptively fast when it was required of him to do so.

Once in the staff room, I removed my uniform and got back into my "civvies." I gazed into the mirror, a little irked at what I saw. It was at Timothy's that I first became aware of the peculiar phenomenon known as "hat head." Hours of donning those close-fitting, triangular caps were apt to produce a curious ridge in the hair at a guy's capline, making it virtually impossible for him to venture forth in public unless he first soaked his head and then "re-fluffed" his tresses.

But it was late that night, almost eleven-thirty, before I finally locked up the place and the three of us went our separate ways. Not really anticipating any further encounters, I'd dispensed with the usual head-soaking ritual and had left for home at a brisk jog, "hat head" be damned. The day's labor had worn me right out; by the time I hit the vast stretch of beach I was completely winded, and had to slow it down to a walk.

As I came within sight of the old house, my pulse quickened involuntarily. The old place seemed to bear so many secrets, and I had grown accustomed to almost daily reports of strange goings-on from Harvey.

His mother had mailed us the two ancient, cast iron keys, and I slid one into the lock now. It took more than one determined twist before I was able to open the door. Stepping inside, I was able to perceive in the darkness a couple of vaguely defined shapes embracing on the couch. One of those shapes I recognized as Harvey, who sprang up like a jack-in-the-box upon seeing me. I was about to apologize for so rudely entering my own house at midnight after nine-and-a-half hours of stress filled hell on the job without his kind permission, when he seized me tightly with both hands, and bawled,

"Carl! There was a break-in here today! Someone stole the landlord's old chest!"

"What?"

I dashed downstairs, with Harv and his lady friend hot on my heels. Sure enough, the chest was nowhere in sight.

"Anything else missing?" I asked my friend.

"Nope. None of our valuables. I don't understand it."

One thing was certain: whoever the culprit was, he or she had clearly entered from the ground floor. The cellar window was shut tight, and there was no evidence of any additional footprints in the soft muck under the back porch.

Damn it, I shoulda boarded that cellar up long ago, I thought, and silently berated myself for my procrastinating ways. *Moron! Imbecile!*

I hastily prepared some sandwiches, and the three of us sat around the kitchen table. I took a good look at Harvey's chick in the revealing glare of the kitchen light, and noted a little enviously how great looking she was. I poured her and myself tall glasses of milk. Harvey had a beer.

"When do you suppose this happened?" I asked.

"I was out from three to six this afternoon, so the misdeed in question must have occurred within that time period," answered Harvey loftily. Obviously the guy had seen his share of grade Z detective flicks.

"You know," I ventured, "it just may be that Davison (the landlord) dropped by himself and picked up the trunk. After all, it's not something I would feel too comfortable leaving in a leased-out house."

"Do you guys have any idea what was inside the chest?" the girl asked, out of the blue.

Harv and I exchanged nervous glances.

"No, it was locked," Harv replied quickly.

I breathed a sigh of relief. It seemed in our best interest, for the time being, to keep the little matter as confidential as possible.

The girl left around one-thirty in the morning.

"Cute," I remarked, after she had gone. "Why didn't you introduce us?"

"I didn't catch her name," Harvey replied nonchalantly, and abruptly he changed the subject. "I'll just bet this is the work of Robinson's Rowdies," he intoned, sounding rather like Batman this time. "They've been waitin' for a chance to bust in."

"Either way, Harv, I'm going to phone Davison in the morning and —"

"Have you gone completely insane?" he cried. He proceeded to follow me around like an annoying toddler as I attempted to clean the place up. "He's a Satanist, Carl! What do you think he's gonna do to you when he hears his trunk's vanished? You might end up in a trunk of your own!"

Not to be outdone, my reply sounded as though it were lifted from an archaic mystery serial of the early forties: "It's a risk I'll have to take. I'm determined to get to the bottom of this nonsense once and for all."

Much too wound up for sleep that night, I tossed restlessly on my bed. I was able to attain a semblance of inner peace after methodically weighing, in my mind's eye, every plausible explanation for the trunk's disappearance. The explanation I came closest to accepting was the one having to do with Davison returning unannounced to the house. The fact that no door had been forced and nothing had been sacked (except for the trunk), lent a degree of credibility to my assumption, or so I felt.

But Davison had to have seen the king-size perforation in his basement barricade. Why, then, did he not leave an eviction notice behind, or so much as a letter of reproach? Indeed, when one dwelt at any length at all upon the issue, the evidence seemed flimsier in support of an untimely visit from Davison than it did in encouraging the notion of a home invasion by the Rowdies.

So was I back to square one again with regards to the trunkful of satanic playthings? I simply could not account for its disappearance. Perhaps Lucifer himself had become attracted to its almost palpable aura of evil, and had teleported the thing back into the infernal pit of Hades where it so rightfully belonged. The theory was no less far-out than some of the others I was dreaming up.

Bewildered (and not a little overcome) by hours of fruitless deduction, my brain responded the only way it knew how: by shutting down completely for the duration of evening.

The baffling, contradictory issue of the trunk was all but forgotten the following morning, in my mad scramble to reach work by ten a.m. As usual, I'd awoken late (heavy night and day shifts, when aligned back-to-back, were most intolerable!)

I decided to postpone the phone call to Davison until that evening, after work. It would give me several hours in which to formulate some sort of game plan, one I could adhere to throughout what was bound to be a terse and disagreeable conversation. Assuming Davison knew nothing of the trunk's disappearance, it would be a delicate task indeed to A) gently divulge the matter without sending him into a state of ungovernable panic, and B) extract as much useful information as I could out of the ensuing discussion.

But did I truly believe I would find nine hours of solace at Timothy's in which to ponder the direction and significance of a phone conversation? Easter Saturday was proving as hectic as Good Friday, especially when one factored in the "merit" of my fellow workers. Working behind the grill that afternoon was none other than that loveable father-and-son duo, Toby Sr. and Toby Jr., while I was given the ignoble job of serving customers.

The younger Renwald had apparently inherited much from his father, although there was barely a quality between them that could be construed as positive. They did share such unflattering traits as belligerence, maleficence, and flatulence, and both were exceedingly foul mouthed.

Wherever Toby Jr. went, his big, ugly dog Jeremy was sure to follow, and that Saturday was no exception. Jeremy would often pass his master's workday snoozing in the back somewhere, an absolute study in serenity, while the rest of us scurried around like stir crazy, amphetamine-charged hamsters in a cage. While I may not have warmed to the humans around Timothy's, I quickly grew attached to that oversized mutt.

Like his master, however, Jeremy did seem afflicted with a marked attitude problem. If left to his own devices, he would on occasion wander out front and attack customers.

It happened twice that Saturday, and a number of times after that – and the outcome was always the same. The elder Renwald, if present, would come barreling out of the cooking area toward the site of the disturbance, arms flailing wildly, and demand that the 'mad dog' be seized by the humane society. Toby Jr. would subsequently appear out of nowhere, and – after savoring for a few seconds the spectacle of his immense, snarling, spitting canine holding its half crazed victim at bay – proceed, halfheartedly, to call Jeremy off.

As I said, it was my misfortune that day to have been designated as the order taker, the drink procurer, and the food hander outer. By comparison, the two Renwalds were nestled comfortably within the confines of the cooking area, shielded to a large extent from their insufferable "public."

However, they proved completely incapable of working with each other, particularly in such close quarters. Both were determined to do the cooking, which was preferable to the more complex task of preparing buns and readying the food for pick-up. All day long the two fought, their profanities often drifting out the pass-thru and reaching the keen ears of the customers, who found the exchanges most amusing. Well, some of the time.

The most embarrassing moment that day – for me, anyway – occurred while I was in the midst of taking a genial, middle-aged gentleman's order. Suddenly, I heard Toby Jr. exclaim with disheartening clarity: "Just take a look at that chick's fish and chips! Just look at them! You've burnt them to a f**cking crisp, you idiot! Why, they're nothing but little, charred…blobs! We can't serve that shit!"

Aghast, I couldn't help but steal a look at the "chick" in question, who was waiting patiently for her fish and chips over in the pick-up area. It was obvious that Toby Jr.'s lack of candor had her a good deal agitated. I lowered my eyes in shame, and gamely resumed taking the order of my customer.

"God damn son of a bitch!"

Now it was the elder Renwald's turn, and his outbursts had the explosive force of Howitzer cannon fire.

"You good for nothing little punk! I should have fired you years ago! You'd be nothing without me…"

"It's getting a little tense back there," I cracked sheepishly, too ashamed to look anyone in the face. "God damn son of a bitch" was Mr. Renwald's pet phrase, and I'm sure I heard it uttered a million times while in his employ.

The day was a series of awkward, horrible confrontations. If the two assholes behind the grill weren't somehow involved, the customers were. I felt I was being suffocated – swallowed alive, even – by these overpowering legions of creepy people.

"Break time" was pretty much out of the question on days of this sort. Having skipped breakfast that particular Saturday I was faint from hunger, and not entirely certain I would make it to the end of my shift. The irony being, of course, it was a restaurant in which I was working, and I was reminded of the immortal words of Samuel Taylor Coleridge:

Water, water, everywhere,
nor any drop to drink.

"The Case of the Missing Trunk" had temporarily retreated into the deeper, darker recesses of my mind, as I had little time at work to grant it even the slightest consideration. I was, however, learning some pretty sobering facts about my fellow man.

For years, I'd been taught to accord everybody – from the lowliest, drug-wired street urchin to those holding supreme positions of power – a substantial measure of respect and dignity. But I seemed to be encountering nothing but arrogant, greedy, doltish louts at Timothy's, whom the prosperous times had jaded almost beyond belief. Certainly they were the very antithesis of the noble, long-suffering heroes who had so inspired my life up to that point.

I looked with amazement upon the many miserable families I served, wondering why some of the young men had opted to marry so conspicuously beneath them. I mean, Good Lord Almighty, their own lives had barely begun, and already they were saddled down with an obnoxious wife and veritable multitude of screaming, red faced children – the eldest of which, I'll wager, was the regrettable consequence of a one-night stand gone awry. I wasn't opposed to the nuclear family by any means, but I believed the time for a wife and kids was when one was well past forty years of age and had made his millions. How ridiculously simple it would then be to acquire both a lovely house and lovely young wife, and really settle down to enjoy thoroughly one's declining years!

Yes, sir, I had it all figured out.

Large families were generally desirable customers, as they tended to order large amounts of food, but taking their orders was often the worst kind of torture. You'd think the head of the household would've had at least a vague idea of what his kids wanted by the time he'd moved through the line. But rarely did we encounter a father figure with the foresight or intelligence to have prearranged the order in its entirety. Some misguided simpletons would even ask their two-year-olds what they wanted to eat, as if the kids had any idea whatsoever. What was worse, they would at times ask the toddlers to order for themselves. How are you supposed to translate, "gaagoogeegaagaa?"

47

If I'm coming across as an ill-tempered dolt, swollen with hate, then I fear it is a fallacious picture I've been painting. It's just that I'd been hideously miscast as manager of Timothy's, and was consumed with loathing for the role. Away from work I was actually an affable fellow, waiting wistfully on the beach for my ship to come in, my head full of absurd and unattainable dreams. The romantic in me concedes that the Robinson's Pt. of the early eighties was an incredibly ethereal place, and that to enter this world was to step back at least three decades in time. (Of course, it has lost much of that precious magic over the years. The water is no longer pure, and, like most places on this earth, the steady encroachment of man has taken a horrendous toll on the environment. Says the ill-tempered dolt!)

But we're getting a little ahead of ourselves. There was nothing magical about Timothy's Take-Out − not then, not ever. It was a grimy, stinking sweatshop. And at no time were magic and enchantment *less* in evidence than on Easter Saturday, 1981.

Conspicuous by her absence that evening was that dark blotch on the face of all that was feminine, Margaret the supervisor. She had been scheduled to work from six to close. As fate would have it, I was the patsy selected to continue working until what time − if any − she chose to grace the establishment with her resplendent presence. Like many at Robinson's Pt. she had no phone, and it was therefore next to impossible to account for her tardiness. Seething with anger and resentment, I prayed for the worst.

It never rains but what it pours. The two Renwalds were replaced by one man − one very small, old, and decrepit man. You know who I'm talking about. I stuck Rupert behind the grill, where I felt he could do the least damage; having not yet realized that if the man had a forte it was more in the line of serving customers and preparing beverages. Unwilling, however, to stick anyone with those loathsome duties if I could help it, I resolved nobly to continue taking and handing out orders myself.

It was while attempting to hand out orders that I really appreciated having Mr. Renwald around. I lacked the vocal 'oomph' necessary to belt out order numbers well, and was constantly calling on him to do it. The old boy was a human air raid siren, and when in good voice even people across the street could hear him intelligibly. It was his sole talent. Rupert, on the other hand, was no great shakes in this regard. His anguished croak was no more audible than my own.

That Saturday, I reluctantly entered into my ninth consecutive hour without a break. This was back when I actually considered nine hours a long time, you understand. Pretty soon, I'd be regarding such a shift as practically a day off.

Renwald's unique conception of all that being a restaurant manager entailed was precisely that: a unique conception. I wasn't bestowed with any weighty obligations, nor was I entrusted with anything of value. I was merely required to work about double the hours of anyone else, doing much the same thing they were doing. Although the work was monotonous for the most part, there were times when it could be absolutely nerve-wracking. I could seldom turn my back without feeling the steely, pitiless gazes of the customers boring into it, etching the phrase, "Why aren't you serving me asshole," across the span of my latissimus. Little pieces of my soul began going out with each and every order. Were these customers blind to the fact that, while they were so innocently consuming their hamburgs and fries, they were in effect devouring my soul? Before long, I had none left. None at all.

Margaret finally did show up, about eight-thirty I think, and although her excuse for being late was both dubious and uninspired (a sick aunt in Owen Sound), it hardly mattered. I was just thankful she appeared when she did, as I could feel my rubbery legs and tenuous hold on sanity simultaneously giving way.

In my haste to leave the restaurant I had forgotten to change, and was halfway down the street before I realized I was still bright orange. Now I had quite familiarized myself with most aspects of my job by that time, but still had trouble coping with the fact that I so strongly resembled one of Snow White's dwarves. Trying to appear inconspicuous (!), I slunk back into the store, weaving in and out of line like a gigantic orange checker, on a roll.

When I finally reached the beach house, I found to my dismay that Harvey was not there. I'd completely psyched myself up to make the cryptic call to Davison by that point, and was counting on Harvey to provide the guy's phone number.

I temporarily shelved the phone call idea and entered the kitchen, intending to respond to a more urgent demand: hunger. Stuck to the door of our old fridge was the list of rules Davison had left us. Sure enough, he'd scrawled his home number at the bottom of the page.

But hang on a second. That last digit seems a trifle faint…Is that a two, an eight, or perhaps a seven?

I recall substituting everything on the friggin' telephone dial for that final numeral before finally getting hold of Davison. But such was my determination to clear up once and for all this whole, preposterous muddle.

49

I quickly introduced myself, and cut right to the chase, confessing both our surreptitious entrance through the cellar and the disappearance of his trunk. I did not mention the fact that we had broken into the trunk and were quite aware of what it contained.

I thought I'd anticipated Davison's every response beforehand, but still his reply caught me off guard. In fact, I was floored by it.

"I don't know what yer talkin' about, lad. I didn't board up the cellar – 'cause there weren't nothin' of value in the cellar. No trunk, no nothin'!"

"What about the upper story?" I pressed. "It's boarded up as well."

"Yeah, yeah, I laid a sheet of plywood across it, sure, but it ain't nailed down or nothin'. Just what the hell have you fellas been doin' over there, anyway?"

With Davison professing his ignorance of the entire affair, I was left more perplexed and apprehensive than ever. If he truly did know nothing, I reasoned, then it would be best for him to remain in that blissful state – at least until I was able to sort things out for myself. We concluded our conversation, but only after he had extracted a solemn promise from me to inform him immediately should anything further transpire.

Seconds later, I was ascending the staircase leading to the concealed second floor and attic. As Davison had mentioned, the slender wooden sheet was not fastened down in any way, and I was able to lift it up with relative ease.

There was nothing at all incriminating about the second floor. Most of the rooms were bare, save for a few skeletal bed frames and the occasional disembodied light fixture. In the attic, I stumbled across some fascinating relics one usually associates with a house of this age, but again, nothing out of the ordinary.

Nevertheless, something was distinctly "not right" about these forbidden regions of our home. The rooms were stark and hollow. The unnatural stillness of the air seemed to generate a sensation of extreme melancholy; it felt as though some heart wrenching tragedy had taken place up there somewhere. Despite it being a relatively humid night I had come to feel distinctly chilled, and wondered if I was not experiencing the "psychic cold" parapsychologists speak of.

Having finally convinced myself that clandestine visits had NOT been paid to the attic or the network of small rooms on the second floor – not in that decade, anyway – I returned to the comparative cheeriness of ground level. Able to contain my hunger no longer, I rustled up every last tidbit of food from the kitchen, and arranged it all like a richly spread smorgasbord in front of the TV.

The set was on its best behavior, and I was treated to an hour of professional wrestling. The "sport" was pretty big in these parts, if the frequency with which it cropped up on our TV screen was of any indication. Harv and I had been indifferent toward the phenomenon at first, though I as an aspiring muscle-builder had always possessed grudging admiration for the gigantic athletes. We ridiculed the contrived bouts and inept officiating without cease, until the day we woke up to discover that we'd established virtual mental directories of our favorite heroes and villains. It wasn't long before we started ducking parties and the like, just to catch the stupid matches.

To my great dismay, virtually the only other shows offered on our television's lone channel were agricultural reports of one sort or another, and they ran virtually "twenty-four seven." It astounded me how much of a production they were able to make out of the recitation of hog and cattle prices!

But I digress. After a none-too-inspiring episode of "wrasslin'," I tossed my dishes into the kitchen sink, straightened up what needed straightening up, and ventured forth on a midnight stroll of sorts.

The night was fabulous, with a soft breeze blowing in from the sea. On nights like this it was easy to imagine our house as being no longer ugly, no longer dilapidated, but rather a shimmering palace in Asgard, a Utopian paradise set far from the congested hovels of the peasants. God, how I treasured my little strip of beach!

After padding barefoot along the shore for about a half-mile – not toward town, but in the other direction – I suddenly, impulsively, dropped to my knees. From there I just lay back in the sand, gazing at the firmament above. Its bright moon and well-defined stars glistened in primordial splendor.

I pondered that which is usually pondered beneath such a sky. Girls (in my case, Radiance, Radiance, RADIANCE!), how insignificant we all are, how it all began, timeless subjects like that. Alone there on the beach, I reaffirmed my goals in life, crass as they were at the time.

In certain respects my goals have not changed at all. As elusive as they've proven to be thus far, fame and fortune are still foremost among my long-term priorities. And someday, as a means of offsetting my eternal crowd phobia, I should like to purchase a country estate and "get back to nature" (although not to the extent of denying myself any modern convenience!). I had read about ex-Beatle Paul McCartney buying up tracts of farmland in the vicinity of his Scottish home, and, despite the millions upon millions at his disposal, continuing to live simply and close to the earth. That is my plan as well. Now if only I had one-tenth of Paul's fortune (or one one-thousandth of his talent!)

But how in God's name was I to realize my grandiose ambitions working in Timothy's Take-Out ten hours a day? The excitement of relocating to a resort town, of taking on a strange job and stranger house, had obviously sidetracked me. I was no further along the heady road to success than I'd been as a youth in Toronto (or, for that matter, as a newborn baby in the delivery room!).

And then the insecurities came creeping back, insidiously at first, but then welling up with abandon, exposing my deficiencies, forsaking their ruinous onslaught only after having reduced me to a quivering, neurotic hulk.

I lay flat on my back in the sand. Looking up, I imagined I saw the constellation Perseus there in the night sky. Ah, Perseus. Once despised and considered a laughingstock on the island of Seriphos, his immortal exploits (and timely wielding of the slain Gorgon's head) had forever silenced the cruelest of his tormentors. How I longed for similar acclamation!

I struggled to my feet and looked out to sea, as far as was possible in the encompassing darkness. I listened with pleasure to the reassuring sound of the swells as they made their way slowly to shore. This is what made all the crap worthwhile. The rotten job, the imbecilic tourists, the intrusive Rowdies, the manic funhouse I called home – they all could be tolerated so long as the lake was nearby. It was my one precious, tenuous link to the past. The quaint shops and atmospheric old buildings lent Robinson's Pt. a rustic flavor to be certain, but the inhabitants of those buildings and proprietors of those shops were "eighties" to the depths of their stony little souls.

Staring out over the water I could commune with all my old buddies, all my boyhood idols from beyond the apparent realm of time and space, whether that person was Alexander the Great, Cuchulain (the fictional "Hound of Ulster"), my one-time sweetheart Rosalie Krane, or Vincent Van Gogh, in whom I'd found a kindred spirit. So what if it's only Lake Huron we're talking about? It was there then, and it's here now.

Harvey was still out when at last I returned home, a few minutes ahead of the "witching hour." I was growing accustomed to his late night excursions, but at the same time could not help feeling a little nervous about them. It was my nature.

To maintain my sanity on this particular occasion I set right to work, tackling several menial chores I knew would be distracting. I did all the dishes, a task I normally tend to leave until food particles begin crawling around of their own volition, and I completely dismembered what was left of our jagged cellar door obstruction.

It was the latter task, of course, which set the old thought processes in motion again, and I started agonizing over just whose damned obstruction it could have been, and just whose trunkful of playtoys lay – or had once lain – in our cellar. Why had the trunk been there to begin with, and who had returned for it? Why had they taken nothing else, and how had they gotten in? Quite an assortment of questions, I must say, comparable in their complexity to those put forth by the Sphinx.

And what of the landlord, if indeed you could be kind and address him as such? Evidently, he'd not been anywhere near the place in months, and had not an inkling of its current sorry condition. I was relieved to learn that he was probably not a Satanist.

And where the hell was Harvey? He hadn't taken the car, though, truth be told, he seldom did – not in this fantasyland, where a leisurely stroll was infinitely more rewarding than motoring about like some detached sightseer. Presumably, he was serving as the very centerpiece to somebody's debauched, orgiastic drinking spree (the sort of activity I tended to avoid like the plague).

Harvey and I had been drifting apart of late. In fact, the rift had been perceivable almost from the day we'd moved in together. No one was really to blame, although upon reflection I suppose it was more my doing than his. I was out so much of the time (working my ass off at Timothy's, mostly), and would return home more often than not haggard, exhausted, and just looking to crash for a few hours.

It was true also that Harv was running with his own circle of friends at the time, none of whom had taken to me with any degree of affection. Par for the fucking course, as I saw it. I had not a fraction of my chum's beguiling charm, and simply did not fit in – anywhere. What a dreadful stick-in-the-mud I must have seemed to the gregarious Harvey.

I slipped into my orange-colored pajamas (which bore an uncanny resemblance to my work clothes) and began flicking off all the clunky, arthritic light switches in the house. All, that is, but one.

Not to wax unduly poetic, but "the washroom light burnt bright all night." We usually left it on this time of year, not because we were skittish wimps in need of a nite lite, but as a damned ingenious method of combating the annual resurgence of mosquitoes and black flies. The mindless little creatures were drawn to the gleaming bulb, to the extent that they would tend to disregard their snoring quarry just yards away. Of course, it did mean having to shave and brush one's teeth in Insect Hell the next morning, but the tranquil night's sleep this method ensured was well worth the trouble.

It was practically out of instinct, then, that I proceeded to the washroom that evening to check on the "trap." As it was terribly warm in the house I filled the sink with cold water and commenced dunking my head a few times in succession. I happened to gaze up at the light after so doing, and became instantly enthralled with the antics of a clever spider that was constructing his web near there.

He appeared just to be finishing it, when BAM!! A fat housefly flew into the wispy core, and was soon thrashing about helplessly. Aroused by the frenzied activity, the spider inched steadfastly toward its victim, and the curious drama reached an abrupt conclusion when he pounced upon the hapless fly, seeking either to mummify or devour it. Impressed by his resourcefulness, I permitted the eight-legged marauder to live – at least for the time being – and turned my attention elsewhere.

Apart from the gentle lapping sound of the waves outside, the house was still as death as I slid into bed. I dimly recall, before sleep overtook me entirely, a rattle from the front door, the urgent whispering of my friend Harvey, and the higher pitched giggling of someone I did not know but would like to have known.

Nothing particularly noteworthy occurred for about a month after that. Mother Nature heralded the arrival of May with profusions of daisies and buttercups, and the lake literally sparkled under the ubiquitous spring sun.

Yes indeed, Robinson's Pt. might have been taken for a Garden of Eden that year, were it not for the festering hellhole of Timothy's Take-Out in its midst. Yet Timothy's was no Tree of Knowledge, enticingly sheathing its evil designs in a covert attempt to seduce The Chosen. Quite the contrary, it was just one of several local fast-food outlets clamoring for its slice of the fast-food pie.

For some inexplicable reason – even today it confounds me – we appeared to do more business than all the other comparable eateries *combined*. On nicer days especially, the people made for our restaurant like those damned mosquitoes made for my bathroom light bulb. Or, as Toby Jr. more expressively maintained, "like maggots to a rotting corpse." Why they were so willing to put up with the slow moving lines, the excessive heat (we had no air conditioner), and the sullen staffers was anybody's guess. I suppose they could have been attracted to the spectacle of a father and son hurling frightful avowals of hatred back-and-forth in public. All I knew for certain was that Renwald was getting rich off these ridiculous people, and I, for all my effort, was not.

Why didn't I get out? Well, I had a great deal of pride, and I wanted to prove to both Renwald and myself that I was equal to the work. At first I was constantly trying to revolutionize various outmoded edicts that to me made no sense. It was only after I'd realized that both my hands were inexorably bound that I abandoned all thoughts of reform, and channeled the greater part of my energies into the very act of surviving, of toughing out those excruciatingly long hours.

It was on the final Sunday in May that I again encountered a few "Robinson's Rowdies," perched practically upon my doorstep. As Harv and I had long believed these assholes to be the true owners of the trunk, I decided to confront them.

These guys in no way resembled a "typical" gang, even by 1981 standards. They had a straight-laced, almost scholarly appearance, although even the frailest of the lot looked to be a good two hundred pounds. It was this preponderance of hulking beef, coupled with the fact that they rarely spoke, that made them seem especially terrifying.

Following the theft of the trunk, the Rowdies had made themselves scarce for a while, and this seemed to confirm our every suspicion about them. *Now that they've seized what they'd waited so patiently to seize*, I mistakenly assumed, *perhaps they will finally leave us in peace.*

So imagine my surprise when I first opened the door that lovely Sunday morning (with every intention of heading directly to work), only to behold the execrable Rowdies poised motionless in various sites about the front of the house like a bunch of grotesquely overgrown lawn jockeys.

I staggered backwards in astonishment, briefly regained my composure, then lost it again as I began cursing and threatening them with every sort of abuse – absurd when one considers my rather precarious stance at the time as one little dude against seven big ones.

But I didn't care. Loner that I was, I despised those who were so insecure they felt they had to become part of a gang, and then atone for their humiliating loss of identity by making miserable the lives of honest people. "I know all about you guys," I declared, hoping to badger them into speaking. "You got what you wanted, now get out of here! You're never using our cellar again for your pathetic games. It's our house now!" With a shudder, I recalled the blood-like pentagram on the cellar floor.

The ruse worked. The apparent leader of the clan seemed infuriated with my "impertinence."

"You don't know what you're saying!!" he exploded. "This structure has been consecrated for the master, and as such is his alone! You are the intruders here, but we will allow you to depart unharmed *if you leave now!!*"

"You twisted fuckers," I began, but stopped short. While the head Rowdy had been so eloquently delivering his ultimatum, the sun had been glinting off his left ear, enough to momentarily draw my focus. As he turned his head slightly, it became chillingly obvious just where his allegiance lay, and I felt my stores of bravado and righteous indignation dissipate into nothing.

For, attached to the bastard's ear, was the most hideous adornment one could possibly imagine: a tiny, inverted crucifix, made of silver.

All the dudes had one.

"If your 'master' is so crazy about our house," I challenged, "then why didn't you guys rent it for him? Between the lot of you deadbeats, I'm sure you could handle the monthly payments!"

"What the hell is goin' on?"

Startled, I spun around in time to see Harvey pop his towhead through the partially open front door. Once he recognized our callers, however, he darted right back inside the house without a further word.

The Rowdies never did respond (in a tangible way) to the question I posed, and it was around then that they began to disperse, following their "leader" back to whatever rock it was they'd crawled out from underneath. The sight of the upside-down crosses had taken most of the starch out of my ire as well, and I said little to the departing Rowdies, except to mockingly suggest that they return on a more appropriate date on their calendar, like Halloween. The head Rowdy visibly flinched at this, and his ensuing mumblings were probably curses aimed in my direction.

And that was the extent of the confrontation. I was glad I stood up to them the way I did; it was certainly an uncharacteristic display of mettle on my part. Normally, you see, I was a very quiet and obliging sort of person, who would have to be viciously goaded into even *contemplating* such a testy display. But I suppose even pacifists have their limits. Now if only I could have asserted myself in similar fashion at work.

Speaking of which…

* * *

In order to keep my full-time co-workers straight in your mind, it is necessary only to associate them with their most distinguishing attribute. Old man Renwald, for instance, could best be described as a flint-hearted miser.

His decision not to install "costly" air conditioners left Timothy's a veritable inferno in the summer months, and my programmed response to whining customers was always, "just be thankful you don't have to work here." The blazing grill and searing hot grease did not, understandably, do much to alleviate the soaring temperatures; we were pretty much immersed in sweat from the second we began our shifts.

Renwald was divorced. For all their apparent wealth he and his son lived alone in a squalid little cabin, not even on the water. Perhaps the divorce weighed heavily on young Toby Jr., I'm not entirely sure, but if he had one distinct characteristic it was his extraordinary cruelty.

Human suffering and despair seemed to provide Toby Jr. with his only real gratification in life. For example, his favorite television shows for the longest time were those ghastly, late-night entreaties for the relief of famine in the Third World. Far from ever being moved to make a donation, he considered the graphic depictions of death and misery light entertainment, and would faithfully tune into as many of the shows as he could. I could just see the guy, while the poor souls lay dying before him, contentedly munching from an enormous bowl of sour cream-and-onion chips (his favorite snack).

And woe indeed to the customer unlucky enough to have a pissed-off Toby Jr. cook for him. I vividly recall an instance where the local barber received a particularly atrocious meal from Toby and later retaliated by giving the callous youth one of the most ridiculous haircuts I've ever seen on a human being.

As for the others, well…Rupert really didn't have anything in the way of a distinct personality anymore. He was just old. When festooned in the Timothy's colors, he cut a hysterically funny figure to say the least. Since his head was so small, he was obliged to wear only the tiniest triangular cap we had in stock, and even this after a while would slide down over his head like a teepee, and completely obscure the upper portion of his face. Nevertheless, the cap was set-aside in the storeroom with the understanding that it was Rupert's alone. Not that it was in much demand. It would have looked like a *yamuccah* on anyone else!

It was clear that Margaret and I would not progress much beyond our current ignominious relationship. The term "knit picking" would have described our sour supervisor dead on; the less said about her, the better. Of some consolation to me was the fact that she seemed to be relatively indiscriminate in her hatred.

David, the "Superhero," was an enigma, and could not be pigeonholed with the same facility as the others. He appeared friendly enough on the surface, excelled in his work, and was quite a good looking fellow, yet the rest of the staff seemed to hate him, or at best were totally indifferent to his presence.

I, however, refused to take the miraculous prodigy for granted. Just as working alongside Rupert and Toby Jr. – who as employees were positively weighted down with deficiencies – could be a kind of hell, working alongside the Superhero was sometimes sheer inspiration. Whenever this guy was around, a serene sense of calm prevailed, even amidst the most frenzied lunch rushes. He could do it all, and simultaneously.

All modesty aside, it is my belief that when the Superhero and I joined forces, we formed the most devastating one-two combination in the business. We were the Ruth and Gehrig of fast-food service. On many occasions I witnessed the Superhero literally leap over the counter in order to assist some old lady laden with food. After responding to her profuse declarations of gratitude with his patented "Dudley Do-Right" smile, he'd jump right back into the fray, and, without missing a beat, resume taking orders at that characteristically matchless pace of his.

As terrific an employee as David was, he didn't put in half the hours I did. How he spent his time outside of work was a mystery. Since nobody knew where he lived, and no friends ever called for him at Timothy's, it was the general conviction of those I worked with that he was some sort of undercover spy.

There was one particular day – or, more specifically, one particular *moment* – in early June of '81 that I recall with particular clarity. I was just winding up a dreadful ten-to-seven shift, having serviced enough fuck-faced dickweeds to last me a lifetime. As usual, I'd bent over backwards to ensure these wretches at least a halfway decent dining experience (no mean feat, what with the inglorious duo of Toby Jr. and Rupert manning the battle stations out back, routinely botching every order to come their way).

(Author's note: Forget about that moment in early June. We'll put it on the backburner for a while. I want to vent!)

Admittedly, there were legitimate complaints from time to time, which I handled with professionalism. To the majority of the patrons (and much of the staff), I extended a front of nauseating and unrelenting cordiality. I was pleasant, affable, helpful – and totally superficial.

The minute a customer began to harp upon anything frivolous, however – or attempted to rile me through horseplay – my true feelings would surface. I would struggle to suppress the overwhelming urge to forever blot out the source of my annoyance. Consider the case of the pathetic old bitch who, in a fury, tossed her Hamburger Deluxe upon the countertop claiming it wasn't wrapped tightly enough! Good freakin' grief! I mean, what can you do about people like that, other than line them up against a brick wall and blow their brains out! Should I have informed her that her burger had been wrapped by one whose manual dexterity had expired some twenty years hence?

Humiliated, but exerting self-control, I re-wrapped the damn thing myself, and thrust it back at her, silently awaiting her next move. As I had figured, my gesture of reconciliation wasn't enough to satisfy the harridan, and she insisted a new burger be cooked. This I'd anticipated as well, and I coolly returned the unwanted burger to head chef Toby Jr., whose deep-seated hatred of these kinds of people, incidentally, made me seem like Mary Poppins.

"Let it sit," I instructed, placing it gingerly under the heat lamp. After what seemed like an appropriate amount of time, the very same sandwich was sent back to the woman, who stalked triumphantly out of the store with it. I congratulated myself on my duplicity – I mean, diplomacy!

But this was merely one isolated instance, gleaned from among thousands. I had a tough time relating to the many pampered buffoons I encountered, and would go so far as to say I was ashamed to be classified in the same species with them. Their fall from grace appeared to have been such that they'd been effectively reduced to mindless puppets, addicted to all manner of base and temporary gratifications (like fast food!)

The old lady's poorly wrapped burger was hardly the momentous occurrence of early June it was my original intention to inform you of; if I in my disconnected ramblings have misled you, I do apologize. Perhaps now, however, you have some idea as to the extent of my mental deterioration around that time.

A trio of nuns had just placed their order, which I'd been particularly beneficent in receiving. Nuns could unveil piety in a water buffalo! Convinced that the good women were somehow attuned to the cesspool of burgeoning evil within me, I was understandably ill at ease in their company.

Toby Jr., obviously wishing to confer for a bit, was gesturing frantically at me from the back. Rather than stick the nuns' order form through the pass thru (as was customary), I took it personally to him. Not out of any burning desire to help Toby, you understand; I was just grateful to escape, however briefly, the self-righteous, self-pitying muggings of the customers. As it turned out, Toby Jr. and Rupert were indeed in deep shit, but no more than usual. When I returned out front it was with four cumbersome packages of food hanging precariously from various parts of my person.

I was in good voice that night, as was sometimes the case, and all four parties responded when I sang out their numbers. (In an effort to fortify that frail voice of mine, I had begun to emulate the methods of the Greek orator Demosthenes, stuffing pebbles into my mouth and screaming for hours over the din of the waves.)

Anyway, back to the "magic moment." Jeez, how I digress! I returned to my unenviable post, and another round of pandering, patronizing, and out-and-out ass kissing. I had an odd habit of never looking customers directly in the face, concentrating instead on their hands, and there was something vaguely familiar about the pair before me now. In my years at Timothy's I had seen all kinds: some large and calloused, others soft and feminine, still others missing a few digits or mutilated by fire. But no hands ever managed to captivate me quite like this particular set. As I marveled at their extraordinary beauty, and heard for the first time the melodic, bell-like voice of their owner, I felt compelled to look upward.

Radiance!!

Completely flustered by the vision before me, my jaw dropped, as did the pen through my fingers. Radiance had returned!

And summer was upon us.

CHAPTER SIX

It was most fitting that dear Radiance – who possessed a loveliness that was, in itself, almost divine – be immediately preceded into the store that day by a trio of nuns. As she bent down, giggling, to retrieve the pen I had dropped, I attempted in vain to control my trembling limbs.

She handed me the pen, which I took without so much as a word of thanks. Quite overcome by dizziness, it was all I could do to remain on my feet. "Haven't I seen you somewhere before?" I finally managed, doing my best to sound nonchalant.

"Yeah-h-h. Allie and me met you in the spring. We're going to be working here too, over the summer."

She spoke in fascinating, lilting tones, drawing out her words much the way a little girl would. She gestured to her left, and sure enough, there was two-ton Allie, flanking her much the way a mammoth bodyguard would. They were like Fay Wray and King Kong, standing there.

These precious few seconds with Radiance were enough to restore, if only temporarily, my good nature and sense of decency. For the first time ever, there was joy to be had in working at Timothy's.

Suddenly, however, no one was speaking. Radiance's bashful gaze had alighted upon the tips of her shoes, and Allie stood in silence, quivering slightly like the huge clump of gelatin she was. If the customers behind them were growing edgy I hadn't noticed, preoccupied as I was with the adorable blonde I could have leaned over and kissed, whose very existence I had begun to question in recent weeks.

Yet there she was, in living, breathing, huggable, squeezable color, more ravishing in life than in any of my fantasies. She had the face of a beautiful child, the voluptuous body of a woman in her prime, and, to be sure, a more alluring combination did not exist.

Radiance and Allie made their way to the back of the store. As no work schedule had been posted that week *per se*, they boldly decided to ring up Renwald Sr. himself for their respective starting dates.

I'd no sooner started back into my order taking, when out from the back popped Toby Jr.

"Who's the moose, Carl?"

Ever the pessimist, he had somehow managed to entirely overlook Radiance, having noted only the undoubtedly startling manifestation of her comrade. Halting my poor customer in mid-gesture, I endeavored to explain to Toby – as thoroughly as I could under the circumstances – the precise nature of the girls' business there. Upon learning that they were not out to rob or sabotage us, Renwald's obnoxious whelp put an abrupt end to our conversation with one of his inimitable dry heaves, and went to rejoin Rupert and the inevitable accumulation of burnt food out back.

The girls reappeared before long, and I gallantly swung up that portion of the countertop affording passage back into the order area and ultimately out of the restaurant. Allie said nothing to me in passing, intent as she was, I suppose, in maneuvering her bulk through the somewhat-less-than-expansive cleft. Radiance did utter a breathless "Bye, Carl!" and it astonished me that she had actually remembered my name.

I completed what remained of my shift that day in the highest of spirits, but just as I was about to leave Toby Jr. drew me aside, and hastened me into the cluttered little storeroom. After rummaging for a time through a huge box filled with various miscellaneous items, he produced, to my horror, a large pistol. I immediately recognized it as no less an instrument of destruction than a .44 Magnum.

And it was loaded.

"Ain't it beautiful," Toby purred, stroking the thing with almost a sexual fervor. "Those chicks were damn lucky..." he continued, but was too absorbed in inspecting his weapon to end his statement coherently. I, too, was rendered incapable of speech, but mostly out of fear. I made up my mind then and there never to get this kid pissed at me – for any reason.

I am not what you'd call a gun person. It's not so much the gun I detest, but rather the frightful power guns lend to us weak-limbed, weak-minded creatures. And here Toby Jr., a weak-minded creature if ever there was one, had in his possession only the most powerful handgun ever created! He sternly forbade me, there in the storeroom, to reveal it's existence to anyone – above all his father, whom he assured me would drop dead of a heart attack the second he learned it was on the premises.

Toby needn't have worried. The way he was waving that gun at me, I wasn't about to tell nobody! Ironically, it was around this time that a grudging sort of friendship between the two of us began to take hold. Despite this "tentative camaraderie," the image of that loaded .44 Magnum hovered above my head like the proverbial Sword of Damocles. I might have been the closest thing to a friend Toby Jr. possessed at the time, but I saw the dude for what he was: a dangerous, unpredictable maniac, capable – indeed, *more* than capable – of firing a gun off whilst under duress.

The disturbing introduction to Toby Jr.'s firearm was hardly enough to eclipse the news of Radiance's arrival. I doubt that the announcement of World War III could have taken precedence! I was obviously madly in love with this girl, a fact made even more apparent when, for the first time, I found myself contemplating in earnest such horrifying concepts as marriage, little cottages with white picket fences, and babies.

To accompany the good in life, there is invariably some degree of bad, and it was certainly true in this case, wherein "bad" was exemplified by the unwelcome swelling of our ranks with Allie and Glenda. The ensuing week was a nightmare of me repeatedly banging my head against the wall in my attempts to teach them what I'd always assumed were elementary skills: cooking, cleaning, order taking, sweeping…By week's end I was convinced – convinced that between Allie, Glenda, and Radiance, there was not one fully functional brain. As I remarked to Harvey, only partly in jest, after a particularly frustrating training session, "I'd have an easier time of it training chimps to do the work. Were we that stupid as teenagers?"

"It's the parents' fault," Harvey offered. "All that acid they dropped in the sixties mutated their kids somehow."

It seemed as plausible an explanation as any.

I tried to be forgiving of my feeble-minded young charges, especially Radiance, and I never scolded, never lost my temper. I came close, when I discovered that Glenda had used tile cleanser to polish the windows. Or when I found Allie watering the flowers out front – a commendable undertaking to be certain, but all the flowers in Timothy's were made of plastic.

Clearly, the girls had forgotten everything they had learned the first day. What I had originally intended as a two-hour "refresher course" was of necessity lengthened to ten hours. I found myself coming in at the crack of dawn each morning to work with these ridiculous employees, who were by no means ready to be foisted on an unsuspecting public. Needless to say, I wasn't getting a whole lot of sleep, and it taxed me cruelly.

In all honesty, I should have fired Radiance. She was a very poor worker. Luckily for me, she did improve somewhat, but only after an absurd amount of patient, loving instruction on my part (which, it must be said, I was only too happy to provide).

Of Glenda and Allie, who as workers were scarcely better than Radiance, I was also exceedingly tolerant, though I disliked them from the outset. At least Radiance tried; these two were bone headed, bone lazy, and, I'm sad to say, forerunners of a whole new breed of crappy Timothy's employee.

I had another problem with Radiance, of a more personal nature. I never wanted to leave her side. When she called me, I responded, no matter how trivial her request. And, indeed, the most trivial things could prove distressing to this shy, simple, wonderful girl.

She appealed to all five of my senses; she even smelled fantastic! Sometimes, alone in the staff room, I'd literally bury my head in articles of her clothing, allowing the heavenly scent, more potent than any drug, to engulf me for a few moments. Had anyone inadvertently have walked in on me, it would have been humiliating to say the least.

Incidentally, the only girl to wear one of our ridiculous uniforms and actually have it flatter her, was Radiance. Glenda was laugh provoking in hers, and Allie resembled nothing so much as a gargantuan, orange beach ball.

Radiance, however, (whose sexy curves could have transformed a potato sack into high fashion) looked as stunning as ever in those tight, tight orange pants, and the conical cap made her seem not like a simpleton but like a medieval duchess, or countess, or lady of similar aristocratic bearing.

Unfortunately, there were a couple of drawbacks to my ideal woman, that even I in my blindness could not help but sit up and take note of. First off, she was a mere fifteen years of age. Secondly, she did not appear to share, to any appreciable degree, the towering passion that so enveloped me every time I looked her way.

My obsessive love for the girl was quite beyond the comprehension of Toby Jr. "For Chrissakes, the chick's marginally retarded!" he'd repeat endlessly, and it was a statement I found difficult to dispute.

If the addition of Cinderella and her ugly stepsisters to our ranks affected business at all, it was for the better. So crazy were things that May, I was positive we'd reached a zenith in terms of customer sales.

I had no idea.

The days lengthened, the line-ups lengthened, tempers flared, temperatures flared, and around mid June I began to suffer from recurring nightmares.

One of them started out pleasantly enough. I was bounding across a luxuriant vale in ancient Greece, wearing only sandals and a skimpy tunic. The sky was a type of acute blue seldom seen in these smog-ridden times, and the air was sweet with the scent of violets, daffodils, and the lovely narcissus. Oh, what a blessed, enchanted age!

I observed a sparse herd of cattle painstakingly ascending a nearby slope – in search of more abundant pastures, presumably – but no people. Nevertheless, I had such a feeling of worth and purpose, as though immediately before me lay a celebrated goal awaiting fulfillment, or some sort of perilous mission to be undertaken. The gods themselves seemed to be directing my flight, as I had not the slightest clue where I was or where I was headed. This total unfamiliarity with my surroundings spoke volumes; I was no longer Carl, the harried fry cook of Timothy's, I was somebody else entirely…

My new persona appeared vested with near limitless power, and as I tore across the valley floor I threw back my head and let forth a lusty cry, rejoicing in the sheer euphoria of it all.

I may not have been myself, but my new-found sense of confidence and outrageous physical strength left little doubt as to my true identity: Hercules! This realization led to others, and before long I was able to piece together just what had taken place.

I had undergone a metamorphosis possible only in the mysterious twilight zone of the subconscious, having somehow been transformed into my foremost mythological idol – Hercules, the invincible. I seemed to know instinctively that, of his fabled twelve labors, this dream had mostly to do with the eleventh, the daring seizure of the Golden Apples of the Hesperides.

To get within striking distance of the prize in question, it would be necessary to procure the service of Atlas, the Titan, he whom vengeful Zeus had condemned to bear forever upon his massive shoulders no less a burden than the entire universe. Atlas had sired the Hesperides, and was therefore one of the select few who knew the location of Hera's coveted apples.

To reach him, however, meant a long journey southward, and that is where my dream, seemingly already in progress, had actually begun. Being Hercules, I performed many valiant deeds en route, and was amply rewarded by appreciative kings and buxom princesses. But the journey was both lengthy and grueling, even for the legendary strongman I had become, and I did not notice Atlas until I was quite literally upon him, having inadvertently stumbled over his immense left foot.

I gaped with awe upon the colossus. In order to view him in his entirety, I was obliged to lie flat on my back on the ground. Peering upward, I was struck immediately by the big guy's extraordinary attire. He was swaddled tightly in garish, sweat-soaked bolts of orange cloth. His huge chest was heaving furiously, and I felt such pity for the poor, dumb brute and his grievous lot in life.

But then I saw his face. And I, glorious hero that I was, commenced trembling like a small boy who'd just been told a frightening tale. My instinct was to run far away, but my feet were rooted to the spot. I simply could not tear my eyes from that horrid, ghastly face.

It was my own, you see. Prematurely wrinkled, marked by extreme suffering, but unmistakably the face of Carl Fellows. A Timothy's cap the size of a Volkswagen had been unceremoniously plopped on my giant head, and it was not the firmament I bore up but a humongous facsimile of Timothy's Take-Out, lit up like a Christmas tree in the dusky sky.

I fell to my knees, sobbing, at this shocking scene. For the first time ever, mighty Hercules was overcome!

I would never fail to awaken at this precise point, balled up like a fetus in my bed, tears streaming down my cheeks. I was subjected to this strange dream no fewer than four times that summer alone.

I was plagued by another horrifying nightmare, influenced, no doubt, by the demonic pursuits of the Rowdies. I refuse to elaborate on this one, but if you've ever had the sensation of being imprisoned in your bed, terrified to the point where you were incapable of the slightest sound or movement, you know where I'm coming from. Whew! It's freakin' me out as we speak!

Worst of all, I think, was the less-dramatic-but-no-less-unnerving dream of being caught up in some monstrous lunch rush, to which there was no foreseeable denouement. What food I'd prepare would invariably go out wrong and have to be redone; customers waiting to order would join customers waiting for food in unbearable, high decibel shrieking for service. On these occasions I'd actually be serving people and making change in my sleep, waking up flabbergasted (but at the same time intensely relieved) to find it had all been a nightmare. I would then proceed to work, where, of course, an identical scene would be played out – only this time for real.

A situation that never should have existed outside a body's worst nightmare was rapidly developing at Timothy's, and it had to do with that bane of my existence, The Nightly Clean Up. At first, as was my policy, I simply stuck to my allotted portion of the work, paying scant heed to the half-assed efforts of the others so long as my own work was sparkling. Far from being congratulated for my efforts, I would find, tacked to the bulletin board next day, a seven page critical essay castigating not those directly responsible for the disgraceful job but my own damn self for having allowed it to suffice. (I *was* the manager, after all.) The authoress of the detailed dissertations? Margaret, who generally worked mornings, and apparently found no greater pleasure in life than deliberately fucking me over.

I tried to improve the staff's pitiable cleaning skills, but it was hopeless. What the task demanded above all else was the expenditure of some pretty hard work, of which they were incapable. Once again The Superhero and I proved to be the star performers, and the rest could be rated thusly on a rapidly deteriorating scale of shitty to abominably shitty: Margaret (whose Clean Ups didn't come close to matching the preposterous expectations she set for mine), Mr. Renwald, Allie, Radiance, Glenda, Rupert, and, finally, Toby Jr. The latter's cleaning ability was largely undetermined, since he tended to leave five minutes after closing time.

Vowing never again to be a recipient of one of Margaret's venomous notes, I began to spend increasingly long periods of time in the store after close, scrutinizing the Clean Up of the others with a jaundiced eye, often redoing it completely. "Fuck the staff," I'd mutter, my fierce independent streak rising to the fore. "I'll do everything myself!" And so it was, essentially.

My methodical approach proved time consuming and laborious, but I found slogging my way through a late night Clean Up infinitely preferable to being in the front lines, serving obnoxious customers. What sucked was how my sleeping hours were impacted. (If you recall, they'd already been decimated by early morning workouts, nightmares, and the like.) In addition, Margaret continued to post her charming notes, the accusations within growing more ludicrous with each passing day. Obviously they were inspired more by her immense hatred toward me than by anything I may have forgotten to clean, for by that time I was forgetting *nothing*.

* * *

Sometime in mid-June, the staff learned of a swimming competition between some of the local businesses, and entered at Renwald's insistence. As I could have predicted, nobody at Timothy's had the slightest interest in participating. I was no exception (it did, after all, infringe upon one of my all-too-infrequent days off), but the thought of Radiance in a bikini was enough to ensure my presence at the event.

Some of the others were not so obliging, but Renwald was adamant – the competition was an annual one, held on the beach, and apparently Timothy's had always been represented in one form or another (although according to Toby Jr. they had never once made it beyond the beginning round of the round robin styled "tournament"). The contest itself varied: the year before it had been bowling, before that, tug-of-war, but this time out it was a swimming race.

Clearly, the silly thing meant a lot to the competitive Mr. Renwald, and so it became my desire as well to garner at least a respectable placement. But how in God's name was this to be accomplished when our "athletes" included an eighty-year-old man, a three hundred pound leviathan, and various other flabby competitors (like Glenda and Toby Jr.)? I could only hope the Superhero's artistry extended into the world of sports.

At an impromptu meeting staged early one afternoon at Timothy's – when most of the staff happened to be on the premises – Renwald enlightened us further.

"We will meet on the beach at six-forty-five a.m. Saturday morning," he pronounced, "and all will be required to wear the compulsory Timothy's uniform over their swimming trunks."

A chorus of groans and gagging noises arose from the captive audience.

"You'll wear your uniforms and wear them with pride!" he reiterated heatedly.

"Land sakes, Tobias!" Rupert blurted suddenly, much to everyone's amazement. "Nobody else at these contests gets gussied up –"

"I have made my decision," Renwald interjected, cutting off Rupert as though he were an impertinent child.

* * *

Saturday, six forty-five a.m. Decked out in full Timothy's regalia, and feeling about as self-conscious as it was possible to feel, I made my way fearfully toward the largish gathering on the beach. As far as I could make out, none of my "teammates" had arrived yet. What was worse, virtually everybody present was dressed either in regular street attire or swimwear. When I spotted a triangular, orange-coloured cap bobbing about in their midst, I hurried gratefully over. It was Glenda.

"Hi, Glen," I murmured good-naturedly.

She made a soft kind of grunting sound, and turned away from me. Resisting the impulse to slap her fat little face, I looked around to see if any more of our gang was approaching, from anywhere. Thankfully, the somewhat more articulate duo of Renwald and son had located us and were heading over.

I wasn't thankful for long. Mr. Renwald, for some inane reason, felt the pressing need to align us into single file formation, shortest employee to tallest. The only discernable advantage to his humiliating gesture was the fact that Radiance would be in front of me, affording me a hopefully unobstructed view of her "bod," as she peeled out of her uniform. My heart leapt with excitement.

Soon everybody was present and accounted for, with the glaring exceptions of Radiance and Allie. And what a ridiculous sight we were! Try to picture it: groups of attractive, contemporary, casually dressed young people, chatting gaily and freely among themselves, just generally having a good time. Then, off to one side, the Timothy's Take-Out morons: orange flood pants, orange t-shirts, orange dunce caps, all in a row, geek upon geek, our grim faces positively burning with resentment and shame.

A portly fellow, clipboard in hand, strode to a makeshift microphone stand. I scanned the beach for any sign of Radiance, amazed at how many people were now on the scene. (I was unaware that the event had become, in the eyes of residents and tourists alike, practically a ceremonial ushering-in of summer.) Suddenly, out of one of the numerous vehicles parked so haphazardly along the side of the road, there clambered Radiance, big Allie, and what I assumed were the latter's parents, if heredity had indeed played a role in Allie's proclivity to stoutness.

That they had no difficulty in finding us was probably due as much to our bright orange color as to the fact that I was jumping up and down while gesticulating wildly, like one marooned on a desert island.

The chubby guy at the mike started into his spiel about the prestigious nature of the contest, its distinguished history, the fine showing that year, etc., etc., clearly reveling in the fifteen minutes of fame he'd been graciously allotted. He insisted on reiterating rules with which we were all quite familiar and which were, in reality, simple as pie.

There were three buoys floating a reasonable distance from shore. Three of the eighteen teams present were to line up at a starting point in the sand, and then race out, in relay fashion, to the buoys and back. The team to finish first would then be pitted against one of the victors from the other five races, and so it would continue until eventually an over-all winner emerged. The teams were to be restricted to eight competitors, so Mr. Renwald graciously bowed out of ours (although he'd had plenty of offers from amongst our reluctant ranks to do the same.)

And then came the great unveiling. Watching Radiance strip was the most titillating experience of my young life. In my wildest fantasies I hadn't dared imagine this moment. As I removed my own orangey vestments, I prayed my "fervor" would not be too much in evidence!

True to form, Rupert provided some priceless comic relief with his wacky, turn-of-the-century bathing trunks. Glenda, Allie, and Toby Jr. flaunted their lumpy bodies with probably the least amount of modesty and tact, although I was hardly one to stand in judgement, overweight as I was at the time. (I couldn't help it; I was too damn crazy about food to diet, and only my consistent workouts kept my chest larger in circumference than my very flabby midsection.)

The Superhero and Margaret looked surprisingly sleek and fit, but it was Radiance's Marilyn Monroe-ish figure and baby face that stole the show so far as I was concerned. She might not have stuffed into the skimpy bikini of my fantasies, but her plunging one-piece met with my complete and unadulterated approval.

The day was cool and overcast, hardly ideal for a swimming race, and the water was ice cold. As luck would have it (I am being utterly sarcastic here), we were among the three teams selected to race first. Our competitors were the "Smarmy's" team (a rival fast food joint a few blocks from Timothy's) and the local Brewer's Retail (a popular site in any town). Talk about taking the contest seriously, the latter actually wore matching bathing suits.

The first three swimmers took their marks in the sand. Little Glenda, while not quite the shortest employee we had, was first for our team nonetheless. (Rupert was shorter but Renwald understandably chose not to lead off with him!) One toot from the chubby guy's whistle and they were off. Glenda made it as far as the water, appeared to recoil from something half-submerged at her feet, and commenced screaming hysterically.

Groups of people nearest Glenda hastened to her side, and Chubbo summoned back the other two swimmers with frantic blasts from his whistle. Before long, Glenda was surrounded by inquisitive onlookers.

"It looks like a fish," someone said.

My own curiosity piqued, I too became part of the burgeoning throng, and discovered firsthand the source of her revulsion.

It was indeed a fish – a big, ugly, *dead* fish!

This unfortunate creature, probably a trout, looked to have met its fate at the hands (fins?) of an even bigger and uglier fish, for it was utterly mangled. The head was just barely intact, and the eyes had been lost to swarms of voracious water bugs. (The ghoulish little critters had since moved "downstairs" and were now dining on the soft underbelly.)

Even I began to feel nauseous after a particularly resourceful spectator impaled the fish on a small branch, and cast it into a cluster of rushes.

Meanwhile, Glenda's racking sobs had finally subsided. When she agreed to resume the race, the crowd applauded as though she were an injured football player being carried off the gridiron.

But the damage had been done. When she reached the water a second time, rather than barrel right in in the manner of her two competitors, she pranced and high-stepped around the spot where the fish had been as if picking her way through a mine field. Thus, almost from the outset, we found ourselves pretty much enmeshed in the last place position.

And Rupert's zig zagging dog paddle, while commendable for an eighty-year-old man, in this contest served only to extend the already boundless gulf between second place and the Timothy's team. Radiance and Margaret did give a good account of themselves, and watching Radiance arise from the waves did conjure up visions of Venus on the Half Shell, but their efforts were all but nullified by Toby Jr., who swam with the alacrity of a dying slug.

It was up to the Superhero and myself, then, to somehow resurrect the fallen Timothy's team. The role was not new to us. Being shorter in stature I was next up after Toby Jr. – that is, assuming he ever returned from his leisurely swim. As I waited, I engaged in the same rigorous warm-up routine I preceded my weight lifting marathons with, doing everything but sprouting fins and scales in an attempt to "get psyched." And when at last Toby Jr. came limping in, I was away.

I have always been a strong swimmer, with endurance rather than speed being my forte. But damned if I wasn't flying now! My form was impeccable as I reached out for the buoy, touched it, then came streaking back to shore, stumpy limbs a-pumpin'. Regrettably, the term "streaking" is only too appropriate when describing the latter portion of my flight.

I knew I shouldn't have worn those baggy, voluminous bathing trunks. There hadn't been any appreciable elasticity in the waistband for about two years. Given the torpedo-like velocity of my breaststroke, I suppose what happened next was inevitable.

My form may have been impeccable, but it was also completely exposed as I launched into a final, high-powered drive towards shore. I'd practically scrambled up onto the sand before having realized I was stark naked! Quicker than you can imagine I was back in a foot or so of water, crying out for my work pants.

The mental miniatures on my team were either not able to fathom my request for trousers at such a time, or simply did not hear me howling. And so, much to my embarrassment, I was forced to exclaim, for all to hear,

"Because I lost my swimsuit somewhere around the buoy!"

I felt like drowning myself amidst the ensuing laughter and applause. My orange pants were finally tossed out to me, but already precious seconds had been lost before our next competitor – the Superhero – was able to "take to the lake."

But take to the lake he did, drawing gasps of amazement from spectators and competitors alike with his measured, powerful strokes. Of a more streamlined build than I, he was that much faster in the water. Using this distraction to my advantage, I slipped back in line, back in amongst my fellow orangies. My efforts to evaporate met with failure, however, when the Superhero arose from the surf twirling my bathing suit around his index finger.

Thanks to David's glorious run we still had a chance – if our clean-up swimmer was Mark Spitz. As it was, that position went to the largest and heaviest of our crew: Allie. She swam at an excruciatingly slow pace and blew our "lead," but I was just astounded she was able to remain buoyant. I had half-expected her to sink like a stone.

The Smarmy's team had no trouble defeating us, but in turn we handily defeated Brewer's Retail. In this contest within a contest, however, second place did not cut it, as only the winner would be advancing further. Renwald, clearly disappointed by our early elimination, forbade us to break rank until an overall winner was declared, despite this being possibly the least significant event in sporting history.

I spent most of the time gazing dreamily at Radiance, who was still before me in line, and every bit as mesmerizing when viewed from the rear.

Why was I acting this way? I had sworn off women at the world-weary age of nineteen, convinced that they would forever remain something of an unattainable luxury. I was just too damned ugly and shy to ever become a lothario like Harvey, and of necessity had diverted my energies toward a more realistic goal: the amassing of great wealth and fame.

Great wealth and fame? Yeah, right!

But I was nothing if not a diehard fighter when the chips were down. I managed to convince myself, as the contest wore on, that it was indeed within the realm of possibility to have both money in the bank and Radiance by my side. And not necessarily in that order!

Mercifully, the tedious affair laughingly referred to as "Ontario's Number One Sports Extravaganza" drew to a close sometime around eleven a.m. I can't even recall which team won, which gives you some idea how thrilling a competition it was. Even the gods seemed relieved when it was over; the threatening cloud cover withdrew immediately upon the crowd's dispersal, leaving in its wake a glowing and effervescent sun.

I had no sooner started for home than there arose from behind me a very familiar, very distinctive cackle. The irrepressible Harvey had apparently – and for the first time in recent memory – awoken before noon, and from the way he was alternately pointing at me and dropping to his knees in fits of spasmodic laughter, I gathered he'd been around to witness what would one day become known as "Carl's Nautical Nightmare."

"Good effort, good effort," he gasped, between otherwise indecipherable ejaculations.

"Give it a rest, Harv. All I want to do is get home, get outa this gay uniform, and relax."

"You must be kidding," he yipped, turning serious all of a sudden. "Look around you, man!"

Flocks of sun worshippers, a goodly portion young, nubile, and female, seemed to be advancing on us from all directions. Harv's demeanor had shifted accordingly. If there was one thing my happy-go-lucky friend took seriously, it was the pursuit of the fairer sex. He approached his craft with all the deadly intensity of a leopard stalking a springbok. If he did appear to be joking around with a chick, it was likely an utterly calculated joking around, intended only to bring about her capitulation.

Wordlessly, Harvey produced two pairs of very dark sunglasses, and we spent much of the day wandering up and down the beach like a couple of old perverts, lasciviously ogling the preponderance of jiggling womenflesh. Every so often, Harv would stop to chat up a couple of good looking prospects; on these occasions, I'd typically linger far behind, taking no part in the awkward, meandering tête-à-tête that formed the basis of his attack.

Still, it was a fascinating thing to observe the pick-up artist in his element.

Rejections that would have left me incapacitated for weeks Harv dismissed with total nonchalance, and for this I admired the little guy to no end. If he thought the dark sunglasses worked to conceal our lecherous intentions, however, he was mistaken. Our drooling tongues gave us away.

* * *

The Irish explorer Shackleton once described Antarctica's fearsome Beardmore Glacier as "the blackest, most horrible place on earth." Obviously, the man had never been to Timothy's. The stifling heat, non-existent breaks, and back-breaking "Clean Ups" were bad enough, but it was the human element – the simpering customers and staff members – that made it all quite beyond endurance.

I've unleashed enough tirades regarding the questionable mental capacity of our patrons, and in doing so have admittedly been chomping on the hands that fed me for two-and-a-half years, so I will now vent some of my wrath upon the nut jobs I had to work with.

If you'd gazed up at our lovely menu board anytime that year, and then had lowered that gaze just a tad, you likely would have encountered the "official" staff photo of 1981. Chances are the silly, pathetic looking figures peering out of that photo would have done much to alleviate your impatience with the slow service, or any feelings of discomfort induced by the oppressive heat. Who would not double over, convulsed, at the sight of Rupert, Toby Jr., a furiously scowling Margaret, and huge, stone faced Allie – all captured for posterity in the same photograph? It looked like a convention of freaks. I don't know what I was thinking as the shutter clicked, but I too was caught at my absolute worst. My heavily lidded eyes and protruding tongue had combined to give me a strange, mongoloid appearance.

The centerpiece of this gruesome picture? A fey, gossamer, fairy princess wearing the expression of one who'd inadvertently stepped into a den of ugly hobgoblins and was now condemned to wander forever in their midst.

With the exception of the Superhero (and possibly Radiance), our staffers had in common three most unflattering traits: selfishness, stupidity, and sloth. Each trait warrants exclusive consideration.

SLOTH: simply put, an unwillingness to work and a predilection to cut out when the going gets tough, this is the most glaring and overwhelming of the aforementioned "deadly sins." Of all the bullshit I was choking down at the time, covering the candy asses of my fellow employees was the most unpalatable. Like I didn't have my own damned burdens to worry about! We're talking here about pussies – of both sexes – who felt a solitary sniffle justified phoning in sick, or that a good television show was reason enough to skip out of a shift. And upon whose shoulders would their neglected workloads invariably fall? My own, of course.

Nowhere did sloth rear its ugly head with more regularity than in the nightly Clean Up. The turkeys I worked alongside tended to coast through Clean Up the same way they coasted through everything else in their lives. Because this particular work was to my liking, however, I was considerably less indignant at the prospect of making it a one-man-show than I was, say, the preparation of the food. (I was no Superhero, although by the same margin he was not the plow horse I was.)

SELFISHNESS: a big, ugly, debilitating disease, a true product of these godless times, and not even the Superhero was immune. Needless to say, most of the Timothy's crew was suffering through its advanced stages! And, dear me, at no time was pure, unadulterated selfishness more in evidence than two or three minutes following the posting of the weekly schedule.

One of the first rules I had attempted to establish upon arrival at Timothy's was in regard to sick days and time off. "You may have all the time off you wish," I declared, "provided you inform us at least a week and a half ahead of time. If you simply must have off a day you are already slated to work, you are then expected to find a replacement."

"Failure to comply," I added imperiously, "will result in, if not dismissal, then at least a drastic reduction in working hours."

I was justifiably proud of my little rule, as it was quite in keeping with my "ask no quarter, give no quarter" philosophy of life. I expected it to be obeyed as I myself would have obeyed it, which is to say, without question. (Personally, I did not even see the need for such a rule; what few days off I would require that year I arranged for weeks in advance.)

The butt-holes at Timothy's, however, with that ungodly talent of theirs for flipping everything upside-down and shredding to pieces every ostensible vestige of logic, transformed my decree into the most maligned, ridiculed, and otherwise abused since the time of Judge Roy Bean. And the preordained punishment for those who ditched work with neither warning nor provision – punishment I was only too willing to administer personally – was never administered, period. We couldn't afford to, as pitifully understaffed as we were that summer. Renwald and I just had to grin and bear gross infractions that no self-respecting establishment would tolerate for a second.

I needed a fucking computer to help me draw up the weekly schedule, although I doubt that one sophisticated enough existed on the face of the earth. I could easily envision a spanking new unit, worth millions, its sole function to create a serviceable work schedule for Timothy's Take-Out, Ltd., commence smoking, beeping, and convulsing with fury even upon its trial run, in its wretched attempt to cope with bushels full of demands for time off and myriad other "special considerations."

More selfish than our shithead employees were some of the *parents* of our shithead employees. It was easy to see where Glenda and Allie had acquired their revolting "laissez-faire" attitude. The parents did appear to be supportive of their daughters (indeed, the girls' 'decisions' to work had probably come at their insistence), but for some reason the girls were only permitted to work at the parents' convenience, and not when they were needed. Is it any wonder, then, that from such irresponsible, wholly undisciplined predecessors sprung "workers" the caliber of Glenda and Allie?

STUPIDITY: Even sweet Radiance had to come under fire sooner or later, and this is her category. I've accused her of neither selfishness nor sloth – not because I'm hopelessly biased where she is concerned, and not because I still carry a torch for her after all these years. Radiance always tried her hardest, and did the best she could with the limited faculties at her disposal. It took her hours to clean up at night, and often her work was no better than that of her bone-lazy co-workers. The one occasion she failed to show up for work was the result of a honest-to-goodness mix-up, and never was there a more tearfully apologetic employee afterward. Okay, so she was quite possibly the thickest kid I've ever attempted to train; the quality that placed her, in my opinion, among the top three employees at Timothy's was her amazing sincerity. And since she was summering at Allie's cottage, there were in her case no obnoxious parents to deal with (although, for the life of me, I just could not visualize the two people that brought this fragile creature into the world as being anything but wonderful).

I'm talking as if "Stupidity" was somehow confined to Radiance, when, in fact, very few at the store possessed an I.Q. much above ten. For example, while I retained a certain perverse respect for Mr. Renwald and his heartless, penny-pinching ways, the man was a complete oaf in the kitchen, and I dreaded the days I had to work alongside him. With that bellowing, blustering, highly-strung personality of his, it was possible for him to screw up food orders from behind his desk in the office! An aura of frenzied chaos surrounded him at all times, radiating its destructive energy in all directions.

Margaret's earthworm mentality was somewhat concealed by her abrasive, domineering character. Rupert, by way of comparison, wore his rapidly diminishing faculties on his sleeve. However you chose to look at them, one fact was beyond dispute: they were pretty sorry individuals.

The date was July 7. Mark it well. In one sense it was a typical July workday, fraught with irate customers, hair-raising emergencies, and incompetent staff members. Radiance and Glenda were the chefs that day (contributing to the word "inept" whole new dimension), while I was out front, fielding the inevitable complaints and dreaming up yet another excuse to approach my crush.

There was magnificence about Radiance quite beyond words. Several times that day patrons returned their charred burgers and skimpy portions of fries to the counter, demanding to speak with the "stupid dipshit cook," only to be confronted with a bashful, blushing, cow-eyed goddess. Radiance would make the most of her beautiful eyes as she stared, trembling, into those of her detractors. The customer who originally sought to castigate her would end up tenderly consoling her, and would exit the building beaming, but blind to the fact that he had been duped – however innocently – into accepting sub par food.

A tremendous downpour, not entirely unwelcome, all but halted the procession of customers into the store from about ten o'clock onward. Normal people might find torrential rain depressing, but we underlings at Timothy's positively revered it. Even the mighty Superhero would gratefully acknowledge the reprieve created by a severe thunderstorm, and of the many hilarious anecdotes told about Timothy's over the years, surely one of the most hysterical and oft repeated relates to the Superhero and his love of the wet stuff.

One particularly busy spring day, the tempo in back of the store was even more frenetic than usual (possibly due to the fact that there were only two of us working!) On perhaps my sixtieth dash to the walk-in cooler I just about ran down my co-worker, David "Superhero" Gardner, who – get this – was hopping about the kitchen, alternately raising and lowering his head, whilst emitting some of the strangest, most guttural sounds I've ever heard. If I hadn't known better, I would've sworn he was attempting some weird approximation of an Indian rain dance!

I think my just having seen him shook him up more than our near-collision, for he returned to his post immediately, his face red as a beet.

That ridiculous incident shed some new light on the Superhero as far as I was concerned. I'd formerly thought of him as a slightly deranged schizoid type, living out some confused, long-repressed fantasy, perhaps wrought from the Saturday morning cartoons of his boyhood. To see him skipping around the kitchen the way he did only strenghthened my conviction that he was mentally ill, but in his desire to see a rainstorm develop at least he was exhibiting more fundamentally human tendencies!

Forward to the evening of July seven. The sheets of rain that had brought business to such a standstill quickly escalated into a full-blown deluge to rival The Flood. Radiance and I were delighted, and I suppose Glenda was as well although it was difficult to tell with her. In any event, we were able to begin Clean Up a full hour earlier than expected, and that was reason enough to be in high spirits. But it was almost as if the restaurant, unaccustomed to such blatant displays of elation, felt a compelling urge to put things right...

By approximately ten thirty p.m. a host of vaguely familiar faces had assembled in the customer area, each identifiable by the small, inverted crosses in the respective left ears. Goddamned Robinson's Rowdies! I briefly considered running out back and imploring either Radiance or Glenda to serve them, but it was a little too late for that. I just prayed to God they had come for food and not my hide. After all, even devil worshipers get hungry now and then, do they not? I greeted them as I normally greeted those I dislike, by feigning incognizance.

"What'll you boys have?"

The fellow I'd long believed to be the group's ringleader stepped forward, casually gripped the edges of the counter, and smiled down at me.

"Your house, dear fellow. Your house."

If I had any illusions about my silly orange uniform serving to conceal my identity, they were quashed at that moment. "Guys," I pleaded, "I thought we'd been all through that."

The head Rowdy, patronizing smirk still etched upon his face, rotated his head a few degrees, and issued a silent command to one of his littermates behind him. It was rapidly becoming apparent that this was a set-up, and I blanched at the thought of having been trailed to work on at least one occasion by a Rowdy "scout."

Acting upon the head honcho's unspoken instruction, a big, fat, eunuch of a Rowdy hoisted a meaty leg high into the air – like a dog about to take a piss – then C-R-A-C-C-K!! He put it straight through one of the store's large, low-stationed store windows.

"Radiance, Glenda, call the cops!" I cried, and leapt over the counter like a Musketeer. I knew I stood an excellent chance of being killed, but I also knew I was more than capable of taking one of them to hell with me. And I didn't particularly care which one.

What followed was truly remarkable. Thank God there was no one else in the store. The first Rowdy I could get my hands on (a relatively inoffensive chap, compared to some of the others) I began to frenziedly stab with a small spike normally used to impale discarded order forms upon. Needless to say he began to squeal like a stuck pig, and the other eight-or-so Rowdies converged upon me at once.

Miraculously, perhaps because I was so much shorter than my accosters, I was actually able to inflict more punishment than I received. I bulled my way through the clumsy mob, swatting that wicked little spike back and forth, until finally I was seized by the leg and unceremoniously pitched through yet another store window. What I did next will always be (if only for myself) a source of great humiliation and shame.

Without so much as a thought for Radiance, Glenda, Renwald, or the day's take, and with no fewer than nine irascent Rowdies on my ass, I determined discretion to be the better part of valor and ran away into the night. Hercules would have stood and fought. Thor would have surely held his ground. And when finally I did reappear, after cowering for several minutes deep in the woods behind our store, I imagined I heard the mocking taunts of both heroes from somewhere far, far above.

CHAPTER SEVEN

The guys at Turners Gym were constantly after me to exchange my weights for boxing gloves. I was an avid fight fan, but my actual experience in the manly art of fisticuffs was limited, extending only to some half-hearted sparring sessions with the fellas, and the launching of imaginary hooks and uppercuts at the pros on TV.

What the hell was it those gym rats saw in me? I was short, squat, and slow-reflexed – as unlikely a boxing candidate as had ever straggled into that place. But I was growing weary of their persistent harping, and eventually a compromise was reached: I would fight *one* bout, but only if allowed to train for it with weights.

"But you'll get murdered!" a gangly, dark complexioned kid roared, and he proceeded to rattle off a slew of aerobic activities I might consider – not one of which held the slightest appeal for me whatsoever. It seemed that all the boxers present echoed his sentiments, but where my beloved weights were concerned I was adamant.

"Not to worry, guys, I'll adjust my workouts accordingly," I offered, by way of yet another of my patented compromises. "I'll get more into circuit training than strict powerlifting, and I'll do some work on the heavy bag. But my strength is really all I have."

They had no choice but to accept my radical training strategy, if they ever wanted to see me box.

I've wondered many times since then why I let 'em talk me into fighting, but it appears that I wanted it to happen (if only on a subconscious level) at least as much. That hideous July seven evening, so fresh in my mind, was likely the premiere catalyst.

Ah yes, July seven. I still recall creeping like some kind of frightened rodent back into the restaurant, after I was good and sure the Rowdies had departed. I remember being aghast at the sight of the shattered windows, and relieved at the sight of Glenda and Radiance huddled together in the storeroom/staff room out back. As I'd expected, neither had called the cops (the closest O.P.P detachment operated out of Port Radcliff), but at least Glenda had emptied the till. She'd done so whilst the Rowdies and I were engaged in our little game of tag out front.

Of course it was up to me to inform Renwald of the damage, and I think the worst part of the whole night was having to listen to him sob over the phone. I didn't much care for the man, but my heart went out to him in this instance. Nothing was more sacred, in my skewed opinion, than the relationship between an employee and his boss, and I alone had been responsible for bringing all this grief down upon his head. I was eventually able to square things somewhat by replacing, at my expense, one of his shattered (and uninsured) store windows. As damaging as this gesture was to my pocketbook, I think it did much to restore Renwald's shaky confidence in me.

* * *

I was spending every spare second in the gym, in preparation for my big fight. My decision to rely on weightlifting in lieu of more traditional training methods was hardly popular, but I was comfortable with it.

What I was considerably less enthused about was the prospect of shedding a dozen or so pounds in order to fight in the "light heavy" division. I had to take care not to sacrifice even the slightest smidgen of power in the process. Three months of mega-caloric Timothy Burgers (and other fat-laden Timothy's products) had bloated me to frightening proportions; the forthcoming weigh-in – by then a mere two weeks off – called for some especially drastic dieting measures on my part.

My pugilistic escapades notwithstanding, life plodded forward in routine fashion through the dog days of early July. The riotous goings-on at Timothy's, however, seemed to escalate in intensity every hour of my every shift. There were times I expected the whole damn store (which I never for a moment doubted was anything less than a living, breathing entity) to go completely off it's rocker, and either explode or implode spectacularly.

As always, the idiocy of our clientele proved a wonderment to behold. Never, ever, would I have believed that people could be so incredibly stupid. I'd had this crazy idea that man's intelligence was the one thing that distinguished him from the so-called baser life forms of the earth. Read on, friends, and see if you don't draw the same conclusions I have drawn.

Immense signs hanging from the ceiling divided the counter space at

Timothy's into two basic sections, and were about kindergarten-level in literacy: "Place Orders Here," and "Pick Up Orders Here." Many folks attempted to order from the latter section, of course, which I could live with. Their stupidity made me wince, but I could live with it. It was the JACKASSES hovering in the no-man's land in-between sections who really pissed me off. Perhaps they were attempting to project their orders telepathically???

The complexity of our menu boards appeared to overwhelm many people. They would gaze up at them with the most tortured expressions on their faces, as if the very act of placing an order was causing them physical pain. For some, the process proved to be too much altogether – their simple brain circuitry would overload and short out. They would exit the store empty handed, eyes glazed completely over, after having waited in line for as much as three quarters of an hour!

And then there were the deaf mutes. Any compassion I felt for these particular customers would evaporate the second one of 'em attempted to "mime out" an order. I don't care for being suddenly engaged in charades, especially with a roomful of strangers looking on! Truthfully, dear reader, if you were similarly afflicted, would you not carry a pad and pencil everywhere, thus eliminating completely the need for such embarrassing public displays? Likewise for those who have not learned the language, although in my experience a heavy Irish brogue can be as indecipherable as Swahili.

According to Toby Jr. every customer was a fucking asshole; I'll be a little more charitable and place the statistic at ninety-five per cent. Every once in a while I would stumble upon a fine human being amidst all the garbage, and so grateful would I be for the opportunity to serve one, it was sometimes all I could do to refrain from reaching over the counter and hugging him or her profusely.

To my surprise, I found this small but glittering percentage to be almost exclusively Oriental, and I take my hat off to these beautiful people now. They epitomized everything I'd ever aspired to with their polite, subservient bearing, and nose-to-the-grindstone approach to work. I stood in wholehearted awe of their alleged technological proclivity, as I had not a trace of it myself. And how could anyone rightly exclude from a list of Asian virtues those delectable females, with their straight black hair, skin like porcelain, and lovely, near-perfect features?

Usurping Harvey as my best buddy and semi-constant companion around this time was ugly, dumpy Toby Jr. Our first actual in-depth conversation was held after hours at Timothy's following the regrettable "Robinson's Rowdies" incident. Although I was somewhat taken aback at the topic of discussion – Adolph Hitler – Toby's declaration that the German dictator was his number one idol surprised me not at all.

Taking great pains not to offend my new-found friend, I concurred that Hitler was indeed a shrewd and resourceful fellow, whose rise from guttersnipe on the streets of Vienna to supreme warlord of much of Europe marked quite possibly the greatest human "power surge" of all time. Although this admission seemed to please Toby Jr., I realized that the discussion – if allowed to continue much longer – was going to degenerate into a very heated debate, if not fisticuffs. For Toby Jr., in my opinion, was just a little too quick to write off Hitler's barbaric slaughter of those he considered his inferiors. Also, Toby was unable to validate to my satisfaction Hitler's blunder of waging a three-front war when he did.

Nevertheless, some affinity between the two of us must have existed, because the next evening we found ourselves at Robinson's Rodeo, checking out the strippers. (I made damn sure they were female this time, having no desire to walk in on "Ramrod Randy" and company again.)

I may have had little use for the regular bars, but strip joints were another matter entirely. Although I will probably never find it within myself to respect a girl who peels down to nothing before hoards of sexual deviates two and three times her age, well...if she insists on removing her clothes in public, you can bet I'm going to watch, too. Viva la difference!

On this particular occasion, however, Toby Jr. and I sat well back from the stage, engaged in some lively conversation regarding – of all things – the Rowdies' recent attack on the store. Toby was unveiling some pretty astonishing bits of info.

"From your description of these guys, C.F., you're talking about the rovin' gang of devil worshipers that's been terrorizin' this community for ages."

I took another pull on my beer and sat back, intrigued. I'd not mentioned the Rowdies' attempts on my house to anyone, considering them my own personal business. But I was determined to extract as much information as I could from the unwitting Toby.

"Farmers from all over the place report animals missin'," he continued, "and later the carcasses turn up in the damndest locations, drained completely of blood. People are safe enough, especially in the summer when there's so many of 'em, but more than one's reported getting' waylaid in the middle of the night and practically beaten to death by a group of big, big dudes."

I was staring fixedly at Toby Jr.'s ugly face, which the dimness of the light did precious little to obscure. His long, thick hair stuck out of his head at the wackiest angles, and his numerous pustules and blackheads oozed and popped like a chain of active volcanoes. "What about the cops, Toby?" I inquired. "Surely they've been on the gang's ass – "

"The cops?" he snorted. "What did the cops do when they finally showed up at the restaurant? Nothin'! No one knows where the gang comes from, man! It's freakin' mysterious! They did manage to haul one of the bastards into the station once, but the others sprung him like it was the Wild West or somethin'! Anyway, the whole thing is played right down. No one wants to alarm the tourists."

At this point, a gorgeous, semi-clad stripper on her way to the stage eased herself provocatively around our little table, commanding for a few seconds our complete and undivided attention.

"You know," Toby remarked, after she had passed, "I only wish you woulda had Jeremy with you the night those fags showed up. Now there's an animal that can kick some ass!"

As concentration was rapidly becoming a problem, we dispensed with the chit chat and made for "Pervert's Row," (that ring of chairs immediately surrounding the stage) and the remainder of the evening was devoted to the obvious, and obviously displayed, charms of the girls. An unexpected highlight came in the rotund form of an intoxicated gentleman a few seats down from us, who had apparently resolved to "possess" one of the girls stripping that night.

The object of his affections was seated on a chair in the middle of the stage, slathering skin lotion all over her body. As our overheated hero undid his fly and scrambled up onto the apron, the bottle of lotion slipped from the hand of the suddenly terrified performer. The resultant, rapidly expanding pool of cream on the stage floor proved too formidable an impediment for the tubby fellow, and he slid right off his feet. By then two immense doormen had ascended the stage from either side, but they too lost their footing in the gunk, upending both the girl and her chair in the process. The entire party careened into the laps of several front row patrons, to the delight of virtually everybody in attendance. Toby in particular practically split his sides laughing, but I was not so much affected. The whole affair just too closely resembled my waltz with the Rowdies a few nights previous!

Lying in bed that evening, I thought of Toby Jr., and how his remarks about Robinson's Rowdies seemed to be tinged with grudging admiration. The evil little bastard certainly possessed all the qualifications to be a Rowdy himself, except overt size. Like his idol before him, Toby struck me as a guy whom even his closest confidants would be fools to trust. I hung around with him primarily for the prestige of having two whole friends (although to see Harvey and I together during that period, you'd never have believed we were anything but the most casual of acquaintances.)

The absolute bane of my existence continued to be the store itself. Working in it, as I alluded to earlier, was a little like taking an active, conscious part in your worst nightmare.

Timothy's was on shaky ground, literally, as it had been constructed upon a spongy, putrid amalgamation of swampland and garbage dump. So badly did the rear half of the building list, it was forever threatening – just like California – to break apart and slide away.

Every once in a while the great fryers would boil over like Vesuvius, coughing up not only scalding hot cooking oil, but remnants of burnt fries, long-dead fish fillet corpses, and the like. On these occasions, no matter how busy the restaurant was, our customers would be all but forgotten in the mad dash for cover.

Because the oppressive summer heat had a tendency to thaw 'em out, our uncooked onion rings required more than mere frying; the bloody things had to be *nursemaided* to completion, lest they permanently adhere to each other in the hot grease.

From the drain in the kitchen sink, there arose a stench like a decomposing body.

Containers of food would be delivered with lids so tight you needed explosives to get them off.

You get the picture.

In addition to the everyday occurrences listed above, something bizarre was going on with respect to the nightly Clean Up. Normally, I worked nights and Margaret the supervisor days, an arrangement I found, for the most part, acceptable. Yet even during the relative serenity of Clean Up her waspish influence could be felt. To put it bluntly, I worked like a fucking slave to please that woman, having transformed what should have been a straightforward janitorial ritual into a three hour orgy of blood, sweat and tears, all in a futile attempt to stop her notes from coming.

Yet come they did, these notes, with disturbing regularity, lambasting me for the most outrageous faux-pas imaginable, and it was when they ceased having anything to do with reality altogether that I decided to confront the miserable bitch.

I *decided* to confront her. I didn't actually get around to it...

As if to compensate for my spinelessness, I continued, doggedly, to put heart, soul and gonads into the hallowed Clean Ups. I'd become something of a classical music aficionado, and the restaurant would reverberate to the thundering overtures of Wagner and Rossini as I wearily went about my business.

The real horror of Timothy's was not all this mundane, day-to-day crap, but rather what the crap was doing to me as a human being. It was almost as if the store was destroying every last vestige of commiseration and human decency I had remaining, in an unholy attempt to turn me into another of its machines! But therein lay my chief merit to Renwald, I suppose. I was a machine that *never* broke down.

So utterly disgusted had I grown with my fellow beings, all I really wanted to do on my days off was to get away from them. Fortunately for me, there was no lovelier retreat than Robinson's Pt. in the summertime.

The only thing benefiting from all this negativity was my weight training. Not only did the prospect of my first boxing match seem to ignite a fire within me, so did my hatred for the "good people" of Robinson's Pt., a community whose ratio of assholes per square foot rose to unprecedented levels in the summer months.

At Turner's, I was shocked to find my fellow pugilists wagering on the outcome of my battle-to-be as if it were the Fight of the Century, particularly since knowledge of my opponent was sketchy at best. All we knew for sure was that he hailed from Kingcardine (where the fight was to be held), boasted a very respectable record (9-0-2), and was quite tall (six foot one inch.)

As to whether I'd get flattened a few seconds into Round One or survive an initial shellacking to provide a respectable challenge to my opponent, the camp was divided. They were betting on how long I'd last, not on the possibility that I might win. As far as they were concerned, that possibility did not exist!

The interest generated by my impending boxing debut was likely due to my image at Turner's as a solitary, somewhat eccentric strongman, of whom not much was known. I was viewed as a guinea pig of sorts in a fascinating experiment – the pitting of a raw brute with zero experience against a seasoned competitor, six of whose nine victories had come by way of knockout.

Six days before The Test, I was feeling fine, and loving every minute of the attention. It hardly mattered that many of my associates were anticipating a lopsided slaughter – I believed I could win. But an analysis of my fighting ability, conducted by no less of a boxing luminary that Mr. Joe Turner himself, was anything but encouraging.

The crusty old goat minced no words. I was far too heavy for my height, and had an embarrassingly puny reach. I was short-winded as fighters go, and totally bereft of grace. He was very concerned about my eyesight as well. I had to remove my gas-permeable contacts in order to box, and without 'em I was about as myopic as it was possible to be.

Turner wasn't alone in his assessment. His scathing report seemed to be the general consensus, and, remember, we're talking about the guys who'd goaded me into this in the first place!

Had they taken the time to observe a few of my sparring matches, they might have been a little less hasty to criticize. Did they think I was blind to the fact that I had no experience? It was *because* I had none that I chose only those sparring partners who would look upon our practice bouts as being real and pull no punches. And I've gotta say, in each bout I managed to hold my own.

So quick was the gang at Turner's to pass judgment on my limitations, they failed to acknowledge that I might actually have had a few strong points. True, I was about as flexible and maneuverable inside the ring as a Sherman tank, but I was also capable of blasting people away like one. I had a great chin, tremendous willpower, and, perhaps most importantly, confidence in myself.

I must have looked like a pretty ridiculous light heavyweight, however. (Technically, I didn't even qualify as one; as late as four days before the fight I was still too fat.) By no stretch of anyone's imagination would my incongruous physique lend itself well to a ten round slugfest. I had great strapping shoulders, a barrel chest, fat stomach, and toothpick legs! Worst of all was my dwarfish stature: five foot, six inches. I would be facing a giant by comparison.

The day immediately preceding my fight was memorable only for its embarrassing moments. I woke up cursing the bright sunlight, such a loathsome enemy on the days I had to work. My shift was ten-to-eight that day – my workmates, Toby Jr. and Allie. The writing was on the wall.

It began promisingly enough. I arrived to find Toby Jr. seated in the kitchen devouring a triple-pattied Timothy Burger, big Jeremy at his side. Allie was at the sink washing dishes, and the aroma of Toby's little snack was obviously getting to her.

"That smells so-o-o good," she whimpered, trying hard to concentrate on her dirty saucepans.

I caught Toby Jr.'s eye, and could not help but notice its malevolent glint. I watched as Timothy's heir apparent tore a small chunk from his burger and then leapt dramatically up onto his chair. The sudden movement brought Jeremy to his feet also, and when Toby commenced waving the morsel of food in a circular fashion, his pet responded in kind, twirling like a hirsute Barishnykov. Toby tossed the scrap into Jeremy's mouth.

"Allie, do you want a piece?"

Allie turned to face her tormentor, who was still up on the chair, dangling more of his meat. Her eyes begged him to cease and desist, but the subtle attempt at communication was lost on Tobes.

"Just two little spins, sweetheart, and the remainder of this delectable burger is yours. Jeremy, STAY!"

The animal, having none of Allie's issues with self-respect and self-control, was more than willing to dance for a second piece. But damned if big Jeremy wasn't unceremoniously shoved aside by even bigger Allie, who advanced upon Toby Jr. with mouth agape, like a giant flounder. She put Toby's mutt to shame with her acrobatic spins, and then ravenously bolted her prize.

It was Allie's day to be humiliated. About one-thirty that afternoon she had me dashing out front like Carl Lewis in response to her shattering screeches. "What's wrong?" I asked breathlessly, more annoyed at her indiscretion than concerned about her welfare. Her response was to fling herself upon me and sob; I felt as though I were slow dancing with an elephant seal.

The source of her trauma was typically absurd. A woman with a small, swaddling bundle in her arms had approached the counter to order a hot dog and coffee. Allie had peered curiously into the bundle, no doubt expecting to see the pink, wrinkled face of an infant. What she did see was the dark, wrinkled face of a Capuchin monkey, and the critter immediately made a grab for her bulbous excuse for a nose.

I've no doubt it was a startling encounter, but did it really warrant Allie's hysterical display? In any event, we did have fun afterwards, feeding the simian sprite tiny portions of banana and pear, all the while marveling at its amazingly dexterous little fingers.

On days like these – when the sun bore down with such merciless intensity

– keeping the restaurant doors propped open was absolutely essential if we wanted to keep breathing, and the occasional breeze to drift our way was considered a gift from God. Less desirable things would blow in too, of course, and I'm not just referring to customers.

The store became a haven for every conceivable variety of insect. Clouds of fruit flies hovered over anything sweet, clouds of mosquitoes hovered over anything human, and houseflies were pretty much all over the place. In the summer months, emptying the parking lot garbage cans was a terrifying experience due to the hundreds of wasps that called them home.

It wasn't enough that they found their way into every human orifice; many species seemed to derive no greater enjoyment out of life than burrowing into people's food, or splashing about in their soft drinks. A word to you budding entomologists: If you wish to rock the scientific community with a profound new discovery, just hang around Timothy's for a few days. You'll find what you're looking for eventually. Incidentally, a favorite past time of Glenda's (when in one of her "upbeat" moods) involved killing unwary flies with one of our large spatulas, and gleefully announcing to anyone within earshot the latest grisly tally.

On the day before my fight, Toby Jr. was suffering through the final stages of a heavy cold, and the store echoed to the sound of his intermittent sneezes. (A classic illustration of his idiosyncratic sense of humor would be for him to saunter up to a hamburger I was so carefully garnishing, stare at it dizzily, and then deliberately and maliciously sneeze all over it.) I was understandably terrified of catching his bug, since in less than twenty-four hours I would be in the freakin' ring throwing punches.

Afraid of delivering a piss-poor performance, I had told no one of the bout, not even Harvey. If I was to fuck up, I determined, better to do so in the company of strangers! But the fight did provide me with plenty to think about while at work, and you need plenty to think about putting in the kind of hours I did, otherwise you go mad.

I resorted to much mental meandering in order to slog through my shifts with faculties intact. I often envisioned myself as a Negro slave in the Deep South, shackled to the grill, forced to cook for the white folk. The sorry plight of these original African Americans had long been a source of inspiration to me, and frequently while cooking I would spontaneously burst into a few choruses of "Darlin' Cora," "Sylvie," "John Henry," or some lovely spiritual.

Bring me little water, Sylvie
Bring me little water, now
Bring me little water, Sylvie
Every little once in a while
© Huddie Ledbetter, Paul Campbell

It goes without saying that I also fantasized about Radiance. The prospect of asking her for a date might have unnerved me, but I was able to derive considerable gratification out of merely imagining what the date would be like.

And then there was my dream about being rich. Believe it or not, it was a dream I was making some effort to pursue. I had a great many interests outside of work, which one by one I was endeavoring to transform into big bucks.

Where were we? Ah yes, the eve of my boxing match. My grueling shift might have come to an end, but the day itself was far from over. I was under more stress than ever back at the beach house. In my attempts to persuade an indifferent Harvey to loan me the car the following evening, I had come dangerously close to bursting some blood vessels. Only when I casually (and untruthfully) mentioned that I might have a "hot date" did the tide begin to turn on my behalf.

"You got a date, Carl? A date? You got yourself a date?"

"Is it that hard to believe?" I asked wryly.

From that point forward I was home free. For if Harvey had anything resembling a goal in life, it was to see his lovelorn buddy co-existing happily with a woman. Any woman! Unless, of course, the woman in question happened to strike his own fancy, which is why I never spoke of Radiance in his presence.

I never spoke of my upcoming fight in his presence either, and felt bad about having to borrow the car under false pretenses. But Kingcardine was a good twenty-five miles away, and the fellow who was to act as my cornerman had no transportation, apart from his skateboard.

Harvey suggested we go out to eat, and I readily agreed. (Anything to secure the use of his chariot, you understand.) We hit "Smarmy's," a local fast food joint, at about nine-thirty p.m.

Harv swaggered in as if he owned the place, with yours truly close on his heels. The little restaurant was packed, but the staff appeared to be functioning with efficiency and professionalism. I wondered what their secret was.

"Hey, Carl!" Harv exclaimed suddenly. "Don't that chick work at your place?"

Tentatively, I followed his gaze. It was Radiance! How did Harv know about her? It was at this point in time that I took complete and utter leave of my senses.

"Watch and learn," I advised my pal, and proceeded to sneak up stealthily behind the beautiful girl. She was standing all by her lonesome, some distance from the counter, presumably deliberating over what to order.

Damn you, Harvey, and your legions of amenable wenches! I only wanted to prove that I, too, was capable of interacting intimately with the opposite sex!!

Radiance remained oblivious to my presence until I was practically upon her. Quite intoxicated by her pristine, little-girl fragrance, I thrust my arms out, meaning to embrace her from behind…

"Radiance! Guess wh – "

With an intensity completely belying her soft young form, she whirled about, drove her thick-soled saddle shoe deep into my right shin, and then nearly took my head off with a wicked, open palmed blow to the jaw. I cried out in pain and surprise, staggered backwards a bit, and fell on my ass.

Radiance was there in an instant, tearfully begging my forgiveness, cradling my pulsating noggin in her silken, supple, sleeveless arms. Reluctant, at first, to say too much (lest my aching jaw break into pieces!), I simply gazed upward, entranced by her huge blue eyes, the lily white skin surrounding her nostrils, and the wisps of golden hair tumbling over her forehead. (She had an unusually high forehead, which would wrinkle up like a puppy's when something puzzled her.)

I still consider Radiance the most glorious thing in all creation. The only girl to even remotely approach her in terms of physical beauty is a certain green-eyed blonde who crops up with some regularity in those naughty Italian films shown late at night on cable.

"God, Carl, I'm sorry! I didn't know it was you…"

I struggled to my feet, oblivious to the deathly silence gripping the store and the many eyes trained our way.

"It's okay, Radiance," I assured her. "But where the heck did you learn those commando techniques? Listen, I was an idiot. It was entirely my fault. Can I buy you supper? Wanna eat together?"

When in the presence of an alluring female, I tend to babble.

"I'm with Allie and her parents," Radiance said, gesturing out front.

"Okay. Well, see ya!"

Having no desire to order anything from the smirking waitress, I grabbed Harvey, and ushered him out of the store before he had a chance to protest.

"All I ask of you, Harv," I implored, "is that you exclude her from your list of potential conquests. Promise you will."

"Is she the one you're taking out tomorrow night?"

"Yep, she is," I responded quickly. "She's the one."

Harvey shot me an exaggerated wink. "She's all yours, pal."

"Uh…anything the matter, Harv?" He seemed terribly introspective all of a sudden.

"I've been giving it some thought, Carl, and, well…I've decided it would be best for me to move back to Toronto."

His announcement came as no surprise. I knew he wasn't happy at Robinson's Pt., although Lord knows he had reason to be. I knew he missed his friends, parents, and the hustle and bustle of the big city.

I also knew there was more behind his desire to take leave than homesickness.

Frankly speaking, he was scared shitless of the Rowdies. He lived in fearful anticipation of their every move, and was finding it increasingly difficult to remain at the beach house alone. The tragedy being, of course, that he was absolutely right to fear these psychopaths, who struck like thieves in the night only to disappear just as furtively – and seemingly right off the face of the earth.

We climbed into the car. Harvey stretched his arms as luxuriously as the sloping windshield would permit, then declared with a heavy sigh,

"Ah, well. I suppose I'll stay the summer."

It was my turn to sigh heavily, only with relief. For reasons that are still unclear to me I had decided to stay indefinitely at Robinson's Pt., and had no intention of relinquishing the beach house until it was absolutely required of me to do so. The longer Harvey was contributing rent, the longer I could hang onto it.

"What are *you* planning to do?" Harvey queried, as adept at reading my thoughts as always.

"Well," I mused, "Renwald has offered me forty hours a week throughout the winter, and I think I'll take him up on it."

"What do you find appealing – the steady work?"

"Nope, not so much that."

"The money."

"Nope. Not much to shout about there, believe me." (I won't embarrass Renwald by disclosing the actual amount of my weekly paycheck; "paltry" about sums it up.)

"Radiance, then?" Harv was obviously becoming exasperated.

"Nope." Granted, I was crazy about Radiance. What began as simple, one-sided infatuation had quickly blossomed into full-blown, unrequited love. However, as she would be leaving Robinson's Pt. about the same time as Harvey, there was just no future in it.

"The beach," Harvey wailed. "The @$#! beach!"

"In the winter it'll be tundra, Harv. What's so appealing about tundra?"

"Okay, you got me, Carl. What's so damned attractive about Timothy's Take-Out outta-season?"

I grabbed him by his shirt collar and screamed at him shrilly. "Did you not hear me, you imbecile? Forty hours! I'll ONLY be working forty hours. A wimpy little forty-hour work week! Ya-hoo-ooo!"

I hopped out of the Grey Ghost and began dancing feverishly around it. "What'll I do with all the free time? Ya-hoo-ooo!"

I leapt up on the tarnished hood and pointed dramatically at Harv, who, aghast at the attention I was drawing to myself, was trying to inconspicuously slink down beneath his steering wheel. Impulsiveness was his area of expertise, not mine. He was totally uncomfortable in the role of straight man, a role I'd assumed so many times in the past. But, on this day, I could have cared less. The people leaving Smarmy's already considered me an asshole for the episode with Radiance. As far as I was concerned this gave me carte blanche to act however I damn well pleased while still in the vicinity of the place. So, yeah, I did go a little berserk, but only because there was so much I'd repressed over the last few months.

However, when I began shrieking at the top of my lungs words to the effect of, "I am free from bondage," "my weary servitude is at last coming to an end," "I am no longer a slave," etc., Harvey decided enough was enough and regained control of the situation as only he was able. He started up the car, shifted into gear, and sped toward the exit. Yes, I was still on top of the damned hood, but only for a moment. Seconds after he tromped on the gas I flew off, landing heavily and painfully on the gravel below.

I had taken my lumps that evening.

My "friend" eventually returned for me. Thankfully, he did not attempt to drag me off to some nightclub or the sleazy rathole of some dorky cohort. We drove home in silence, Harv undoubtedly still a little shocked by my vitriolic and wholly inexplicable performance outside Smarmy's. My silence was more the product of my futile attempt to contain my thoughts, which were coming fast and furious but were not particularly profound.

Interestingly, these "mental conferences" I occasionally hold with myself are often mistaken for acute shyness. I have always been an independent creature, but it was my exposure – via Timothy's – to the world at large that taught me to turn inward, to rely exclusively upon myself for pretty much everything. Whoever initially claimed, "no man is an island" may well have been correct, but I believe I've come closer than anyone to being the sole exception.

Once home, Harvey went straightaway to bed, while I, absolutely ravenous, went straightaway to the refrigerator. I passed on the week-old Chinese food (although that stuff can sit for six months and still taste great), passed on the detumescent celery stalks, until a half-empty jar of spaghetti sauce made its overture to the chef in me. A sumptuous spaghetti dinner for one sounded perfect. Joyfully, I set about the task, invigorated further by a stiff breeze that blew in from the lake.

Every so often, one stumbles into a setting like this. All the ingredients for a memorable evening will likely be present and will have meshed splendidly: a pretty sky, a gentle breeze, a late night, an old house, and a large body of water nearby.

It was with a light heart, then, that I proceeded to sift through stacks of putrid, slime-ridden dishes in our kitchen sink, searching for those utensils least contaminated, and most practical for cooking spaghetti. I approached the hot water tap with particular apprehension. The bloody thing would engage me in a kind of auditory "Russian Roulette" every time I so much as twisted it a fraction, forever threatening to emit a horrendous "phaug-g-g-gh!" and scare the hell right out of me. However, this night the tap was mute, and, surprise of surprises, clean water came out of it! It was the last thing I was expecting.

After cooking and straining the pasta, I dumped it back into the pot, and began adding anything I could find: pepper, tomato sauce, string cheese, horseradish, Tabasco sauce, etc. After some ferocious stirring, I trucked the whole shootin' match into the front room, and attacked it like a hungry bear.

Ah, the joys of bachelorhood!

Halfway through the meal I sensed something was amiss. Never mind that I'd already devoured three slices of bread, almost a pound of spaghetti, and was guzzling from a second bottle of diet cola! Something was not right with the picture. Outside, the stars continued to gleam enchantingly, but then, like a ton of bricks, it hit me. Music! To do this night of nights justice, some rhapsodic strains were definitely in order. Reluctantly, and feeling some twenty pounds heavier than when I first plopped down, I arose from the chesterfield and sauntered breezily toward the vast collection of LPs belonging to Harvey and I. They were stacked neatly inside four or five milk crates "borrowed" from Timothy's. I approached the first crate and began flipping through records, the majority of which were greatest hits compilations from such diverse artists as the Who, the Guess Who, Jethro Tull, the Beatles, Cat Stevens, and Abba.

The night demanded something above and beyond the realm of simple pop/rock, however, and in the final crate I found it: Debussy's "La Mer." I placed the record gingerly upon the turntable of Harv's sophisticated sound system, and then blindly flipped a bunch of switches, hoping to activate the proper components. Miraculously, I succeeded. Turning the volume down low so as not to disturb my slumbering buddy, I returned to the couch, stretched out upon it in such a way that my head was but a few inches from the left speaker, and force-fed myself the remainder of the spaghetti (now waxy, viscid, and cold.)

You might be questioning my sanity by this point, shoveling wagonloads of food down my throat on the eve of a big fight. But there was method to my madness, in that it was customary at that time to "carb up" before particularly intense physical activity. My only concern was that I might have overdid it and blown the 175 pound weight limit.

But this hardly seemed important as I reclined languidly on the couch, allowing the soothing music to wash over me as if it were Lake Huron itself. In these blissful surroundings, what image should pop into my head but that of Radiance, some twenty feet tall, dressed as she was earlier that evening when I encountered her at Smarmy's.

With both eyes closed and a goofy smile upon my face, I replayed the scene in Smarmy's over and over in my mind. Not the part where I crept up on her like a dolt and was deservedly decked, but immediately afterward, when she was cradling my head in her arms as though it were her newborn child. Rapturously, I recalled those gorgeous blue eyes staring down into mine, wellsprings of absolute innocence, exuding tenderness, compassion, and – dare I say – love.

And yet, I had a sinking feeling I was no one special in her eyes. She was just by nature a kindhearted person, who would have accorded the same "TLC" to anyone foolish enough to do what I had done. (Not that I was ever likely to know for certain; I could not even bring myself to ask her for a *date*, let alone goad her into a true confession!)

I'll tell you, though, by the time I rose from that couch I knew exactly what I was going to do to bolster that wretchedly unilateral "romance" of ours. I'd hit upon the plan whilst fighting the inclination to drift blissfully into the land of Nod. It was something I had experimented with before, on other beautiful women, with absolutely no degree of success. For some reason I was still convinced of its effectiveness.

The plan, in essence, was to disclose – in as discreet a manner as possible – my strong feelings for Radiance, to everyone but Radiance herself. The news would inevitably reach her, of course, and that was the intention. From that point on it would be up to her. If she felt the same, she would likely respond at some point. If she wasn't interested, I wouldn't ever hear from her. Needless to say, I did not have a great many dates as a young man, not while employing this ridiculous strategy. But it was better than no strategy at all, and what was really terrific about it was that there was no risk of actual rejection occurring, at least not the devastating kind that my sensitive ego was incapable of handling. Even in the worst-case scenario – if the girl did not respond – you could always choose to believe that she did indeed fancy you but was just too painfully shy to do anything about it. It was much easier to live with than what was presumably the truth.

I woke up bathed in sweat, and awash in early-morning sunlight. Cursing myself for the lassitude I'd displayed in falling asleep fully clothed on the sofa – with shoes still on and contacts still in – I stumbled to my feet and attempted to focus my bleary eyes on our small clock. It appeared to be floating in mid air. There was no mistaking what it had to say, unfortunately: ten to ten! I had precisely ten minutes in which to sprint four miles, if I was at all concerned about reaching work on time.

To declare that the magic of the previous evening had vanished would be to understate the case infinitesimally. Reality bore down on me with a vengeance this morning, as if trying to compensate for having lost its grip the night before. I scrambled out the door, not even troubling to lock it behind me. Such a lapse in judgment, with those nasty Rowdies about!

But my thoughts were elsewhere as I sped along the shore. Did I think I would win my fight that evening, after having been so effortlessly dispatched by a girl of fifteen? Did I think I'd so much as remain on my feet?

Did I think?

My musings were enough to send a sudden chill up my spine. Any feelings of genuine fear dissipated upon arrival at Timothy's, where hatred was the operative emotion, always.

It was about this time in my life – with the emergence of Toby Jr. as my new bestest buddy, and with Harv on the verge of strolling nonchalantly into the sunset – that I began to undergo an alarming attitude adjustment. The young fellow I'd taken it upon myself to reform was clearly influencing me with far greater effectiveness! Toby and I were more alike in some ways than I cared to acknowledge.

As it turned out, I was about five minutes late for work that morning. At an establishment where employees would routinely duck out of their shifts without so much as a syllable of forewarning, it was nothing to be ashamed of. But it did mean a tortuous day serving customers, as the coveted positions of cook and "bun person" had already been snatched up by Glenda and the Superhero, respectively. I know the Superhero would have traded with me had I asked him, and probably would've done a much better job at the counter, but it never occurred to me to ask him. That kind of pathetic, last minute jockeying for position may have been common practice amongst some of our employees, but it went totally against my principles and was actually repellant to me.

Grimly, then, I slipped into my ignominious orange uniform and joined the dismal conga line shuffling in and out of the walk-in cooler, endeavoring to "psych" myself for the onslaught of customers I knew was just minutes away.

It was hard to accomplish, this mental preparation, and I felt defeated from the start by the clothes I had to wear. I had worked so hard in the gym to construct the kind of forbidding physique that would automatically discourage assholes from hassling me, and here the effect was just about nullified by my ridiculous uniform, which seemed to literally scream out, "Take a look at this geek!!"

Surely mighty Conan never had to put up with this kind of garbage, I'd often think, but took heart in the "fact" that even Hercules had been subjected to similar indignities (while in the service of Queen Omphale of Lydia), such as having to dress in women's clothing, and being made to spin wool at the loom.

Things went pretty smoothly over the busy lunch hour, as they were inclined to do while the Superhero was around, but I must confess I would've paid a king's ransom to have been Glenda that day. Working alongside David, she had far and away the least to do. I, by way of comparison, had to struggle just to keep the contents of my stomach in place, as I was besieged by what was surely the greatest assortment of imbecilic pinheads ever to have crossed my path. How I deplored them!

I hated everyone: old people (reputed to be so wise, though I saw no evidence of it), the insufferable preppies and yuppies (who, with their arrogant attitudes and shallow lifestyles almost made me pity them), and, of course, that strange, boorish, beer swilling Neanderthal of our day (he of the derogatory expletive, dubbed "working class swine" by one who was surely in a position to know – Toby Jr.!)

And every last one of us hated kids. Even Radiance's pert little nose would crinkle up in disgust if there happened to be a rambunctious one on the premises. And woe to the child who approached Toby Jr. for anything! Toby could contort his facial features in a most terrifying manner (as if his usual countenance wasn't gruesome enough), and was hardly discreet about it, to the horror (and enduring trauma, I'm sure) of many, many youngsters.

The Superhero seemed quite tolerant of kids, on the surface. But he could be a hard guy to read at times. His Dudley Do-Right smile seldom if ever wavered, although on certain occasions those perfect teeth looked to be clenched together pretty tightly!

But, you know, it's funny…In the midst of all the bad apples were a few genuinely good eggs. Scant few, but enough to prevent me from losing all faith in mankind as a species. How I adored these charming people! They'd obviously had my sort of upbringing, with particular emphasis having been placed on the development of qualities such as courtesy and refinement. Unlike myself, however, they seemed to have adapted fully to life with their idiotic contemporaries.

I was having a difficult time of it, as you must be aware of by now, trying to contain my unadulterated disgust for these "contemporaries," who appeared to be bumbling through life with no mental dexterity to speak of and atrocious mental health. To my thinking, they were comprised of just two groups: those running society's proverbial treadmill, and those who'd recently fallen off. Perhaps Toby Jr. and I were spending too much time together, perhaps the steady diet of Timothy Burgers was making me hyper aggressive, I'm not entirely sure…Whatever the case, I'd begun to take sadistic pleasure in baiting customers who dared approach me with illogical complaints.

Beneath that baleful exterior of mine I could feel the old, affable, bear-no-malice Carl clawing to get out. Getting out was actually less difficult than staying out, as one kind word from somebody was usually enough to have me beaming and gurgling like a contented infant for the duration of my shift. Away from the workplace, some classic old tune on the radio or sentimental movie on the tube could attain the same result.

Working at Timothy's during the tourist season was rather like playing defense on a crummy hockey team: most of the time the play was in your end, and it was often frantic. But every so often someone would "clear the puck," and you'd have a few seconds to regroup, get hold of yourself, regain your sanity, have a meltdown…On the day of my fight, Glenda took advantage of just such an occasion by dashing off to the "powder room," the Superhero hot on her heels. I sauntered back at a more leisurely pace, to say hello to the recently arrived Toby Jr. and Jeremy. Tobes was a record twenty minutes early for his seven o'clock shift.

"You can always tell when it's Glenda's time of the month," he commented, by way of greeting.

"Who do you have the misfortune to work with tonight?" I asked him, knowing full well the answer to that one.

"Uh, Radiance and my dad, I guess. That senile old fart Rupert phoned in sick again." (While I tended to be a little more forgiving of the "senile old fart" than I was some of the others, to Toby he was just another stupid kid, to be insulted mercilessly every time he faltered.)

"Isn't that Radiance gorgeous?" I cautiously proceeded, roughly caressing Jeremy behind the ears.

Toby's response was precise and to the point.

"The Radiator? Yeah, I'd love to fuck her! What a body!"

I could have slapped his fat face. So utterly ethereal was Radiance in my view, the mere thought of sex with her was, for lack of a better term, *beyond me*. It was as vague and incomprehensible a concept as the limits of the universe, or the meaning of life. Luckily for Toby a resurgence of hungry customers beckoned, and I was once again called to duty.

I was through for the day soon after, and in the midst of changing excitedly into my street clothes. I say "excitedly," because Radiance was in the building, not because I had a boxing match in less than two hours.

She did it to me every time: transformed my stalwart legs into jelly, accelerated my normally sluggish heartbeat, and, with an ease that was almost frightening, stripped away the otherwise impenetrable game face I so often wore.

I prayed I'd run into her that evening, the abuse to my circulatory, skeletal and nervous systems notwithstanding. Perhaps I'd be the lucky recipient of an inspiring comment, glance, or inadvertent touch – something of a positive nature to take into the fight with me.

My prayers were about to be answered. Radiance had purchased a birthday card for Allie before her shift, and wanted me to sign it. Now secretly I despised Allie, and would not have signed a condolence card in the event of her *demise* voluntarily, but at Radiance's tender behest I wrote a lengthy passage in the birthday card, as though Allie and I were the best of friends. I would live to regret it.

"Oh, that's great, Carl!" Radiance gushed, as she glanced over the corny platitudes I had scrawled. "Allie'll love it!"

"You have a good night, honey!" was out of my mouth before I had a chance to edit it.

She blushed considerably upon hearing herself referred to as "honey," and cast a gaze somewhere in the region of her nervously fumbling fingers and genitalia. Significantly, she made no attempt to dash out of the kitchen, or even to back away a few feet.

"I want to apologize again for sneaking up on you last night," I babbled, willing to say anything if it meant prolonging our delightful tête-à-tête.

At that point, Toby Jr. appeared suddenly from behind a small partition, and wailed, "Radiance! Customers!"

That was the extent of the conversation between Radiance and me. It had gone pretty well, all things considered. At least she hadn't physically attacked me this time! In fact, I left the store both convinced that she genuinely liked me, and astounded by what I'd perceived as fiery sparks emanating from our closely aligned bodies!

Needless to say I practically flew home, despite the beach's being about as congested, in terms of humanity, as one could imagine. It was the height of tourist season, and the scene along the shore was reminiscent of a vast, grossly overpopulated walrus colony. I was concerned that the hallowed strip of beach in front of our house had been similarly violated, but by the time I got to within half a mile of the place the number of beachgoers had dwindled dwastically and dwamatically.

When I got home, Harvey was there. Excited about my impending "date," he'd actually laid out some of my finest clothes on my bed! The poor guy wanted so badly to see me bonded to some female, I had not the heart to tell him that my date was, in fact, with a man, and within the confines of a ring not too unlike the "squared circle" he had come to know through the world of professional wrestling.

If he truly believed I was whisking Radiance away for dinner and dancing (I only wished it were true), Harvey must have be gotten damned suspicious when I popped my head into the fridge upon leaving, and commenced gobbling everything up like some distraught bulimic.

And he should have known by then that the only dancing I ever did was on roller skates.

I clambered into the Grey Ghost, backed her onto Lakeshore Road, popped a well-worn Beach Boys cassette into the well-worn cassette deck, and then sped toward Turner's. I was inappropriately attired to say the least, looking more like a headwaiter than a boxer. At the rate I was perspiring beneath the fancy trappings, I figured I would have no trouble making weight for the fight!

At the gym, I was both disappointed and a little relieved to find an entourage of two awaiting my arrival. The old building was otherwise deserted, and I found it amusing that – in spite of the hoopla and brisk wagering of recent days – none of the real loudmouths had elected to so much as see me off. The two guys present were willing to accompany me, however; one to act as corner man, the other, presumably, to verify the results of my fight.

The latter fellow (I never did learn his name) was built along the lines of a Toby Jr., which is to say, short and dumpy. He appeared to be of aboriginal descent (Mississaugan or Chippewan), although he may even have been Hispanic – I wasn't in the mood to play twenty questions. In any event, he sat in the back of the car en route to Kingcardine, and scarcely uttered a word for the duration of the trip. His companion, however, more than made up for his painful reticence, and mine.

This guy I knew well. He was a tall, angular, pimply-faced youth named Stephan, who made a habit out of getting involved in everybody's business but his own. Only his soft-spokenness precludes my classifying him as one of the aforementioned loudmouths. He fancied himself a "trainer-manager" of hot amateur prospects, and had gone so far as to style his hair like that of his idol, Don King! While King wore, and continues to wear, his outrageous coiffure with some degree of panache, Stephan resembled nothing so much as a badly frightened sea anemone (although the look did compliment his jittery, loquacious personality to a tee.) Stephan was, however, one thing that Don King could never be: Caucasian. His pasty skin tone served only to further accentuate his explosive dark mane. Not only was it difficult to take this goofy-looking chatterbox seriously, it was tough to look him in the face for more than five seconds without breaking into fits of hysterical laughter.

And chatter he did, all the way to Kingcardine, condensing one hundred years of boxing history into a forty-five minute harangue, dwelling with particular affection upon the careers of his two favorite fighters: Sugar Ray Robinson and Marvelous Marvin Hagler. I longed to inject some pugilistic philosophy of my own into the one-sided discussion, but could not get a word in edgewise.

I was somewhat familiar with Kingcardine (having relatives there to this day), and thus had little trouble reaching the YMCA on time. As the three of us traipsed from the car to the impressive new building, I was grateful for the encroaching twilight and how it concealed my suit pants and silk shirt. Harv's resplendent selection was embarassingly gaudy, and the tattered attire of my companions was only drawing attention to it.

Stephan, who on more than one occasion had led fighters to this place, ushered us down a flight of stairs and through a maze of corridors. He was swinging my duffle bag around like a damned fool, periodically smacking it against the multi-colored brick walls. The other chap and I followed quietly, marveling at the gigantic new facility, which I couldn't help but compare to our claustrophobic little gym at Robinson's Pt. The halls were, for the most part, deserted, although every now and again a polo shirted preppie would skip by, clipboard or whistle in hand.

We eventually located two locker rooms, situated on opposite sides of a stubby corridor that led, presumably, to the boxing rings. We chose the less crowded room, and almost immediately Stephan set to work taping my hands up.

"Hang on, man!" I implored my overzealous second. "At least let me take my shirt and tie off!"

Far from delivering a rousing, pre-fight pep talk, both boys confessed that they had bet against me. The fat, olive-skinned one went so far as to encourage me to take a dive in the opening round!

"No freakin' way," I muttered. "What would the point be in that?" But, truth be told, I was getting a bit nervous, particularly after glancing around at the other combatants.

Most had already fought that evening, and some had been beaten into bloody pulps. Watching them grimace in agony as they tried to do up their shirts, I felt the confidence seep from my body like air from a punctured balloon. Those few who had yet to box looked taut, grim faced, and exceedingly well conditioned.

I looked about for my opponent, but there were no tall black dudes in sight. I was convinced, for a few brief, optimistic seconds, that some kind of mix-up had occurred, and that he wasn't going to show. I expressed this notion to my "manager."

"Anyone seen…" Stephan pulled a card out of his denim jacket and glanced at the name of it for reconfirmation, "…Trent Harker?"

"In the other room," a booming voice replied.

So much for my red tape befuddlement theory.

Possessing no boxing trunks of my own, I was compelled to don the same baggy swimsuit that had tumbled unceremoniously to my ankles the day of my "Nautical Nightmare." This time I took no chances, lashing it to my midsection with a few feet of tape.

I weighed in, and was about a quarter of a pound over. However, being the amateur, amateur, AMATEUR event that it was, the officials decided to look the other way. They might as well have; I probably sweated off five pounds just trudging from the locker room to the ring.

If I felt nervous in the dressing room, I felt positively minute in "Ring One," standing there in my silly looking bathing trunks before a crowd of no-nonsense boxing aficionados. My opponent had not yet made his entrance, and there was a fight in progress over in Ring Three. It was a fairly listless fight, if the reaction of the crowd was anything to go by. The spectators seemed more captivated by the sight of Stephan clambering up into my corner. (My other helpmate, evidently too timid to join us, stood just outside of the ring, his chubby face barely visible between the mat and the first rope.)

"Don't just stand there like a stiff, Carl," Stephan whispered sharply. "Limber up, stretch those muscles, get your blood pumpin'!"

I complied, wordlessly, hoping the sudden activity would do something to alleviate my heebie jeebies. It almost did; about halfway into my warm-up I began to loosen up a considerable amount. In fact, I'd about managed to cajole my racing heartbeat back within the range of normalcy when Stephan slapped me on the back, and said jubilantly, "Well, guy, you'll probably get murdered tonight, but it'll sure be fun to watch!"

I almost choked on my Gator Gum.

The fight in Ring Three was over, and the referee, who also happened to be the sole sanctioned judge, had delivered his verdict. Now he was on his way to

Ring One, and he reached it about the same time Trent Harker did. Their combined appearance was enough to send me scurrying back to my corner.

"What the hell have I gotten myself into?" I cried to Stephan. "I can't hit this man! What did he ever do to me? I ain't no fuckin' boxer! Look how tall he is! Holy shit!"

Stephan responded with an equally disjointed verbal barrage.

"Calm down, Carl! Mellow out! You can always take a dive, right? Use your strength, guy! How do you want the ref to introduce you? You got a catchy alias to use? Hooo wee, feel those vibes – its fight night!"

"Just give the referee my regular name," I sighed, and plopped down upon a diminutive stool that had seemingly materialized out of nowhere. I was promptly fitted with a most uncomfortable piece of headgear, which Stephan's sidekick assured me was both compulsory and essential for my well being. It was the first time I had ever worn such a contraption, and I wasn't thrilled about the way it restricted my already restricted field of vision.

While Stephan stood with conviction in the center of the ring, befuddling the poor ref with his aimless prattle, I struggled to insert my outsized mouthpiece, which had apparently been designed for Carol Channing. As I was doing so, I peered beyond Stephan and the official to the opposite corner, where my feinting and weaving opponent was being massaged vigorously about the neck and shoulders by one of a battery of trainers. The robe he wore was splendid, and I believe "Hurricane Harker" was embroidered into the back. (I, personally, had longed for a sobriquet involving either wolverines or tornadoes, but for the life of me could not find a way to work them satisfactorily into my given name.)

Even without contact lenses, I was able to see very early on what type of guy Harker was. He was an arrogant jerk. When he saw me glancing his way, he gestured effeminately with his left glove, drawing a few scattered titters from the crowd. He turned to acknowledge the "titterers," raising that left paw high in salute, and, naturally, they burst into enthusiastic applause.

A real hometown hero, I thought to myself, no longer concerned about hitting him too hard. *We'll see how tough you are a few minutes from now, buddy!*

The ref introduced us with theatrical flair, and motioned us to the center of the ring. As I expected, Harker towered above me, but he appeared very willowy. Seldom one for protracted eye contact, I chose to fixate subserviently upon my rival's boots; in doing so I could feel his stony glare searing into the top of my head. When the time came to touch gloves in a gesture of good sportsmanship, he abruptly pulled away, once again humiliating me in front of the buzzing assemblage. As I returned to my corner, wondering how people could be so bloody cruel, I felt something warm trickling down my back. The hometown hero had spit on me.

I was ready to fight.

"DING-G-G!!"

Equally intent on tearing the other limb from limb, Harker and I met in the middle of the ring, and immediately my longer-limbed opponent began peppering me with jabs. I had no real defense as such, and deliberately opened myself up even further to allow for Harker's stinging right cross. Having reasonably assessed Harker's strength in this fashion, I was ready to launch an attack of my own

However, in addition to being an excellent tactician, Harker was extremely light on his feet, and therefore a difficult target to hit. For the remainder of the first round I continued to press, but it was he who landed the punches (and accumulated the points.) Nevertheless, when the bell sounded and I clumped wearily back to my corner, I was greeted with abject disbelief.

"Fan-bloody-tastic, man! You made it through the round!" Stephan shrieked joyously. "He didn't even faze you! Listen, you might even have a chance – some of those punches you threw spun you right around!"

"And why do you think that is, Steph? He's too damn fast!"

My other collaborator, apparently no longer self-conscious, had scrambled up into my corner to join us. "Cut the ring off on him," he urged, "then take the bastard's head off!"

"Do either of you have any water?" I asked. "I'm parched."

"Sorry."

"DING-G-G!!"

Not surprisingly, Harker came into this round showboating for the people, convinced I'd never be able to tag him in a million years of trying. But I took the advice of Stephan's friend to heart, and advanced on the cocky dude a la Joe Frazier, in an effort to trap him in one of the corners. I had to pay the price, of course, which came in the form of numerous thudding blows to my chest and stomach, but at length I was able to back Harker into the ropes, and that's when I caught him with my first good punch of the fight – a ponderous left hook to the head. He seemed ready to crumble, but then the bell sounded to end round two.

Far from appearing disconsolate at the prospect of losing their wagers (Stephan bet I would fall in three), my two companions gave every indication of being delirious with joy. I paid scant attention to them, however, as I sat upon my stool, wheezing like Rupert after a particularly frenetic lunch rush. Instead, I blissfully recalled the sensation of finally having pasted that jerk-off Harker, and the marvelous "AAAAAH-H-H-H!" that the blow had elicited from the crowd.

Something extraordinary occurred within me between the second and third rounds of that scheduled-for-six-rounds fight. It was triggered, I think, by the realization that here was quite possibly the ideal outlet for the frustrations I'd been besieged with of late, frustrations borne out of my nerve-wracking confrontations with the Rowdies, my Echo-and-Narcissus relationship with Radiance, and doing business with mindless bungholes sixty hours a week.

Why deny it? I enjoyed nailing Harker with that shot, I enjoyed the attention I was receiving, and I enjoyed the fact that I was doing exceptionally well for a man who had never fought before. Hell, I even enjoyed getting hit! Not that I'm a masochist, you understand. It's not the pain that I delight in, but rather the act of sneering audaciously at said pain. (An example: What might well stand as my finest achievement whilst in Renwald's employ was wrought exclusively over a certain two week period in May of '83. I was tormented at the time by a ghastly disorder of the stomach, which very nearly took my life and from which I am still suffering repercussions. Yet from May eleventh to May twenty-fifth – when the physical manifestations of my ailment were most pronounced – I put in no fewer than 136 hours at work. At the risk of sounding boastful, a lesser man would have been flat on his back on a damn hospital bed! How ironic that the shiftless Timothy's employees, who were inclined to phone in sick at the drop of a hat, were likely the source of my gastronomical discomfort.)

It was this confidence and grittiness that I took with me into round three. By then I was a veritable fount of negative energy, and "Hurricane" Harker was every wretched scumsucker who had ever set foot in Timothy's Take-Out, past or present.

He didn't stand a chance.

Precisely fifteen seconds into the round, my opponent collapsed beneath a flurry of punches, blood streaming out of his left nostril like spilled milk off a tabletop. He remained prostrate on the canvas for some time after the eight count, and I was glad, since I would almost certainly have found a congratulatory hug in this instance more difficult to administer than the feeblest blow.

CHAPTER EIGHT

It took me several days to come down from the high of that stunning KO victory. In my euphoric state I hastily made arrangements to fight again, and was duly granted a bout sometime in mid-September.

As usual, I allowed my imagination to run rampant. My fantasies grew increasingly grandiose, and increasingly preposterous. I dreamt of challenging Michael Spinks for the light heavyweight crown, raking in millions upon millions per fight, and accompanying my girl Radiance to glitzy celebrity functions. That last fantasy was easily the most compelling; how could Radiance possibly resist the advances of a world champion?

By mid August, however, neither Radiance nor the sport of boxing was governing my thinking to any appreciable extent. The countdown to Labor Day was on, and never had there been a day more eagerly anticipated, by anyone. To me it signified more than the mere transition into fall; beyond the seventh of September there would be no more crowds, no more twelve-hour shifts, no more Glenda, no more Allie, and only limited exposure to Margaret Humes.

On the evening of August eleven, I had an unpleasant phone conversation with Glenda's parents. They were no longer permitting her to work past ten p.m., having suddenly decided it was too dangerous for their "little angel" to walk the one, well-lit block back to their cottage at night.

Listen, bitch, I felt like saying to Glenda's mother, *if anyone deserves to be bludgeoned, strangled, gangbanged, and hacked into little bitty pieces*...But, in the end, I had no choice but to accept her inane edict. Business at Timothy's was still hot and heavy, and the old miser who ran the place would not hear of taking on more staff so late in the season.

You know, I would have expected something like this of big Allie's parents, but I'd met Glenda's a few weeks prior to the mother's phone call and their conservative appearance had fooled me into believing that they were straight-laced, reasonably diligent adults. However, they were young, and, as I was finding out, only too representative of their generation, a generation to whom anything resembling a work ethic was abhorrent.

Okay, so we're short one body from ten o'clock on. It could be worse. Someday I'll be rich and famous, and will be able to look back on all this and laugh. God, how I'll laugh!

Toby Jr. and I were tighter than ever during this period. And I think I was exaggerating when I told you that Radiance was no longer utmost in my thoughts.

It took a bit of detective work, but I eventually located the cottage where Radiance and Allie were spending the summer. Sometimes, after downing a little hooch, Toby Jr. and I would pay a visit to it in the dead of night, boldly scampering right up to the windows in search of my ladylove. We'd make a point of checking the clothesline out back for any intimate apparel worth filching, and retaining as a beloved keepsake. All we ever did find, if I remember correctly, was a mammoth pair of undies – undoubtedly Allie's – and neither one of us wanted to touch those.

We made a habit of dropping by on garbage night, so we could heist a few bags of trash upon departure and tote 'em discreetly back to Timothy's. While sifting through the malodorous contents, Toby Jr. would kid me about my "Tainted Love," a popular song of the day. We were not altogether certain if taking somebody's garbage constituted theft, but felt at the very least we were giving the collectors a break. And it's true – you would not believe the things some people throw away!

One night of "refuse rustling" held more surprises than Toby and I had ever bargained for. Again, it was sometime in mid-August, and the two of us had just come off the night shift at Timothy's, where we'd been working with Radiance, of all people. Toby had been particularly annoying throughout the protracted Clean Up, blabbering endlessly about Hitler, and doing very little work. I recall wheeling on him in exasperation at one point, and declaring,

"Hitler was so great, huh? Why, then, did he not crush Britain when he had the chance? Why did he not lay waste to Stalingrad when he had the chance? Why did he abandon Rommel in Egypt the way he did?"

"He cracked up," Toby Jr. offered.

"I'll say he cracked up!"

Toby had been silent for a good while after that. Fearing I may have hurt his feelings, and uncomfortably aware that he kept a loaded revolver in one of the back rooms, I'd striven to make amends, primarily by acknowledging what had admittedly been Der Fuhrer's considerable political acumen.

Shortly after three a.m., Toby and I set out for Radiance's, big Jeremy trotting alongside us. Now that I'd shed my Timothy's uniform, the dog – as stupid as he was gargantuan – appeared somewhat confused as to my identity, and would not stop snarling menacingly in my direction. It was almost as if he'd been conditioned from the day he could walk to attack anything that was not orange. He behaved himself well enough once we reached our destination, snooping about the grounds with as much enthusiasm as Toby and I.

As usual, there were no great discoveries to be unearthed, and no startling revelations to be had. After a few minutes of worshiping the ground Radiance must surely have trod upon at one point or another, I motioned to Toby that it was time to leave. We snatched up the three bloated sacks nestled together at the foot of the lane (as if pilfering trash in the middle of the night were the most common activity in the world), and hightailed it back to Timothy's. At some point during the course of that return journey Jeremy re-emerged from the tangled growth at the side of the road, looking for all the world like a great, fawn colored bear, and scaring the living shit out of us.

I immediately reprimanded myself, as Timothy's Take-Out came into view, for having left the lights on in the order area. It was not like me to be so negligent. Say what you will about my plodding Clean Ups, they were ultra thorough; I seldom forgot a thing.

Or was something rotten in Denmark this night?

Toby bent down and whispered something to his dog, which promptly bristled and began slinking stealthily forward (well, as stealthily as a 200 pound canine can slink!) Toby and I, a little less courageous, inched cautiously across the parking lot, clutching those bags of garbage to our chests as though they were bulletproof vests. The light emanating from the order area had transformed the store into a veritable beacon; whoever our intruder was, he wasn't very smart. It was that particular deduction that rekindled for me senescent thoughts of Robinson's Rowdies.

Were they not content to have free reign over my home? Had my brazen refusal to vacate prompted them to invade my place of business as well? To the best of my knowledge the Rowdies always traveled *en masse*; why, then, was at least one of the contemptible bastards not visible through the glass? There was no hint of movement in the store, which would have suggested to me that the thieves had come and gone, had not Toby Jr. gently nudged each door and found it to be locked.

It was up to Jeremy to shed some light on this most perplexing mystery, and he didn't let us down. It was in response to the animal's terrible howling and baying that our startled culprit came tearing out of the back and, inadvertently, into full view.

"Well, I'll be dipped," Toby Jr. bawled. "It's Margaret!"

It *was* Margaret, and, judging by her look of horror as I alternately rattled the door and tapped upon its glass surface, she had yet to recognize us.

"It's me, Marg, don't panic!" I sang out. "I got Toby Jr. with me! And Jeremy!"

Still that look of shell shocked terror; if she hadn't been moving around, I'd have sworn she was in a catatonic state.

Perhaps the sight of Toby's massive canine was serving to intensify her fear. Jeremy had literally burst into the store behind me (after it had occurred to me to unlock the restaurant door with my key!).

Or perhaps Margaret was simply up to no good. She had the look of a person who was attempting to conceal something.

Toby Jr. obviously suspected the latter.

"Ask her what the hell she's doin' here!" he murmured.

"Okay, What *are* you doing here, Margaret?"

We observed her fearful expression transform into one of unadulterated guilt. She sought to avoid my gaze, and responded to my inquiry in a hoarse, barely audible squawk.

"I left my purse out back, earlier today."

"Did you lose it back there?" I inquired, sardonically. "It's taking you long enough to find it. Perhaps Toby and I should have a look-see, whaddya think?"

Jeremy, obviously knowing a pernicious viper when he saw one, was growing more distressed – and unstable – with each passing second, until finally it became necessary for his master to put him out. Toby and I then accompanied the unwilling Margaret to the back of the restaurant.

What I saw there, while excruciatingly sad, sure helped to explain a few things. It appeared that Margaret had been rising at four-thirty on certain mornings and trudging some three-and-a-half miles into town from wherever it was she lived – for the express purpose of desecrating my painfully scrupulous Clean Up work. Had I still an actual heart it might have shattered into thousands of pieces at this frightful realization.

And it looked as though she'd been lining her pockets with substantial portions of Renwald's stock into the bargain.

I gazed at Margaret, shuddered, and wondered how one so fashionably attired and impeccably made-up could seem, at the same time, so utterly vile and repellent. Why the hell couldn't everyone be like Radiance and me, refreshingly unpretentious and virtuous to a fault? Thievery is such a detestable crime, yet over the course of my "career" I was forced to confront Allie, Glenda, Toby Jr., and various others with that very charge.

Small wonder I used to daydream constantly of life in the Mesozoic Era, when the world was young and sweet, floriferous and luxuriant...Even in these fantasies Radiance would invariably take center stage, most often as a blissed-out, primordial Eve to my Adam. We'd dance together under a Jurassic moon, feast upon the flesh of the sauropods, and above all remain a childless couple, thus sparing the world from the ravages of mankind.

Whether or not I'd be truly happy in such a setting is difficult to say. I don't like to admit this, but deep down I think I do need people, if not for companionship then at least as something to transcend.

Did I demonstrate transcendence over Margaret that morning, when I sat her down amidst her artificially induced quagmire of carnage and force-fed her my interpretation of a stern-yet-compassionate message? Hell, yeah!

"I can't believe what I'm seeing here," I began, examining with exaggerated distaste the littered floor and tarnished steel. I moved to within inches of where she was sitting to deliver the remainder of my soliloquy, and in so doing felt the tiniest flicker of sexual desire. "You realize, of course, that I could have you fired for what you've done this morning, especially with Toby Jr. here acting as my witness."

Toby, who for the last little while had been leaning against the massive cooler door glaring venomously at Margaret, nodded his head exaggeratedly in a gesture of assent.

"Why do you hate me, I wonder?" I continued. "Whatever I've done to you, I'm sorry."

It was obvious that the shock of our untimely appearance was wearing thin, for Margaret already seemed back to her brusque, dour, and extremely annoying self. Aware that something in the way of affirmative action would just have to be taken if I was ever to get the upper hand of this bitch, I presented her, right then and there, with an offer she could not refuse: "Due to your ignorance and childish petulance, Margaret, it is unlikely that we shall ever become friends. I'm more than willing to accept this, believe me. And I won't exact much-deserved retribution by firing your ass. Unless, of course, that's what you want."

"Hell, no," she quickly exclaimed.

"I though not. All I ask of you, then, is that you put an end to this nonsense of besmirching my Clean Ups and criticizing me afterward in print. Agreed?"

"Yes," she replied wanly.

"Do you want us to walk you home?"

"That won't be necessary. Just call off your mutt, Junior!"

We reentered the front area. Toby did what he could to preoccupy Jeremy, while Margaret made a beeline for the door.

"Oh...Carl?" she called, just before stepping outside.

"Yes?"

"It took a great deal of 'besmirching,' believe me."

I suppressed an urge to vomit up my dinner.

Margaret and I were to have our petty differences after that – they are hard to avoid when two such disparate personalities interact to any extent – but for the time being I felt as though a giant millstone had been removed from around my neck.

I didn't dwell much on what happened. The moment Margaret departed, Toby Jr. returned with Jeremy and the stolen garbage, and like three depraved ghouls we dove into the nauseating mess, displaying all the fervor of deep-sea divers at the site of a sunken Spanish galleon. As usual, we recovered nothing of interest, least of all proof in writing that Radiance had the hots for me. The latter would've been akin to finding the Holy Grail. (You know those teenage girls, though, always scrawling, "Radiance loves Carl" on books, sneakers, and the like...Ha ha ha!)

* * *

The odd mindless diversion aside, I was keeping pretty busy. In fact, "running myself ragged" might be the more applicable phrase. Between preparing for my next fight, logging workweeks that were stupendous in size, and making time for Harv and Tobes, I scarcely had time to breathe. To stave off complete physical and mental collapse I tried to set aside at least one four hour period each week for myself, exclusively. It was on those occasions that I would retreat into the serene, deliciously cool Port Radcliff library, and immerse myself in books. (My warped idea of relaxation!) Afterward I might concoct some sort of picnic lunch, and either ramble deep into the surrounding countryside with it, or paddle way out onto the lake in Harvey's "Minnie Mouse" dingy.

Although I did a fair amount of hiking, Lake Huron was far and away my favorite plaything. I called it the Great Healer. After being beaten black and blue in preparatory sparring (I deliberately chose heavyweight partners whom I knew could knock me senseless with a single punch), after "OD-ing" on stress after a particularly heavy shift, or even to recover from a night of heavy drinking with my hollow legged buddies, I went not to a physician or analyst but directly to the water. It would proceed to work a bona fide miracle upon my battered form, sometimes within seconds. I have always been in relatively good health, yet the exceptional recuperative power my body exhibited during this period astounds me to this day.

Although it hardly bears mentioning and is actually a painful thing to recount, several of us did embark on a little excursion into Barrie around this time, where a traveling funfair of some repute had touched down for a day. If I remember correctly it was Allie who suggested we go, and it was no mean feat to stuff her, Radiance, Glenda, Toby Jr., and myself into Harvey's "Grey Ghost" – sizable as the old jalopy was. It was the first and last time Allie ever set foot in the car, but the shocks were never the same afterwards. I would not be exaggerating if I were to tell you that she took up roughly two-thirds of the capacious back seat.

I don't think five words were spoken on the way over. Toby Jr., so garrulous and outspoken with me, was about as animated in the car as a plastic cup. As far as I was concerned, the sole reason I'd agreed to this nonsense was sitting in the back seat alongside Allie – so far removed she might as well have made the sojourn in another vehicle.

Things were no better at the fair. As I could have predicted, we were unable even to locate it for the longest time; the only reason we eventually *did* was because Allie had cajoled me into cruising through the entire city, side street by crummy side street. Ultimately, one of us caught sight of a tent that looked suspiciously "carnivalesque," and so we pulled up.

The fair itself could not be criticized. It was slick and sturdily constructed, rather like a cut-rate Disneyland. But I've always hated this kind of pageantry, with its tackiness and legions of overweight, "touristy" types. And, having been intensely acrophobic since birth, I wasn't courageous enough to attempt even the least threatening ride.

Well – until that afternoon, anyway.

Reluctant to "wimp out" in front of Radiance, I joined my co-workers in line for something called "Death Trap." The line moved slowly, albeit not slowly enough for me. Not only did the ride turn out to be what I loathed most – a damned roller coaster – I was somehow paired with Allie in one of the little cars.

What ensued were five of the most terrifying minutes I've ever experienced. If Allie felt anything resembling a thrill when first I grabbed her arm, it must have forthwith turned to agony as I proceeded to wrench it out of its socket.

At least the weather had been co-operating, but, alas, even that turned against us in time. We had all dressed lightly – Allie a true sight to behold in her pink, terrycloth hot pants – and appreciated neither the rain nor the sudden drop in temperature. We spent a good hour in line at the fair's one food outlet, and our reward was a pizza I could have rolled out to the car as a spare tire.

All of us were still experiencing, to various degrees, the lingering effects of that horrible roller coaster; to soothe our frazzled nerves I suggested we take a nice, relaxing "choo-choo" ride around the park. As we moved through the line, however, certain brightly colored warning signs kept reappearing, to the effect of, "Those with heart trouble embark at their own risk," and "May prove traumatizing to those under twelve years of age." Sure enough, my nice, relaxing choo-choo ride turned out to be a death-defying contraption entitled "Runaway Train," and it was as nightmarish a ride as "Death Trap," if that were possible. When finally it came to an end I made no pretense of walking away unscathed; quite the contrary, I had to be helped back to the car.

Labor Day weekend, 1981, was a mixed bag for me, emotionally speaking. I was soaring and dipping like a manic-depressive through much of it. The weather was lovely, which meant business was booming; yet for the first time ever I was able to derive a little satisfaction out of serving customers. It was their last gasp – they knew it and I knew it – and just the thought of going eight months without ever again encountering swarms of this magnitude made me giddy with anticipation.

I particularly savored the broken hearted expressions of the children. The little bastards had been antagonizing me since spring, and Labor Day was my day to turn the tables. All day long I sang, shouted, chortled, and otherwise alluded to phrases like "SCHOOL TOMORROW!!" and "Gotta get up early for school!" As they watched me burst into gales of demented laughter for no apparent reason, the Superhero and Margaret must have wondered if I was not becoming completely unhinged.

And then there was Radiance. She dropped in that Friday to pick up her final paycheck, and was accompanied by so fair and handsome a youth I knew it had to be a sibling. I thought it charming that the two of them were holding hands, rather than bickering as brothers and sisters so often do. Either he was either very shy, however, or reluctant to venture too close to the repulsive

Allie, who was working cash that day. After a clandestine word to Radiance he returned outside, presumably to join those lying in wait for the next available picnic table.

Radiance, meanwhile, put a food order in with Allie – after oh-so-sweetly beseeching me to trot out back and fetch her paycheck. Of course I dashed back as if my life depended on it, and commenced flipping furiously through the stack of envelopes on Renwald's desk until finally happening upon one marked "Radiance." Something prompted me to take a good look in one of the mirrors before rejoining my crush, and I obliged.

Did I look like hell! My eyes were bloodshot, my face pasty despite the deep tan, and slick with sweat. Worst of all was my hair. No longer short and preppyish, it jutted out from underneath my cap like that of a circus clown. As is always the case when one's hair goes awry there was not a comb in sight.

I was forced to improvise.

There happened to be a partially opened box of plastic French fry picks in the vicinity, and so I raced over to it and dunked my hand in. Aligning four or five of the miniscule tridents into a feeble approximation of comb teeth, I ran them roughly through my hair, shrieking in pain whenever one of the sharp points pierced flesh. I attempted to reaffix my cap with a more rakish tilt, but in the end had to settle for doltish. Feeling more repulsive than ever, I hastened back to Radiance and presented her with her pay. The whole breathtaking flight took maybe forty-five seconds.

Allie lumbered off with Radiance's food bill, giving me a final minute alone with the girl of my dreams. I wanted so desperately to lean across the counter and kiss her, but all I ended up doing was blurting out an effete (albeit heartfelt): "I'm gonna miss ya, Radiance."

"I'll be back next year," she assured me, her eyes darting timidly about.

I could not keep my own eyes off her beautiful face, as it appeared a blush was creeping into it!

Ever the dutiful employee, I tore myself away from Radiance and rejoined Toby Jr. in the cooking area – which was a little like dumping Helen of Troy for Quasimodo. I found the latter hunched over one of the fryers, red faced, snickering, a hand clenched over his mouth to stifle outright laughter. Allie lay crumpled at his feet like a slowly deflating dirigible. She was moaning softly.

"What the hell happened?" I demanded.

At that, Toby's hand shot from his mouth, and I found myself on the receiving end of that noxious, horribly abrasive laugh: "AW HAW HAW

HAW HAW HAW! AW HAW HAW HAW HAW HAW!!"

I managed to extract a semi-coherent explanation from teary-eyed Allie, and it did sound amusing. While squashing through the lilliputian portal leading to the cooking area she'd apparently forgotten to duck, and had whacked her head – hard.

A tiny abrasion was visible over her left eye, just under the hairline, but otherwise the big girl seemed fine. I wish I could say the same for the wall directly above the entranceway, where there now existed an obvious impression of Allie's head. (Question: must her head have been the consistency of concrete itself, to do that kind of damage?)

"Worker's Compensation" notwithstanding, this wacky business generally takes little pity on its wounded. Although she moaned something about wanting to go home, Allie really had no choice but to stay and tough out the remainder of her shift. She rose ponderously, pinned up the crumpled remains of Radiance's food order, and remarked, between sniffles, "Radiance's boyfriend sure is good looking, isn't he?"

"Her WHAT?" I screeched, unable to contain my astonishment.

"Her boyfriend," Allie repeated, looking at me curiously. "Her boyfriend from home. He hitched all the way up from T.O. just to spend the weekend with her. Romantic, huh? I guess he's gonna ride home with us."

Allie returned out front, ducking conspicuously this time, but it was my turn to feel as though I'd been smacked upside the head. What a fool I'd been, pathetically choosing *not* to believe that A) girls of Radiance's calibre had waiting lists the length of city blocks, and B) I wasn't qualified to so much as step in line.

Yet, to me, there were no girls of Radiance's calibre. She was my baby, the most perfect aggregate-sum-total of a woman in existence, and the thought of her with someone else just destroyed me inside.

Normally I'm one to internalize my grief, but Toby had been so much a part of the ceaseless romantic pinings, the garbage raids, the aborted kidnap plots…I felt I just had to share some of it with him.

"She's got a boyfriend, Tobes," I lamented, still grasping the edges of the condiment counter so as not to topple over.

Confiding in an asshole like Toby Jr. is not something I would recommend under any circumstances, least of all in situations when despair and sorrow have cut you down so badly you become like putty in a confidant's hands, ripe to any number of his nefarious schemes. Still, the idea of deliberately botching Radiance's food order did sound like a good one at the time, and I

116

applauded the inner workings of my friend's evil mind.

We decided to send Radiance's portion of the order out perfectly, but to render that of her beau's an inedible mess.

"But who ordered what here? You don't wanna fuck up her chow, right?"

"Toby, you know as well as I that Radiance only takes ketchup on her burger, and detests onion rings."

Every now and again I look back on what occurred next, and my head drops to my chest in shame. Toby Jr. and I did everything but piss on that poor guy's food, and I think the only one to come out of it looking stupid was yours truly. Radiance's boyfriend, gentleman that he was, did not return to give Toby and I the lambasting we deserved, and this only made me feel worse. It was quite simply the sort of juvenile, retaliatory stunt one would have expected of a prepubescent, and although Toby Jr. (speaking of prepubescents) watched with glee as the chap's burger fell to pieces the moment he picked it up, I had not the courage to look on.

I was heartsick at the prospect of going without Radiance for the better part of a year, but at the same time longed to be rid of Allie. The joy I derived from bidding the latter good riddance almost eclipsed what I'd felt upon first learning of Radiance's swain. Allie was nothing but a fat, lazy sow. What was worse, she'd taken the sentimental slush I'd jotted down in her birthday card to heart, and had been pestering me nonstop those past few weeks. How does one go about fending off the advances of a three hundred pound leviathan bent on amour? I was much too polite to tell her what I really thought of her. It had become an uncomfortable mess, to say the least.

I was not particularly sorry to see Harvey go, either. I hadn't the energy anymore to indulge in our customary, elaborately tiered repartee, preferring the more lowbrow humor of Toby Jr. And – perhaps more significantly – when in the company of Toby Jr., I didn't feel half so inferior.

Harvey went out in characteristic fashion – which is to say, with a bang. Several members of his adoring public and I joined forces to throw him a monstrous going-away bash on the evening of September six.

Normally I loathe being in the company of even a handful of people, and have always considered that pathetic, universal chant, "PARTY, PARTY…" a true reflection of man's weakness, his ignominious compulsion to band together in little groups. But Sunday the sixth was to be Harvey's day, and I wanted to give him a send-off he would not soon forget.

That I should have been so integral a component of what was probably the wildest party of all time seems more than a little ironic to me now. If I recall correctly, it was already well underway by the time I'd gotten home from work, and at some point during its latter stages the police showed up, having been summoned all the way from Port Radcliff to do something about the noise. Music had been blaring from Harv's stereo at an unimaginable volume; some contemporary blather with little redeeming value other than the fact that you could hop up and down like a geek to its monotonic dance rhythms.

But there was more, much more. A girl I'd never met before (or have ever seen since) took to wandering dazedly about the house, a battery operated popcorn popper in her arms. Although the appliance was on and blowing popcorn in all directions the girl did not seem the least bit out of place. The following morning, certain sections of the house looked as though they'd received two inches of snow. The crunchy white stuff was everywhere, even in my bed.

Parties of this magnitude are frequently obligated to play host to one or more "weirdoes," and ours was no exception. One of Harvey's more eccentric associates was a fellow named Albert, who, if we were to believe his claim, hailed from a small planet in the system of Alpha Centauri. It was not difficult to see precisely why this man felt he had to cultivate an "alien" personality in order to evoke interest in himself. Short, towheaded, bespectacled, he was in every way a stereotypical wimp. I sat next to him at the dinner table, politely soaking up all his claptrap about the hardships of life on "Zybloon," but remained secure in the knowledge that if there was indeed an alien among us it was my own damn self. Was it not I, after all, who'd vowed to maintain as little contact as possible with the outside world for fear of inadvertantly antagonizing anyone? Was it not I who gazed upon my fellow man with the scientific detachment of a zoophobic taxonomist?

For me the party was neither a good nor bad experience (I could have spent the time more productively elsewhere), but Harvey seemed genuinely touched by the proceedings, and I was glad. He was so much fun to be around, so high spirited – just a hell of a guy – and the only reason I speak of him in the past tense is because I've not seen him since that crazy night so long ago. Come Sunday morning he and his friends were gone, and I was alone in a house that lay close to ruin.

CHAPTER NINE

The next seven or eight months were slow paced, uneventful, and among the finest of my life. Robinson's Pt. had become a ghost town by the second week of September, although the warm weather remained through to the twenty-seventh or twenty-eighth. For the first time in recent memory I was able to tranquilly absorb the sun's rays rather than fear and despise them, and it goes without saying that I spent every available second on the lake.

I'd bought Harvey's car, but he had taken the Minnie Mouse dingy home with him (a mode of transportation I considered almost as efficient as the Grey Ghost, and infinitely more reliable). Fortunately, I'd happened to be in the process of tearing down an old garbage hut behind Timothy's, and was able to construct a sturdy raft from its remains. The raft serves me to this day.

I can't tell you how happy I was to have summer over and done with. Work was a breeze, I was finally getting eight hours of sleep each night, and the town had become like a mythical place. What few bad memories of the summer lingered, were effectively erased by the second victory of my boxing career.

The bout was almost a carbon copy of the first. Once again, a tall, lanky fighter succumbed to a barrage of punches a few seconds into the third round, a hapless victim of my perfectly controlled rage. I'd known all along that my first triumph was not a fluke, and I think my performance in the second fight convinced Stephan as well. On the drive home he treated me to a brief but colorful evaluation of my unorthodox style.

"You don't knock your guys flying like real power punchers do. You kinda tear them down, as if they were sheaves of wheat and you were a giant scythe. It's awesome to watch."

It was this fight that officially ushered in my "Rocky" period. Convinced I'd finally stumbled upon that high road to glory (you know, the one I'd been destined since birth to tread), I plunged back into my training with renewed optimism and vigor. But not only did the road prove much rockier than expected, I was a man traveling on bare, callous ridden feet.

Conditions at Timothy's, meanwhile, had improved to "tolerable," largely because burger-happy vacationers were no longer lined out both doors. Yet certain problems did persist. Toby and his dad continued to fight like cats and dogs whenever they were together, and what few customers we did have continued to wander off like Alzheimer's patients after placing their food orders. It was a phenomenon I found positively intriguing, and have often likened to the mysterious, suicidal impulses of lemmings.

What is this strange compulsion people have to order food, then retreat to an area all but inaccessible to their servers? I must confess, it really began to grate on my nerves after awhile. Whenever the task of ferreting them out befell me, I made damn sure to embarrass them thoroughly: "OH, THERE YOU ARE!! DO YOU KNOW I'VE BEEN LOOKING ALL OVER FOR YOU?! YOU SHOULDN'T HAVE RUN AWAY LIKE THAT! TSK TSK TSK TSK!!"

I went so far as to purchase a bullhorn out of my own personal resources. However, in addition to bursting the eardrums of everyone within twenty feet, it was horribly embarrassing to have to cry into the thing, "Number 364, please!" rather than, "We have the place surrounded!"

But there is hilarity to be found in most anything. In response to the cry, "Number 007!" a dapper figure would invariably approach, looking warily about him, requesting that his order be packaged, "a la carte, if you please." Similarly, those who drew number 000 were often forgettable individuals, to say the least.

More offensive than the lame brained customers, more infuriating than the worthless employees, were the two fellas known collectively as "The InKompetent Kooking Kombo" – Toby Jr. and Tobias Sr. Even Glenda was on a higher emotional plane than these infants, who could not work five minutes together without threatening to cut each other's black heart out. There was never any real violence, thankfully, although old man Renwald would sometimes bounce his son right out of the cooking area with a stiff bodycheck.

I was sick to death of their non-stop epithet flinging – God knows my morale was low enough when in that store – and some days I just felt like grinding Toby and his father into fine powder. Old man Renwald, in particular, would spew vulgarities from sunrise to sunset. Toby Jr. at least needed a reason to cuss (albeit not much of one.)

In general, all was well and good through the sleepy off-season. The notorious Rowdies had become too dim a memory to inspire fear anymore, and what was potentially a far more terrifying concept – that of the restaurant becoming overrun with a bunch of zany, obnoxious junk food addicts – had been reduced, however temporarily, to a mere flight of un-fancy. Toby Jr. and I would get together perhaps once a week, to take in a movie and see some strippers.

Toby could be a riotously funny guy at times, but fraternizing with him on a regular basis did have its drawbacks. One of his boorish, off-the-cuff wisecracks nearly got us booted out of the prestigious "Port Radcliff Cinema" once, though the entire incident seems quite amusing to me now.

What we were doing in that miserable little theatre on such a beautiful evening I'll never know. Some God-awful psychotic-killer-on-the-rampage picture was playing, and it appeared as though at least one nubile young nymphet had been inserted, boobs a jiggling, for every lapse occurring in the storyline. Needless to say the film was chock full of nubile young nymphets! I pretty much fell for the ploy, but Toby Jr. saw it for the cheap stunt it was. Twenty minutes into the film he was fidgeting in his seat; sensing his restlessness, I did my best to whisper a few words of reassurance:

"Take it easy, Tobes. Look, there might be a rape scene coming up."

"Huh!" he spat. "Cunnilingus couldn't save this movie!"

Well! That struck me as just about the wackiest, most hilarious thing I'd ever heard, and the two of us snorted and guffawed through the rest of the picture like a couple of imbecilic thirteen-year-olds. Luckily for us the film was rather sparsely attended, and the few couples to our fore were not exactly concentrating on the screen.

It was more often at Robinson's Rodeo that Toby would cause problems for me, and I was almost guaranteed trouble if I let him get overly plastered. As far as Toby was concerned, alcohol was just one more substance to abuse, and unlike me he could get a little nasty after one-too-many rye-and-gingers. Still, I'd be lying if I said it wasn't fun to get fall-down drunk with the guy, and that I did not look forward to our evenings together.

We were frequent visitors to the Rodeo, but only when they had strippers. Both of us abhorred the "meat market" singles scene, much preferring the sex-charged atmosphere of the Rodeo on a Friday or Saturday night, when naked, big-breasted bimbos were virtually served up for us on a platter. The fact that they removed every last stitch of their clothing was exciting enough, but the thrill to end all thrills would invariably come whenever a girl insisted on singling Toby or I out for special attention. I'm quite certain, for instance, that Toby Jr.'s entire week was made the day a particular stripper commented on his "cute smile." How anyone could have perceived that lopsided, snaggletoothed grin as being cute is beyond me, but Toby, loser that he was, insisted upon wearing it like a grotesque mask for days afterward.

Yes, those were admittedly some fun times. I remember one dancer who was foolish enough to hop onto the stage in bright red pumps and nothing else, and was thereafter besieged with drunken, Wicked-Witch-of-the-West imitations ("I want those ruby slippers! Give them to me!"), the majority coming from two quiet guys turned obnoxious drunks.

The trouble came when Toby decided to go head-to-head with those he considered "working class slime." Robinson's Rodeo was often crammed full of factory workers – especially on strip nights – and although Toby Jr. could easily have been mistaken for one of those people, he professed to hate 'em.

I had no great love for the cretinous numbskulls either, but at the same time I had nothing against them, and did not relish the role foisted upon me as Toby Jr.'s bodyguard on the occasions he got into scrapes. Fortunately, a gargantuan doorman worked the Rodeo most nights, and no one wanted to mix it up with him.

Working just forty hours a week, I found plenty of time for sparring, reading, hiking, and indulging in my latest get-rich-quick scheme: songwriting.

I don't know who or what gave me the idea I was capable of writing good music, but I felt I owed the industry at least one fantastic song for all the pleasure it had provided me with over the years. Also, I wasn't blind to the fact that one monster selling pop single could make you rich beyond your wildest dreams – at that time in history, particularly, when the competition was so poor!

I'm sure most music historians would concur (although perhaps not publicly lest they be deprived of their livelihood) that rock and roll has pretty much gone the way of the dinosaur. To my thinking it had become terminally ill with the advent of disco, and by 1983 was stone cold dead. I can't ever recall using the Grey Ghost's radio, at least not in the manner it was intended. I did spit at it a lot. Thank God the car had a tape deck!

Why have no artists surfaced in recent times to rival the likes of Paul McCartney, Paul Simon, Brian Wilson, Neil Diamond, and Chuck Berry? Even the much-maligned "bubblegum" acts (Monkees, Partridge Family, etc.) have to be considered infinitely superior to anything that has come along in the last twenty years. To those misguided individuals who insist on classifying today's garbage as actual music, I'll concede only one thing:

That, every once in a while, the restless corpse stirs…

On second thought, that's being too generous.

Throwing myself into songwriting with characteristic abandon, I succeeded in accumulating roughly an album's worth of material in a few months. Was I prolific or what? My biggest hindrances (aside from the fact I had no talent) were not being able to play a musical instrument with any degree of proficiency, and having no connections in the recording industry.

Winter arrived about mid-December, pretty as a postcard. Business at the restaurant pretty much ceased, and I traded in my hiking boots for a pair of cross-country skis. As I was still in the midst of my mad songwriting spree and had recently won two additional boxing matches, one could say this was a happy, fulfilling time in my life. I was making what I considered a genuine attempt to reach my goals.

Timothy's, once the site of erupting oil vats, frenzied mob scenes, and terrified employees, had come just about full circle by December of '81, in that it was now an almost boring place to work. (When you become totally engrossed in the meticulous placement of countless little ketchup and vinegar packets, you know you're either anal retentive or stuck for something to do.) Because of some absurd technicality buried within the pages of his lease, Renwald was obligated to remain open, come rain or shine, most every day except Christmas.

I received word that my hours were to be further slashed, and wondered how I was ever going to make ends meet. My tentative solution was to become dreadfully tightfisted. I never drove anywhere I could reach by foot, wore clothes that went beyond threadbare, and allowed my hair to grow tousled and long. (How unkempt I must have appeared to my customers!) With Davison's permission I got rid of the beach house's oil furnace and telephone. The latter I relinquished with a smile, for it had been the bearer of nothing but bad tidings for eons.

All this penny-pinching served only to prolong the inevitable. I was doing what I could to hang onto the beach house, but knew I'd be lucky to have it come spring. Why Davison was so averse to lowering the rent a tad is beyond me; it's not like people were standing in line to rent the place. I could just visualize the realtor's listing for it: "Teetering Old Ruin off the Beaten Path."

I was struck dumb when Renwald granted me about a week-and-a-half off during the Christmas season. After all, the man was not known for his beneficence. When I learned that this extended vacation was to be in lieu of my much-anticipated Christmas bonus, however, Renwald's lack of integrity was preserved! I accepted the time off with a shrug of my shoulders, and hustled home to Toronto to spend it with my family. (I would have preferred having them up to the beach house for a "good old fashioned country Christmas," but they unanimously refused the idea. Perhaps their brief summer visit had not sat well with them...)

It was my intention to sleep through the greater part of this unexpected holiday, but I had difficulty winding down. My folks, who'd once gone so far as to blame my lack of energy on a sluggish thyroid gland, were stunned at the sight of this "new" Carl, some fifteen pounds lighter than they'd remembered, hairier, and utterly incapable of sitting still for more than five minutes at a time.

I was having a marvelous holiday just the same, and wrote on Boxing Day what I consider to be my finest song. (A three-minute ditty titled, "Lost Among Five Virgins"!) I did my best to avoid the wealth of sticky Christmas confectionary, but with bowlfuls of chocolate and peanut brittle in virtually every room of my parents' house it was not easy. My few episodes of over-indulgance were followed immediately by agonizing workouts with an isometric device I'd stored in the basement.

When it came time to return to the beach my folks suggested I take along our dog, Shindig, and I agreed instantly. Not only would he be fine company through the winter, he would have acres upon acres up there in which to romp. When spring began anew, I could return him home, as Persephone was returned to Demeter each year after wintering in Hades. (I suppose Robinson's Pt. in winter is comparable to Hades in some respects, although I continue to find it nothing short of enchanting!)

If my parents had been shocked at my recently transformed appearance, I was positively thunderstruck at the sight of fifty-five pound Shindig as he came barreling out to greet me.

The tiny pit bull with the outsized paws, who'd looked on so forlornly the day Harv and I first set out for Robinson's Pt., was barely recognizable to me now. Muscles bulged out all over him, and he was easily twice as tall at the shoulder as I remembered. He was simply magnificent, in every sense of the word. I think what impressed me most about his appearance were his enormous jaws; they looked as though they could have snapped a two-by-four in half.

I suppose some of you misguided individuals will take it upon yourselves to jump down my throat for harboring such a vicious creature, but the charge that pit bulls are kill-crazy hellhounds is just so much rubbish. We've raised several over the years, and, if anything, they've proven themselves gentler and less inclined to take a chunk out of a person than many breeds. There is no denying that they were genetically programmed to fight other dogs to the death, but is that not more revealing of *man's* sadistic inclinations? Even a toy poodle can be bred to fight – he just wouldn't be as effective a killing machine.

Shindig and I were lucky to reach Robinson's Pt. in one piece, for the weather that day was inclement, the roads frightfully slick. Trying for a cut-off I did not see until the very last second, I veered a little too sharply to the left, and the old Grey Ghost began pirouetting like a ballerina on Dexedrine. I remained curiously detached throughout it all, although quite convinced I was that we were going to crash right through an adjacent guardrail and die. From the get-go I'd expected to come to grief on these roads; now that a fatal accident seemed imminent I was quite relaxed behind the wheel, doing what I could to keep the wheels straight, and almost enjoying the unique sensation.

But it wasn't an unyielding guardrail that put an end to the skidding. The ass end of the vehicle eventually came to rest in an accomodating snow bank that seemed to have materialized out of thin air. When I realized that both Shindig and I were alive (and apparently none the worse for our misfortune), I slumped heavily over the steering wheel. I did manage to blow God a kiss out of gratitude!

Something was distinctly not right as we lurched into Robinson's Pt., however. Shindig sensed it first, whining uncharacteristically before we were even off the highway. Despite it being about two a.m. there was a tension in the air you could reach out and grab.

Something disastrous *had* occurred in my absence, but I did not learn precisely what until two days later. Typically, the information came via Toby Jr.

Robinson's Rowdies had struck again! And, for once, the target had been something other than my house or place of business. I was back to work perhaps five minutes when Toby thrust the December twenty-seventh edition of the "Huronia" in my face, demanding that I read a brief article on page two:

ROBINSON'S PT. – St Tarcisius' Catholic
Church, a one-hundred-year-old structure,
was vandalized and plundered in appalling

fashion early Christmas morning. Father
J.W. Hutchison, who was roused by the
commotion, later told authorities that he
had seen from a window in the adjoining
Rectory "seven shadowy figures" dashing
across the front lawn. Damage is estimated
at 25,000 dollars, and worshipers were
obliged to attend Christmas Day services at
another parish. The incident is still under
investigation.

"And I suppose you think the Rowdies were these 'seven shadowy figures,' eh Tobes?" I muttered, handing him back the paper.

Of course it had been the Rowdies. Christmas Day, God's holy sanctuary...Who else could it have been? Incensed, I marched over to what was left of St. Tarcisius' with every intention (gasp) of getting involved.

Ironically, I arrived on the scene only to find the little church sealed up like a can of sardines. According to a cleaning woman I encountered in the rectory lobby, the distraught preacher had done likewise with himself (in one of the sitting rooms), and was taking no callers.

You'd think I'd have been quite beyond pity by this time, having a job I despised and all, but my heart really went out to this man of God. There were so few good people in this world, and it pained me to sit idly by while one from their ranks was getting the stuffing kicked out of him by the likes of Robinson's Rowdies.

I did sort of grudgingly admire the Rowdies. I admired the way they were able to evaporate into thin air after perpetrating a misdeed. I found their sullen, taciturn air a refreshing change from the self-righteous pomposity I had to put up with at work. Though they did cling rather tightly to each other at times, the Rowdies were clearly rugged and ballsy – down to the last man. And, if their religious leanings were of any indication, they were truly evil, not pallid poseurs.

But not only had I been raised Roman Catholic, I'd been fortunate enough to have made the acquaintances of several devout, non-hypocritical Christians as a child. My own spiritual status was admittedly hazy – I admired and respected Jesus yet did not share his boundless, wholly incomprehensible love of humanity – but this did not prevent me from empathizing with the congregation at St.Tarcisius', which I naively imagined to be humble, pious, and pure as the driven snow.

I did want to help, but aside from anticipating where and when the bastards would strike next (and arriving on the scene with the National Guard) there wasn't a lot to be done. In addition, "out of sight, out of mind" was a principle the Rowdies utilized to great effectiveness; by midwinter they had once again been relegated to the murky backwaters of my subconscious.

In the meantime, things were progressing about as well as I could have hoped. At Timothy's, we'd long since dropped any pretenses of being hard at work on the job, and would either wile away the hours with a good book, or drift in and out of our perpetual game of Snakes and Ladders (during the course of which entire paychecks would sometimes be staked!) Some little kid had left the board game on one of the picnic tables and had never returned for it. We at Timothy's were forever in his debt, for the game had become like a national pastime, luring even Margaret and the Superhero on occasion.

After work I'd sometimes drop by McCoy's, the local supermarket (and one of the few establishments open year round). It was an absolutely charming place to do business, unlike any grocery store I've seen before or since. The hardwood floor would groan audibly as I strode up and down the aisles, and even in the dead of winter there were bins full of beach stuff: swimsuits, commemorative t-shirts, sandals, beach balls, and, that staple of every Canadian winter, sun tan lotion!

The sole cashier was a lady after my own heart. She always greeted me with a cheerful "hello," but never assailed me with the small talk I hated so much. She tallied up my items quickly and efficiently, and never once tried to rip me off. (The fast talking cashiers in the big city – especially in those dreadful variety stores – were constantly withholding items from my bag, items I had paid for. These instances of subterfuge would never fail to sicken me. Is it any wonder convenience stores are getting held up all the time – the gun wielding individuals are probably disgruntled customers only out to claim what was rightfully theirs in the first place!)

McCoy's was a little out of my way if I was heading homeward; to do business there meant having to pass by Timothy's a second time. I was sure to keep a low profile in doing so, to avoid being spotted and dragged back into work for whatever reason. From Timothy's onward, of course, it was the same walk I'd made all summer, although to glance at my surroundings at this time of year you would never have believed it. The main drag, a veritable beehive of activity during the hot months, was now completely deserted, and

I mean *completely*. The ghostlike buildings did provide me with a bit of diversion on my way home – I very much enjoyed leaping from rooftop to rooftop in "D'artangnon-esque" fashion!

The iced-over lake fascinated Shindig, which was understandable. It seemed a page out of my old *Explorers of the Antarctic* picture book. We spent hours playing hide-and-seek amongst the floes, until some concerned citizen (the killjoy) decided to let the cops in on our game. You can imagine my surprise as I clambered up a miniature iceberg, only to behold from its crest three squad cars parked side-by-side on the shore, their respective drivers waving me back as though I were an escaped convict.

On the nights I did not work I was usually at home with Shindig, huddled in front of the ancient, potbellied stove. It was here, at a tiny folding table, that I would attempt to write music, drawing inspiration from the frosted windowpanes, the antique furniture, even the sight of Shindig asleep at my feet. Funny how all the songs ended up being about Radiance, though.

The ditties were coming at a fast and furious pace, which is not to say that they were any good, particularly. I did not have much of a "melodic gift." More than anything my musical aspirations served to creatively and productively pass the time. Still, there was always the possibility of my inadvertently composing something fabulous…

* * *

I've always been a fairly open-minded fellow, even in matters of the supernatural. For example, I freely acknowledge that there may exist a personification of evil some refer to as Satan. In fact, throughout my "Timothy's" years, not only was I convinced Satan was real – I suspected the Rowdies of having unleashed him upon me full force!

Timothy's had been an evil enough place before there'd arisen any talk of a "curse," but a certain eerie sequence of events just cannot be explained any other way. On the morning of March fifteen, Mr. Renwald went out and purchased a kitchen knife with a serrated blade. Those of us who'd grown resentful of having to dice tomatoes and onions with a paring knife the length of a child's index finger welcomed the new utensil. We puzzled awhile over Renwald's uncharacteristic generosity, before putting the entire trivial incident out of our heads. The fact that Julius Caesar had been so treacherously stabbed to death on or about March fifteen hadn't occurred to us.

In the weeks that followed, it seemed that everyone who picked up the knife sustained at least one gruesome injury to his or her hand. I'm not being melodramatic when I say that these gashes and slashes were incurred through no fault of our own...

The evil blade was dubbed "The Saw," and was generally regarded as being some sort of diabolical entity. We were forever misplacing it, only to have it turn up later in the most unlikely places. While I can't speak for the others, for a time I was actually fearful of being alone with it. It was I, after all, who'd sustained the nastiest "Saw-related" injury (the ensuing damage to my pinky finger had necessitated a trip to the Owen Sound General Hospital, and several stitches.) The power of The Saw did appear to diminish over time, and we attributed this to the neutralizing force of "Bundula," the Overlord of the Bun Toaster.

In spite of his regal status Bundula was essentially a creation of Toby Jr. Flipping idly through the pages of the "Huronia" one wintry day, Toby happened upon a photo of a large, scowling police chief with a head the shape of a cinder block. According to the caption below the photo his surname was Palermo, but Toby felt his dark features and liver lips were those of a Far Eastern gentleman, and proceeded to ink in a garish red dot right in the middle of the poor guy's forehead. Needless to say, the bright red spot looked absolutely ludicrous (this being a black and white wirephoto), but still Toby was not satisfied. He neatly clipped out just the head, taped it to the side of the bun toaster, and thus "Bundula" came into being.

From that point on, whenever we stuck hamburger or hot dog buns into the toaster (an ingenious contraption that transported the buns through a hellish inferno by means of a slow moving wire conveyance), we were, in fact, sacrificing to Bundula, who would extract their very essence before ejecting their charred, lifeless corpses.

But even The Great Bundula ceased to amuse after awhile. There were graver matters to contend with anyhow, as winter slid insidiously into spring. A monster tornado was making its way north, the same F10 that struck every spring, and it threatened to completely obliterate my languorous period of repose.

Chapter Ten

I had made several New Year's resolutions, and one in particular I vowed to see through no matter what. If I did not do anything else that summer, I was going to make Radiance mine.

I'd also been curtailing my intake of junk food since the first of January – while continuing to work out *hard* – and by April was looking damned good, if I do say so myself. As a matter of fact, I'd shed so much beef that I planned on stepping into my next fight as a middleweight. (I'm sure that Marvin Hagler blanched a sickly white when he heard this news!) I didn't expect the local contingent of fighters to give me any problems, provided I'd not lost too much power.

As you may already have guessed, the weight had not been dropped for boxing, specifically. I fully intended to woo Radiance away from her walking, talking, Ken doll of a boyfriend. I only hoped they'd not done anything crazy over the winter, like gotten engaged. (I was constantly forgetting she was only fifteen years old!)

But how to induce her capitulation? How to make the girl love me? Months of brooding over the matter had yielded no constructive ideas. All I knew for sure was that I had to try something, or I would forever agonize over what might or might not have come to pass.

Renwald's annual spring meeting, in which he routinely foisted inept new employees on the hapless regulars and pontificated mercilessly about the future, was scheduled that year for March 30. So excited was I – to see Radiance – I awoke ridiculously early the morning of the assemblage, only to spend hours primping and preening in the bathroom. (If I couldn't look perfect, I wanted to come as close as Mother Nature would permit!)

I briefly considered taking Shindig along as sort of a conversation piece, but thought better of the idea (after all, the rather unsociable Jeremy was sure to be present) and set out for Timothy's alone. Whilst in transit I recalled my initial walk upon more or less the same path a year earlier. Had it really been a year, already? If memory served me correctly, the nervousness I'd felt upon that first walk had very nearly induced heart failure, and things had been no better at the meeting itself. Until, that is, I'd caught my first glimpse of Radiance, and forgot what it was to be anything but head-over-heels in love.

I felt little nervousness on this occasion – there would, after all, be fresher faces than mine at the meeting – but at the same time was only too aware of my "odd man out" status around Timothy's. While it's true I had gotten to know Toby Jr., I was barely on speaking terms with most of the others. And so, with the battered old Timothy's signpost looming like a corroborative witness, I promised myself that I would as of that very moment transform, and shed my innate dislike of people like an old suit.

Either in my circumspection I was walking slower than usual or I had misjudged the time the walk would take; whatever the case, Timothy's was chock full of people when I arrived. It had to have been my error, because no one at Timothy's was ever early, for any reason. While most were actually inside the restaurant (it being a trifle nippy out-of-doors), Toby, Rupert, and the Superhero were slouched across the first couple of picnic tables like wallflowers at a high school dance, afraid to mix with the womenfolk, or, for that matter, each other.

I can't imagine anyone being shyer with the ladies than myself, but such was my desire to gaze upon lovely Radiance after having gone all those months without her, I was more than ready to dash right in amongst them. Of course, that age-old macho code of ethics demanded that I be "cool," even if cool in this instance meant sitting outside with the guys in stony silence, freezing my balls off. I did have sufficient presence of mind to sit facing the building, and my heart leapt when I caught sight of Radiance, looking very much like the Radiance of my dreams with her honey hair done up in a French braid and her faded blue jeans a couple of sizes too small, highlighting that incredible ass. (Do keep in mind that this was 1982, several years before the laughable "outsized T-shirt-baggy shorts-dark sunglasses" craze swept the nation, rendering all teenyboppers sexless, and absolute laughingstocks in the eyes of all who refused to bow before the dictates of fashion. It is difficult to imagine anything less flattering to the female figure than the aforementioned attire; nothing, not even the atrocious sackcloth fashions of the Roaring Twenties was less becoming in my view.)

When the time came to get down to business, Allie, looking no less grotesque than she had the year previous, beckoned Rupert, David, Toby and myself inside. The meeting itself passed without incident – until, that is, I went to insert a training cassette into Mr. Renwald's VCR. I fumbled about with the unfamiliar control panel (if you recall, VCRs were still a relatively new concept in 1982), distracted by the thought of Radiance's eyes glued to my backside. Needless to say, I was overjoyed when finally an image appeared on the screen, but that joy turned to mortification when I realized that this was not the recommended "Food Preparation and Handling Instructional Video." Someone (Toby Jr.!) had playfully substituted a hardcore sex film at the last minute, and thus – for a few seconds, anyway – some of the more youthful staff members were treated to what was presumably their first glimpse of graphic humping. While I'd long believed that much practical knowledge could be obtained from working in a restaurant, I never suspected the experience could be a sexually enlightening one!

I was as transfixed as anyone, but managed to shut down the machine before (hopefully) any permanent impressions of the depraved activity were left with the likes of Radiance and Allie. The instructional video was recovered, eventually, and all progressed smoothly from that point on.

We were hours into the meeting before I realized that miserable little Glenda was not there. (Renwald later informed me, much to my delight, that she had quit.) Similarly, I did not really notice the three newcomers among us until the meeting was already well under way, for no one had bothered to introduce them.

All were female. While two were homely in the Glenda-Allie-Toby mold, one was actually quite good looking. Good looking or homely, I was pleased indeed to see our ranks swell by a few bodies. Lord knows we could have done with another six on top of that!

Radiance and I did not actually speak that day, but I swear at one point she looked over at me and smiled broadly. The affectionate gesture choked me up to the point that I was incapable even of reciprocating it. I could only stare back in open-mouthed stupefaction. What an angel!

At the request of Renwald, I stayed on with the new arrivals, conducting their first training session. Although my tone of voice was superficial and controlled, my mind was screaming out a different tune: *Leave this place, girls! For God's sake, get out while there's still time! I beg of you! I beseech you! This place will destroy you, damn it!*

Of the three girls, only one warrants having an in-depth character study made of her at this time, and that is the good looking one I spoke of. Her name was Roxanne, "Roxy" for short. While not quite as pretty as Radiance (was anyone?), she nevertheless had a body that could knock you right into the next solar system if you weren't paying attention, and was not bashful about displaying it.

Roxy belonged to a select group of chicks (and I've known several of this type) who are tallish, voluptuous, slow in their movements, and who project a sleazy kind of charm. She laughed often, and her laugh was most infectious. She and I hit it off immediately, her warm, easy going personality meshing seamlessly with mine, and were it not for my Radiance obsession I might just have fallen for her. As it turned out, we became the closest of friends, seldom seeing each other outside of work but deriving much – I hesitate to use the word – *enjoyment* out of our shifts together. In addition to being closer to my age than Radiance, she was a good deal livelier, and considerably more intelligent. However, even with all of this going for her, Roxy when in the vicinity of Radiance seemed like so much ground up beef to me. There was just no comparison.

If Roxy had a fault it was that she dressed like a whore, although it sure didn't seem like much of a fault at the time. She went a little heavy on the make-up, and preferred her own flimsy, orange colored blouse (which she seldom bothered to button up past her navel) to the standard-issue Timothy's t-shirt. Needless to say, whenever the girl had to bend down for something, I was there, indiscreetly hovering a few paces behind, neck craned and standing on tippy-toe.

A grateful – and, apparently, financially strapped – Roxy went to work a few days after the meeting was held, while most of the younger part-timers left Robinson's Pt. altogether, to return at some point in the summer.

I had my own share of financial woes to contend with that spring, and they culminated in my having to move from my beloved beach house. I would spend the next five months living out of a pup tent, moving from one secluded locale to another. Not as inconvenient a mode of existence as it might seem; on the contrary, it was both enjoyable and inexpensive. The greatest problem I faced was what to do with the cumbersome Grey Ghost. Most of the time it just sat at Timothy's, and it goes without saying that Renwald did not view it as an adornment to the building.

The time had come for Shindig and I to part company. Although he and I had become practically inseparable over the winter, I just had to face facts – he would be much happier romping about back home than sitting out the stifling summer months in my car. Shindig does not exit our tale at this point; come October he would be back, and the following July as well, to play an integral role in the great adventure to come.

Oh yes, I almost forgot...I informed Toby Jr. of my burgeoning fighting career, and he was suitably impressed. He even attended one of my tournaments, the one I had sworn to enter as a middleweight. As fate would have it, I'd not been able to diet down quite far enough on that occasion, and ended up fighting as an extremely light light heavyweight. Nevertheless, I battled my opponent to a split decision that tipped in my favor, and the hard fought victory only reinforced my conviction that I had the potential to go far in this game.

* * *

I have one more anecdote to relate, before I allow the spring of '82 to fade from your consciousness.

One particularly cold and dreary afternoon, the Superhero had a remarkable experience. A panel truck ran over him, and did not kill him.

This, in a nutshell, is what happened: On April 6, at precisely two p.m., Renwald sent his star employee out to the intersection of Seventh and Main to drum up some business. What was unique about this ostensibly straightforward scheme was the fact that the Superhero happened to be inside of a hot dog costume. (Renwald had obtained it for the weekend from a novelty shop in Port Radcliff.) The prospect of remaining completely anonymous likely played a role in David's agreeing to participate.

Anyway, there he stood, at the intersection, waving his arms as best he could (they had been reduced to flipper-like appendages projecting from either side of the "bun.") A few hours of this accomplished next to nothing, although it did make the day of several kiddies whizzing by on bikes. Desperate to attract *somebody* to the store, and probably cold to the point where he was no longer thinking rationally, the Superhero leapt, arms a-waving, right in front of the next vehicle to come along, which happened to be a newspaper delivery truck. Needless to say, the truck steamrolled over him.

I was working that day, and was quickly summoned to the scene. It was horrible; beyond the curious, ever expanding cluster of onlookers, I spotted what looked to be a huge frankfurter lying on the shoulder of the road, thrashing about in agony. There was much blood, which looked for all the world like great gobs of ketchup!

It was when David ceased moving that the more pessimistic folks at the scene began to fear for the worst, particularly the elderly couple that had run him down.

"I'd told George he'd run over a giant somethin' or other," the missus was tearfully explaining to a policeman. "Heck, it looked like the man in the moon! One minute it was in front of the truck, the next minute it was gone. So I said, 'George, stop the truck!' I had to talk him into it, because he thought the bump we'd felt was a pothole! He's been so tired lately, poor dear."

The rest of us were in a quandary as to what to do with the motionless form at our feet. It turned out that nobody knew anything about first aid.

"Kick it and see if it moves," a bespectacled prepubescent advised.

Fortunately for the Superhero, paramedics soon arrived, and I think one young lady voiced what we were all thinking, as they carried him – still clad in the hot dog suit – on a stretcher to their ambulance: "Now that's something you don't see every day!"

Miraculously, David's wounds proved, for the most part, superficial. The bulbous costume had saved his life. What was truly macabre about the entire affair was the fact that it did succeed in drawing customers to our store that afternoon, in almost record numbers for that time of year. The Superhero's painful trial had not been in vain.

CHAPTER ELEVEN

"Hi, can I help you?"

"I want four single burgers and two double burgers…No, no, two singles and four doubles, that's it."

"What would you like on them, ma'am?"

"Three with cheese, and three without."

"Uh…which would you like with cheese on them?" *Idiot.*

"The two singles with cheese! And one of the doubles!"

Oh, forgive me. How could I have been so ignorant?

"Okay, now four I want with mustard, relish, and onions only."

"The four doubles?"

"No, no. The two singles and two of the doubles. On second thought, put that on one single and two of the doubles. The others I want with the works, except for one of the doubles, which I want with mayo and double cheese."

"Now let me double-check this, ma'am."

"Well, I did my best to simplify things for you!"

Yeah, and you did such a lovely job of it, too…douchebag!

"Now these are the drinks I want…"

"Hi, can I help you, sir?" *Nice hair.*

"Smile, fella! It's not that bad, is it?"

"What can I get for you, sir?" *We'll see how wide your smile is after you've sampled Toby's cooking.*

"I'd like a double hamburger with ketchup, onions, cheese, bacon, triple mustard, pickles, and relish."

"Anything else you'd like on that?" *The kitchen sink, perhaps?*

"No, but I want some onion rings, too. And I want 'em crispy! Last time I had 'em here, they were undercooked."

One order of rings, Tobes, burnt to shit! "Anything else you'd care for?"

"A coffee."

"Cream and sugar?"

"Black."

It's your stomach!

"Hi, can I help you?"

"I'll have an order of fries – large."

That goes without saying, tubby.

"And maybe a triple burger with cheese."

Of course.

"Do you have any diet soda?"

Ha ha ha ha ha ha ha ha!! That's priceless!

"Hi, can I help you?" *Fuck you and the horse you rode in on.*

"I want three orders of fish and chips, and my daughter would like the Fun Meal, but don't put any mustard on the burger. And cut it in half. Little Norman wants a chicken sandwich with double mayo, but absolutely no lettuce…Oh, and a large orange soda – no, make that a root beer.

"Okay, ma'am – three fish and chips, a large root beer, one Fun Meal…What did you want to drink with that Fun Meal?"

"A small cola, I said!"

Grrrrrrrrr! "Oh, I almost forgot – what was it that little Norman wanted? The chicken sandwich?"

"Yes, but with double mayo and absolutely no lettuce! He'll puke it up."

Charming.

"Hi, can I help you, sir? Uh…sir? Can I help you with something…maybe? Uh…sir?"

"H-Hamburg."

"I'm sorry?"

"Hamburg…"

"Would you like the single, double, or triple patty? Uh…sir?" *Triple, it is!* "Anything else you'd like?" *Read my lips, chuckles. ANY THING ELSE YOU'D LIKE?* "Right, that's two-eighty, please." *Why, Lord? Why the hell me?*

"Hi, can I help you?" *Jesus, Mary, and Joseph!!!*

"Brucie, you go first."

"I'll have the teensy weensiest little hot dog you have. Mmph! That's quite a play on words, isn't it, Stan? 'Weensy – hot dog'…Get it?"

"What would you like on that, sir?" *Fag alert! Fag alert!*

"A teensy weensy bit of catsup. I'll also get a small moo juice, and I know just what Stanley wants!"

Do tell, pansy. Do tell.

"Large French fries! Am I right, Stan?"

Oh, how lovely!

"Here, I'll get this, Bruce…"

"No, way! It's my treat today!"

"No, I insist."

"It won't do you an iota of good, Stan! I'm paying!"

Here's a suggestion: Why don't both you knob gobblers pay me, then all three of us will be happy?

"Hi, can I help you –"

"YOU IGNORANT SON OF A BITCH! GET THE FUCK BACK HERE!!"

"Er…excuse me a moment, Reverend. I'll be right back."

"Mr. Renwald, what is your problem? We can hear you out the front, you know! I'm serving a man of the cloth, for crying out loud!!"

"My good-for-nothing son just walked out on us. What are we gonna do now?"

"Close early?"

"What was that?"

"Nothing, Mr. Renwald." *Nothing at all.*

"I'm sorry, Reverend. Things are getting a trifle heated back there. Now what can I get for you…"

"Can I help you, sir?" *Whoops!!* "I mean – ma'am…"

And so it began. The big crunch. The merciless onslaught. Call it what you will. Every principal of Eastern philosophy I could think of, I employed, to avoid going insane. I forced myself to hallucinate, latching with desperation upon some idealized vision of my future, or of Radiance without any clothes on. I daydreamed endlessly of big houses, big cars, big tits…(I wanted it all!)

Yet even in my darkest hours – when stress, fatigue, anxiety, and frustration would converge upon me with the pitiless intensity of the four horsemen unleashed – I felt this sense of being nurtured and protected, as though the gods themselves were guiding my steps. I was much comforted by the sensation. But inevitably would come that cry of "Can I place my order here, chief?" and again I would be taken down a few pegs. Such a vicious circle is life!

And then there was Roxy, who in the space of a few weeks had become the most proficient female employee at Timothy's. She may not have been in the Superhero's league, but her very approachability made her much more fun to work with. And on those all-too-rare occasions when the three of us were working the same shift – well, there wasn't anything we could not do.

While Roxy was undeniably an angel of salvation that spring, I did not contract, to any degree, "Florence Nightingale Syndrome," in which afflicted persons have been known to fall madly in love with their benefactors. There were a few reasons for this: Radiance's impending return to work was pretty much all I thought about, Roxy's interest in me did not appear to exceed the bounds of platonic friendship, and I was astute enough to realize that – unlike Radiance – Roxy was a human being.

Roxy's abilities and obvious charm notwithstanding, I'm at a loss as to why our humble eatery was so popular. I'm as fond of junk food as the next fellow, but would likely never have set foot in that vulgar "greasy spoon" had I not worked there. It baffled and exasperated me that Timothy's would become the very nucleus of Robinson's Pt. on hot, sunny days. Need I mention that the working conditions were apt to deteriorate in direct proportion to the rising temperatures? Many was the time I thought, despairingly, *I'd rather crack rocks at Leavenworth than endure this shit a moment longer!* And I meant every word.

Because I had no intention of spending the rest of my life pandering to loutish customers and working among moronic teenyboppers, I put my modicum of time off to good use, dividing it equally between my songwriting endeavors and feverish weight lifting sessions at Turner's. Although I was supposed to be training with my upcoming fights in mind, what really fueled my workouts was my irrational hatred of my job. My muscles were first and foremost a place to hide under, sadly…

Despite my apparent success as a boxer I'd made no real friends among my fellow athletes at Turner's. I had grown to love the sport, but could not live it twenty-four hours a day as they did. Many of these guys were bona fide gym rats, content to hang around the gym from sunup to sunset, whereas I spent comparatively little time there, and took no part in their interminable gab sessions when I was present. Boxing to me was simply a means to an end, not the "be-all, end-all" of my existence.

Turner's Gym, however, was invaluable to me for reasons other than working out. Since I was now officially of no fixed address, it was a place in which I could shower, shave, and brush my teeth!

The Easter season came and went that year without the Rowdies trying to put a stop to it, and I was surprised at this in light of their dastardly deeds on Christmas Day. Curious as to whether or not they'd finally taken up permanent residence in the beach house, I revisited the place on a sunny day in May, creeping stealthily up to the windows and glancing inside. Far from betraying any signs of life, the old homestead was like a morgue, and pretty much as I'd left it except that it was now up for sale. There were no fresh footprints in the sand, save for my own, and although I strained mightily I could detect no sounds of chanting drifting up from the cellar.

May 1982 was distinguishable only for its hoardes of jump-the-gun vacationers, the majority of whom evidently knew of no greater attraction in town than Timothy's Take-Out. Renwald had to have been pleased, but the building itself was suffering from these unrelenting waves of stampeding humans, especially the little washrooms out back.

There was both a men's and a women's washroom. Ironically, our glorified hamburger stand was not even required by law to have 'em – public ones, anyway. You'd think a mean son of a bitch like Renwald would have relished the sight of people looking around in vain for a place to piss, but this was clearly not the case. Our little washrooms remained open for "business," only to endure the most barbarous vandalism imaginable. The ladies washroom did have a delightful tendency to trap children inside of it (thereby exacting a bit of justice for itself, I suppose), but it seems scant retribution for what has surely amounted to decades of abuse by now.

Twice that May were the outdoor "facilities" the center of considerable excitement. Bustling about one busy Saturday I imagined I detected a faint but acrid odor, which I attempted (twice) to trace to its source and failed. Both Margaret and Rupert scoffed at my suspicions, insisting that the overworked grill was responsible. I remained unconvinced, having worked at Timothy's long enough to know what burning meat smelled like. I was eventually proven correct when a small man emerged from the cluster of blubbery, open-mouthed groupers at the counter, to report that the gentlemen's washroom was ablaze.

I could do little but run out, douse the flames, and paste an "out-of-order" sign on the door. I was back serving in minutes, as if nothing out of the ordinary had occurred. After we closed up that evening, all three of us went to more thoroughly assess the damage – believe me when I tell you the sight was not encouraging.

At least the thick limestone bricks had managed to contain the fire. The cause of it all was pathetically obvious, and I was almost disappointed to learn that no foul play had been involved. Some pinhead had dropped a live cigarette butt into a tissue-filled plastic garbage bucket (in fact, the smell of the bucket being reduced to smoldering ash was what had first alerted me to the calamity.)

Our two restrooms never seemed to be up and running at the same time (ever had to snake a toilet?), and a few weeks after our little fire a far more humiliating incident occurred to put the ladies' can out of commission for several days. Once again it was close to dusk on a busy Saturday, only this time I was cooking – the job at Timothy's that arguably best suited my talents – and had as my help-mates Toby Jr. and Roxy. Roxy was taking orders out front, doing commendably well for one so inexperienced, and working alongside of me was supposed to have been the elusive Toby Jr.

I was more than holding my own, despite having a plethora of food orders to contend with, until my train of thought was snapped by a dreadful caterwauling that seemed to emanate from somewhere out back. Suspecting that someone was trapped in the ladies' can, I located Toby Jr. and sent him to investigate. He was back in the cooking area within minutes, grinning from ear to ear, and when I inquired as to the origin of the unearthly screeching (which had not abated), he merely looked at me, still grinning like a jackass, before finally taking me by the arm and dragging me back to see for myself.

At first glance I was able to gauge the predicament: a hysterical teen-age girl had indeed managed to become trapped in the ladies' john, to the extent that neither she nor those on the outside were able to do anything about it.

Several of her companions sat nearby on upturned milk crates, and they appeared to be taking this far more lightly than was the captive.

Toby returned to the grill, leaving me there with all those dopey girls, and I thought I would die of embarrassment. Sobs had replaced shrieks from inside the washroom; apparently the girl was claustrophobic to the nth degree. No locksmith, I ended up removing the entire doorknob, only to find the girl rocking back and forth on her haunches next to the toilet, hands clasped tightly around her knees. She looked every inch the sole survivor of some epic disaster film, and I wondered how anyone could react so hysterically to what was in reality a pretty trifling incident.

Nevertheless, I get kind of a warm and fuzzy feeling about the whole thing these days, largely because of what happened next, once the girl realized she was free. I'd expected an earful, and would not have objected to it, but instead the girl (who was not at all unattractive) flung her arms about me, buried her head in my chest, and wept joyous tears. I was momentarily flabbergasted, but recovered enough of my wits to assume the role of sympathetic consoler, softly stroking her hair, revelling in the unique sensation of her lips pressed against my neck.

The pleasurable embrace ended abruptly, cut short by the frenzied shrieking of the girl's friends behind us. Having had quite enough in the way of shrieking for one day I wheeled about irritably, only to be confronted with the ulcer-inducing spectacle of big, bad Jeremy slowly backing six very frightened teen-age girls across the parking lot and into the forest beyond. But such was life in the nightmare world of Timothy's Take-Out, where disasters tended to occur not in threes, but in sixteens or seventeens. As we were in the midst of the monstrous Victoria Day weekend when the aforementioned disasters took place, they were quickly forgotten.

We entered into June praying for the arrival of our young relief troops. They were still many miles to the south of us, of course, poised for the final school bell. What this translated into were few, if any, days off for yours truly, but it did teach me something profound: Days off were sweeter if you worked for them.

The beginning of June was flat-out wacky. For instance, I came close to tossing a fight due to the histrionics of my "manager," Stephan. I don't mean to appear overly critical of The Brillow Headed One – he was, after all, the only guy in my corner that night – but check this out:

We were in the fourth round and I was having things pretty much my own way, battering my smaller, lighter opponent all over the ring. I had beefed up considerably in preparation for this match, and although the other fellow was putting up one hell of a brave front I think we both knew it was only a matter of time before I caught him.

A minute or so into the fourth, however, it was he who'd caught me, with a vicious head butt that sent me reeling back against the ropes. The referee – who in choosing to officiate boxing matches rather than pro wrestling matches clearly missed out on his calling in life – ruled it an unintentional butt, and this sent Stephan into paroxysms of rage.

"Are you insane, you stupid dork?" he roared. "I could see the butt coming a mile away! He actually crouched down to launch it! You're an asshole!"

I stared down at Stephan pleadingly, making furtive little "cut it out" gestures with my gloves, but to no avail. It was obvious that the highly animated fuzzball was just getting started, and I knew my only hope lay in somehow placating the ref.

"You thought that was an unintentional butt, horseface?" Stephan continued. "How about this?"

To my utter horror, he turned toward the spectators, unhitched his oversized dungarees, and wiggled his bare ass at the stunned official. "Do you think this is an unintentional butt? Well, do you??"

The crowd erupted in a mixture of laughter and applause, and the din belied the sparse attendance. The ref, whose scarlet flush was visible even under the harsh lights, began pointing accusingly in all directions – first at Stephan, then at me, and then towards the hallway that led to the dressing rooms.

I really wanted this fight to continue, if for no other reason than I had it in my hip pocket. By launching that damned head butt when he did, my opponent had sealed his fate as far as I was concerned. I strode over to the corner in which the referee and timekeeper were having words, and carefully, discreetly, let my point of view be known.

Claiming that Stephan was really not my second at all, but merely some dude with funny hair who'd offered me a ride (this was not too far from the truth), I painted myself the bewildered innocent, as dumbstruck as everybody else by his "eccentric" behavior. I assured the ref that I was in agreement with the "unintentional butt" call, and in a very low-key fashion praised him for his clear headedness.

What, might you ask, did all of this slick talking accomplish? Well, not only was the fight permitted to continue, Stephan was ejected bodily from the arena. A satisfying ruling all around!

The remainder of the bout was by no means anticlimactic. The unexpected break in the fighting seemed to instill new life into my opponent, who – to the delight of his handlers, I'm sure – came into Round Five "floating like a butterfly" and "stinging like a bee." I responded to this show of finesse by throwing a succession of roundhouse punches that whooshed dramatically through the air, but otherwise accomplished little. (Well, they did make me look pretty stupid.)

I forced myself to cool down, and attempted to counter his ring savvy with a little of my own. By the final seconds of the round my opponent had ceased to exist as such; I'd reduced him to a rough composite of every obnoxious ingrate of a customer I'd ever been obliged to do business with. By the sixth and final round, the poor bastard was in deep, deep trouble.

There we stood, propped up against each other in the center of the ring, our breathing labored and shallow, trading blows we would have sidestepped with ease a few rounds earlier. But whereas my opponent had quite genuinely run out of steam, my seeming exhaustion was a ruse. I'd saved a little something for just this type of situation. I graciously permitted him to punch himself out, and when finally I saw those big ten-ounce gloves drop to his sides, I opened up with primal fury, knocking him senseless.

Great fighters, after a win, usually appear briefly at a press conference, before getting whisked away to some elaborately staged reception held in their honor. Two hours after my fight, I was still wandering the street in front of the arena searching for Stephan, who had completely disappeared. As a matter of fact, no one I questioned could recall having seen him since he'd been ejected.

The chilly night air was not exactly the best tonic for my overheated body, and I soon called off the search. I had the car, after all, and was not the least bit averse to leaving Stephan stranded. I happened to pop into a local diner for a glass of milk, and it was there I found the imbecile, all but obscured from view in one of the little booths. (His long legs, propped so insolently upon the booth's table, had given him away.) I ran over to him at once, with every intention of raising a stink. But either I was too tired to do so, too polite, or too disoriented by his torrent of chatter upon seeing me.

He was even more garrulous on the drive home. To sum up Stephan in four words: chuckle headed mynah bird. I managed to shut him up long enough to inform him of my victory, at which point a strange light came into his eyes – a sure sign he was drifting back into fantasyland. Before I knew it, he was waging grandiose promotional battles with his nemesis, Don King, and vowing to book me into Madison Square Garden...

With my natural inclination to please, I am regarded as something of a pushover by many. But at the same time I can be stubborn to an extreme degree. Stephan would assume a significant role in my boxing future – over my dead body! For all his glittery dreams of the future, he did absolutely jack-shit in the present, and I knew I was nothing more to him than a potential meal ticket, or free ride, or (insert appropriate cliché here).

To anyone who'd listen to him, I was his "discovery" and he my "manager," though if it were truly the case we had a peculiar business relationship indeed, rarely seeing or speaking to each other until fight night. What I perceived at the time as being adroit career moves I made independently of Stephan or anyone else, although I sometimes did collaborate with old Tom Turner, whom I respected, in selecting opponents. I was no longer in the game "for the good of my health"; it was my fervent wish to turn pro and reap all the honor and glory I possibly could. Had I voiced this to the guys in the gym, of course, they would have laughed in my face.

But if working at Timothy's Take-Out was teaching me anything, it was that I had more dogged tenacity that anyone else on the face of the earth. I intended to exploit this quality to the full, both in and out of the ring.

Speaking of Timothy's, the place continued to exude its own inimitable sense of despair and impending doom. Particularly at this juncture, with the warm weather apparently having set in for the summer, and the month of September hovering veritable light years in the distance. I was frightened of the place, damned frightened; I admit it. Margaret was growing increasingly sour and waspish with each passing day, and I was sick to death of walking on eggshells all the time to avoid setting her off. Rupert, that grand old patriarch of Timothy's, no longer amazed me with his youthful vitality, for he did absolutely nothing at work aside from annoying paying customers with his habit of spending inordinate amounts of time in the gentlemen's washroom. And then there were the customers themselves, whom I was inclined to regard more as decadent, bovine *things* than as human beings. Even when working the grill I could not help but see them, through our little pass-thru. All that was visible from that vantage point, thankfully, were their flabby midsections and fistfuls of currency.

But most of all I was terrified by Mr. Renwald. I'm convinced that the years I spent on the receiving end of his tirades were what turned me into the neurotic creature I am today. He never accused me directly of any wrongdoing – he wasn't that courageous – but he was forever insinuating that

I wasn't doing my job. Proud fellow that I am, those insinuations cut deep!

Even in physical appearance he was horrific. His face was like a death mask, and he was virtually bald except for a startling growth about the ears and back of the head. Although he was short in stature, and on the spare side, it was difficult to see him as anything but a colossal ogre, devoid of humor and of social graces

As a cooking partner Renwald was without peer – for sheer incompetence. Extremely farsighted, hard of hearing, reacting to every little faux pas with bellows that must have sounded to customers out front like those of a cape buffalo being tortured, he was in every way a liability to have around. He did not seem to realize that fast food cooking is largely a matter of precision timing, and that if you pile too much meat on the grill it's going to burn up before you can get it off. While Roxy found the old goat's buffoonery endearing, it was all the rest of us could do at times to refrain from lynching him and stringing him up.

But if June of '82 was memorable for anything, it was for the return of Radiance. Staggering bleary-eyed into work one morning I was surprised to find her, Allie, and the two new employees behind the counter, huddled around a milkshake machine we'd recently acquired. So preoccupied were they with the contraption, oohing and aahing as though it were some priceless museum piece, my arrival went entirely unnoticed. (This suited me fine, as I'd had about fifteen minutes' sleep the night before and looked like shit.) Fearing I may have crashed some clandestine meeting, I ducked out back without a word.

As luck would have it, the girl whose return I'd awaited so breathlessly and for so long was not scheduled to work that day. Neither was her obese friend (for which I was grateful.) This left me with the two new pug uglies, and I wasn't sure I was ready for the two of 'em at once. Their names, incidentally, were Lucinda and Cheryl.

I was able to "inadvertently" bump into Radiance before she left, and a few seconds of gazing into those beautiful eyes was akin to the simultaneous ingestion of nectar and ambrosia. (Or, for those less poetic souls among you – one look at her and I was "up" all day.)

It was indeed a delicious way to start my shift, but Lucinda and Cheryl were on a mission to burst my bubble. To be honest, I don't know how they made it through Renwald's initial interview; they made Radiance seem intelligent. Why trained chimpanzees aren't substituted for teen-age girls in the workplace, I will never know.

Lucinda. It's hard to envision a girl with such a pretty name being scrawny, zit-faced, and buck-toothed, but ours was certainly all of the above. She possessed other shortcomings as well, that even had she been a raving beauty would have ensured her remaining celibate for life: glasses, curly hair, and a voice akin to fingernails down a chalkboard.

Cheryl, while also a dog by any reasonable standard, was a little easier on the eyes. However, in addition to having the mentality of pus, she was very argumentative, questioning my every utterance in a most infuriating manner. What was worse, I think, was the fact that she had a very big chin. I hate chicks with big chins!

What's that, you say? I'm coming down too hard on these poor girls? You wish for an example of their alleged incompetence? I'll be more than happy to oblige. Their collective blunders must number in the thousands, but few were more hilarious (or outrageous) than one that occurred that very first day.

Eager to keep track of all the milkshakes we were drawing from his new machine, Mr. Renwald had devised an ingenious counting method: For every shake we made, we were to drop one domino into a specially marked bowl. Whoever was in charge at the end of the night would simply count up the dominoes. Cheryl, struggling with the complexity of these instructions, never did catch on completely, and for a time was under the impression that the dominoes were to be dropped into the shakes themselves, much the way free prizes are deposited into boxes of cereal. To this day, the thought of an astonished customer dunking his or her paw into one of our shakes in an attempt to discover what had been obstructing the flow of liquid through the straw, and then muttering, "what the hell..." at the realization that it was a freakin' domino, is enough to reduce me to tears of hysterical laughter. Did Cheryl honestly believe that same customer would then be motivated to order dozens of milkshakes in the hopes of obtaining a complete set of dominoes? A truly priceless illustration of her pea headedness, would you not agree? I've got a million of 'em, folks.

Radiance was scheduled to work the following day and I was overjoyed at this, as our shifts appeared to more or less coincide. When I learned that she was to be my cooking partner, I was ready to renounce every negative word I'd ever murmured against Timothy's!

For the first time in recent memory there was joy to be had in crawling out of my pup tent at eight-thirty a.m. in response to my quartet of buzzing alarm clocks (I'd become paranoid about sleeping in.) Turner's would not be open, it being a Sunday, and so I headed directly to the sea to wash up. As was my custom on workdays, I prayed for rain.

The gods were responsive – the rain began to fall as I was cavorting about in the waves. Feeling especially blessed this fine morning, I high-tailed it into work, where my run of luck appeared to be continuing: Radiance and I had been inked in as bun boy (!!) and cook, respectively. Allie would be replacing the ailing Rupert as our "party of the third part," but this did not bother me. One was really no better or worse than the other.

My vow to ask out Radiance (or perish in the attempt) foremost in my mind, I bided my time patiently, waiting for that one truly opportune moment to strike. But it was beginning to look as if no such moment would materialize that day. The problem lay not with any ungovernable glut of hungry people – the heavy rains kept that sort of thing to a minimum – nor was big Allie entirely to blame, although she certainly had a role to play, beleaguering poor Radiance with nonsensical gibberish at every opportunity.

I was the real problem. I simply could not muster up the courage to ask Radiance out. This particular failing on my part was no doubt attributable to disastrous encounters I'd had with chicks in the past – three times I had asked girls out the way a guy conventionally asks a girl out, three times I'd been shot down the way a girl conventionally shoots a guy down. I had my little speech to Radiance down cold, but was vanquished totally by fear, unable to make a move in her direction. I contented myself with standing as close to her as possible as often as possible, savoring her heavenly scent, hoping the nondescript cologne I'd slapped on that morning would have a similar effect on her.

The undisputed highlight of the day came during a slow spell in mid-afternoon. Radiance and I watched in silence as the blimpish Allie bustled about the grill, readying things for her fifteen minute feeding frenz–...er, break. No sooner had she waddled to the back of the store, already stuffing French fries down her throat in the manner of one who has not seen food in weeks, did lovely Radiance turn to me, and in the most unprepossessing of tones whisper the words that shall live in my heart forever:

"Seeing how it's not so busy, Carl, do you think I could get my math book and study a little bit? I have a final in algebra next week, and maybe you could even help me with some of the problems. Unless, that is, you have something else for me to do."

I assured my angel that this would indeed be a convenient time to get some studying done. Although math in any form had always been for all Fellows males a source of much weeping and gnashing of teeth, I offered to help in whatever way I could.

We spent the ensuing thirty-or-so minutes (with scarcely an interruption from out front) wading through a few of the more difficult algebraic equations she might have expected to encounter on her exam. To my astonishment we were actually able to solve one or two. That was one or two more than I'd been able to solve during my entire stint in high school. Needless to say, I had sidled right up to Radiance while all this was going on, and would even have attempted to slip an arm around her had I not been so repelled by what I ran into on page 138 of her text – incredibly lifelike sketches of giant, dripping phalluses, which I only prayed Radiance had not drawn herself. Whoever the artist had been he or she must have had a model posing before him, so realistic were the renderings.

Allie returned after having spent twice the allotted time on her break, although I suppose it could be argued that she had consumed twice the equivalent of a standard luncheon repast. Whatever the case, I was far from displeased with her, and would even have suggested she take another fifteen minutes had not a flock of customers suddenly burst into the store, as if on fucking cue. It was all downhill from that moment on.

The rain that fell so heavily on so much of the district that day, flooding out Timothy's and other buildings whose roofs leaked like sieves, was little more than a fey, tinkling shower by four o'clock. Radiance, Allie, and I looked on in terror as the accursed sun burst forth from its confines, evaporating both the rain and any hopes we might have had of breezing through the remainder of our shifts in the carefree manner we'd begun them.

Believing the interlude of sunshine to be just that – a short break in the stormy proceedings – I dashed outside to change some garbage bags. Legions of wasps were buzzing around in impressive and intimidating formations. Not only had wasps long considered our garbage bins something of an annual vacation triplex, they controlled our trash like the mobsters controlled Vegas, always objecting when an attempt was made to replace an overflowing garbage bag with an empty one. On this occasion they seemed especially pissed. Given the circumstances I suppose their anger was understandable; no sooner do they get out to sample some bright sunshine when along comes this big, goofy looking thing, infuriatingly orange in color, with every intention of making off with their prospective feast.

Small wonder that they attacked with such vigor.

They were on me the moment I began dragging the canful of grungy slop out of the largest of our bins. It was hardly the first time I'd run afoul of the horrid insects – throughout most of the previous summer they had indulged me in their little game of chicken – but this bunch seemed more aggressive than ever, and I wondered if indeed the notorious killer bees had not finally made their way into Canada.

Making no attempt to "rebag" the can, I headed as fast as was humanly possible for the dumpster out back, the bulbous sack of trash slung over my shoulder and at times suspended like a kite behind me. Rounding a corner of the building, my sneakers skidded hard on the gravel, fought valiantly for traction, and ended up airborne. As I was still inside those sneakers, I followed their trajectory, more or less. The wasps, which had been in hot pursuit all this time, caught up with me, and I was stung twice in the neck and once in the ankle. There were no customers in the vicinity when it happened, thank God, but Radiance and Allie had witnessed the entire incident from inside the store.

Bad to worse. Radiance was seated near our walk-in cooler, munching contentedly on an apple, when I came flying by in search of drink cups. Had I been lucid at the time I would have crept across that kitchen floor with the utmost of care, as the ungodly combination of heavy rain and leaky roof had transformed it into a skating rink. But I was preoccupied with poor Allie, who had just mixed a fellow's milkshake and was looking frantically about for something to pour it in. (In these sorts of crisis situations I tended to lose all capacity for rational thought.)

And so, for the second time that day I lost my footing, only this time Radiance had a front row seat to the proceedings. I didn't fall down, exactly. I just kept on losing and recovering my balance, and in this manner slipped and slid past the highly amused girl like a rubber-legged purveyor of the old soft shoe. I don't think she'd figured on live entertainment with her dinner.

The topper came at about four-forty-five. I was out front covering for Allie as I so often did, and was gazing longingly out the window as I so often did, when an enormous school bus lurched into the parking lot, crammed-to-bursting with hyperactive kiddies. Either my brain was flat-out refusing to process this visual or I remained rooted to the spot out of sheer terror; whatever the case, I could only stare in stunned disbelief as the accordion-like side door of the vehicle opened, and a wave of the little monsters advanced on the building as swiftly as their stubby legs would carry them.

The (shall we say, "rowdy") children swept into the store, ran us ragged with all their idiotic requests and bizarre inquiries ("how much does this cash register cost?"), toppled a fragile Muscular Dystrophy collection box (spilling its vast accumulation of silver all over the floor), and then were gone as quickly as they'd come, with only the half-wrecked store as evidence of their visit.

We would have survived the day just fine were it not for the fact that with Radiance by my side I made for a totally imbecilic cook. Perfectly turned-out food seemed less of a priority when she was around than taking care to stare penetratingly into her eyes whenever she asked me a question. As I was ordinarily something of an ultra-dedicated employee, my startling deterioration on these occasions was a testament of my love for her.

"What more could possibly go wrong?" I had to have been asking myself at this stage of the game. I'd been stung multiple times, was aching all over from those ridiculous pratfalls I had taken, was no closer to asking Radiance out than I'd been on the occasion of our first meeting, and had suffered through something resembling a kiddie blitzkrieg.

As if my hand was not crummy enough already, the gods went and slipped me one more useless card.

It was not unusual for me, when Radiance was around, to duck back into the storeroom/staff room for a few seconds of primping and preening before the full-length mirror. (To think I actually believed that a few strategically plucked nose hairs and a few strategically slicked-back scalp hairs could do anything to improve my appearance, amid that cacophony of orange I had on!) Returning to the cooking area after one such grooming session that day, I found the entrance to the kitchen blocked by Allie. She had eased her bulk up against a side of the threshold in what I can only conclude was an attempt on her part to look *coy*, and had pretty much sealed off the threshold in the process. As beefy as I was, I hadn't a prayer of slipping by this most effective human impediment, not in the genteel manner I would have preferred. I stared at her pleadingly, wordlessly beseeching her to allow me to pass.

Instead, without so much as a jiggle of her fat rolls, she asked me to her high school prom.

In the interest of my emotional well-being, dear reader, I dare not dwell upon the ensuing five minutes at length. Suffice it to say I was able to deny the girl's request. It's my belief that Toby Jr. had encouraged Allie every step of the way and had probably even put her up to it, convinced I'd never in a billion years be able to say no. Of course, Tobes should have known by then that when it comes to evasive tactics I'm as canny as any politician. Not only did I end up refusing to accompany Allie to her dance, I did it in such a way that nobody got hurt – neither she emotionally nor I physically!

The following day, July 1 (Canada Day), was no less an exercise in humiliation. The "Annual Summer Games" were being held, the same government-sponsored competition in which I'd lost my swim trunks a year earlier. Although this time out it was an archery competition, the whole affair came to eerily resemble its precursor. We were once again marched out onto the beach in our orange uniforms, amid the same kinds of snickers and catcalls, and made to stand in single file. No disrobing this time, unfortunately.

Our staff members, for the most part, were as inept at shooting arrows as they were at serving customers, and we ended up dead last out of twenty-or-so teams. I must take some of the blame – I was a terrible shot under the most favorable conditions, and on this occasion was dog tired, discouraged at the prospect of summer beginning, and still mooning over Radiance, who was standing just a few feet ahead of me but might as well have been on another continent. Not even caring whether I hit the target, I damn near skewered the announcer my second time up (the same chubby fellow who had presided over the last competition).

There were two occurrences in July of '82 that I suppose could be deemed newsworthy. One was the installation of a long-awaited Timothy's Take-Out suggestion box, while the other was more sinister in nature, involving, to the best of my knowledge, those perennial masters of evanescence, Robinson's Rowdies.

Aside from a healthy dose of comic relief, the suggestion box provided us with little that was remotely positive or constructive. One anonymous writer suggested we submerge all of Timothy's (with the exception, I would hope, of the order area) in about four feet of water, equip our staff with goggles and snorkels, and let the poor souls splash and dunk their way through particularly virulent heat waves. The offbeat surroundings would provide not only respite from the heat, but visual diversion for the customers.

Indeed.

There was another suggestion, equally imaginative, in which exclusive access to the roof of the restaurant was to have been provided by an ornate spiral staircase! Upon successful negotiation of this staircase astonished patrons would encounter a scene out of nineteenth century Paris, replete with patio lanterns and nattily attired violinists. The high paying customers who chose to dine on this upper deck would, of course, proceed to dine on the very same greasy fare that was so readily available to the riff raff below.

Surely the most intriguing suggestion of the lot had us all fitted with leather masks, not unlike those worn by certain pro wrestlers and masochistic sex fetishists. That I actually entertained this preposterous notion, however fleetingly, gives you a clear insight into my deteriorating mental condition as of July 1982. The idea of being completely anonymous captivated me to the extent that I didn't even stop to think about how truly idiotic we'd all look running around with masks on.

Had I a suggestion of my own to drop in the box, it would undoubtedly have been connected in some way to my fantasy of replacing every employee in the store with an android. (Well, I mighta left the Superhero alone; he was already pretty robotic.) Think of it – no temperamental Margarets, no simple Allies or Cheryls, no ugly Lucindas or Tobys…Just a fleet of nameless, faceless androids that never over portioned, called in sick, or dawdled when there was work to be done. Should this kind of technological advance occur in my lifetime, I'd be back into restaurant management in a flash!

As it was, however, I was stuck with a crew the casting director of "Alice" would have envied. The 1982 staff photo went up in place of the old one, and all of the regulars looked just as geeky as before. My feelings for Radiance had now been captured on film; if you closely examine the '82 pic, you'll notice my roving eyes, roving precisely in the direction of her heaving bosoms.

Despite the "fair weather" inclinations of our customers – and what had been some very sluggish off-seasons – I believe that Timothy's Take-Out was the highest grossing fast food joint on the face of the earth back in the late seventies / early eighties. And this includes any McDonald's outlet I can think of! I'd be doing you a disservice if I failed to tell you something of the hellish working conditions I had to endure that particular July.

I'd long since dubbed Timothy's, among other things, "The Place Where Everyone Comes to Eat, But No One Comes to Work." Why are we such a nation of spineless dorkwads when it comes to putting in even part-time hours on a consistent basis? The mighty Superhero himself was out a week in July of 82 with a heavy cold, an ailment I personally laugh in the face of and have worked through many times. My two "fast food flowers," Roxy and Radiance, were out a combined total of sixteen days that month, although they had at least made a token effort to replace their ailing bodies. The others simply did not show up for work most of the time, and gave you only a blank, uncomprehending stare when you tried to explain, in exasperation, that it was irresponsible of them to do so.

At the risk of sounding immodest, I believe that I was the only true bulwark that summer, plugging along day in and day out, at a loss as to why everyone did not share my own brutal work ethic (i.e., show up for work unless you're dead), sacrificing on occasion even that which I held most dear – my days off.

I must give Mr. Renwald credit; he *never* took days off, and had an uncanny knack for knowing, at any given time, precisely what we were running out of and how much of it to reacquire. Of course, he was making all the money, and money is still the most effective stimulus I know of for working like a government mule.

Lurking like cancer within many fast food workers is a condition known as "grill shyness." Most of our staff was afflicted, albeit to varying degrees.

It was pathetic. The moment activity in the cooking area began to heat up (so to speak) my cooking partner would more often than not *dematerialize*, leaving me to face the inevitable whirlwind of food orders on my own. This wouldn't have been so bad had the majority of our simpletons not been "counter shy" as well. All they ever wanted to do, it seemed, was fill and clean – and even at these chores they sucked donkey testicles. Needless to say, the one person who would have been an asset to us grill shy was Mr. Renwald, and he was without trace of the disorder.

I almost always worked nights ("three-to-three" in the summer), and I think my record of having worked the most consecutive Friday and Saturday nights still stands. Margaret, on the other hand, typically worked mornings and afternoons, and although that instance of "fast food sabotage" the previous year had stemmed the flow of handwritten castigation she remained a most vociferous critic of our Nightly Clean Ups.

She didn't realize that the Clean Ups were often one-man shows. Many of the parents disapproved of their daughters working past eleven p.m., and would routinely spirit 'em away seconds after we closed. If this was a deliberate attempt on the parents' part to inconvenience us they were using the wrong tactic, as their wretched spawn was like so much excess baggage at cleaning time.

I went so far as to *encourage* those working alongside me to leave early. Once I had the store to myself I would pop some great cassette into the store's rinky-dink sound system, lug out the heavy-duty artillery (which in this business meant four ply paper towels, buckets of soapy water, baby oil, Windex, and steel wool), all the while prepping myself mentally for what lay ahead. My cassette of choice that summer featured Tchaikovsky's "Marche Slave," which I in my ignorance had taken to mean, "March of the Slaves," and had subsequently adopted as my theme music!

The last thing I cared to do after eight exhausting hours of pandering to assholes was engage in a meticulously conducted four-hour Clean Up, but I hung in there every night, approaching the chore in the same stolid, plodding manner that I approached most everything else in my life. So vivid are the memories of stumbling around the joint at three in the morning, very nearly in a stupor, my ill-fitting contact lens grinding and scraping in a seemingly coordinated attempt to pop out of my head. As if my martyr complex wasn't already huge enough, I even developed "stigmata-scars" – ugly calluses on the palms of my hands, albeit of decidedly earthly origins.

As strange as it may seem (to anyone who isn't obsessive-compulsive), the Clean Ups themselves were child's play compared to the mental hell of shutting the store down and locking it up. One of Renwald's patented cost-cutting measures involved flipping off individual breaker switches at night – as opposed to simply throwing a master switch – so flip 'em off I did, checking every one of the switches on the panel some seven or eight times to ensure that they were in the proper position.

"Stashing the cash" was as much of a strain upon my faculties. In my increasingly futile attempts to assure my disbelieving psyche that I had indeed taken the money out of the till and stashed it away, I'd stare as penetratingly as I was able at the rolled-up ball of cash in its hiding place, concentrating on nothing but where it was at that particular point in time. After nine or ten minutes of such pure concentration, not only would images before me become blurred and drool commence its trek down my chin in crisscrossing rivulets, out of my ears would sometimes erupt geysers of smoke, just like in the cartoons.

Need I mention that, upon leaving the store, I tested each door a trillion times to ensure that it was locked? Or that I often returned hours later, if only to conduct another check?

Sunday, July twenty-fifth was looking to be a typical summer Sunday in every respect: beautiful weather, the restaurant busy beyond even Ray Krok's wildest dreams, and Roxy, Rupert, and myself working gargantuan shifts through to close. The onset of darkness brought little relief from the stifling heat, although the three of us were both hot *and* cold beneath our clammy, sweat soaked uniforms. I was working the counter, and therefore had a slightly easier time of it than those in front of the grill.

If you yourself were to have been a customer that night, the great disparity in sound is what would first have commanded your attention. For starters, you'd have sworn to yourself, as you stood there in line, that a sheep was on the premises, bleating in anguish. In fact, we had traced the rankling noise to the store's solitary electric fan, which had been set in the cooking area lest we all succumb to smoke inhalation. The fan tended to squeak a lot.

From overhead, you'd likely have been subjected to the ranting of various fire-and-brimstone type evangelists, who on Sunday evenings pretty well dominated the airwaves in that part of the province. Because the preachers seemed to have a curious, debilitating effect on our customers, we let them have their say.

Amid these more obvious audiogenic assaults was a true myriad of lesser ones, including the gentle farting sounds generated by the zealous squeezing of empty condiment bottles, and the not-so-gentle sounds of intense bickering among the staff.

Even the major mishaps that Sunday were typical. Renwald was a most inattentive head chef, allowing no less than five weiners to roll off of the grill during the course of his "shift." (The slope of the building simply had to be accounted for when cooking hot doggies; he of all people should have known that.) Another absentminded bit of business on his part had poor Rupert hopping around in pain for close to a minute afterwards.

Evidently – speaking now of the injury to Rupert – Renwald Sr. had at one point just sauntered away from a heap of overcooked food on the grill, as he was known to do from time to time. Having appointed himself head chef for the duration of his employer's absence, Rupert made a desperate lunge for the spatula, failing to notice that it had been cooking along with the rest of the food. No sooner did Rupert pick up the utensil did he drop it again, just a-howling in pain. For the next sixty seconds or so he danced a strange dance the length of the cooking area, clutching his inflamed appendage, continuing, at sporadic intervals, to howl dolefully.

At precisely eleven o'clock, we doused the lights and gleefully displayed the closed signs. As was sometimes the case, however, we were about a fraction of a second too late to thwart a final onslaught of customers. Thus we were obliged to spend an additional twenty minutes accommodating these irritating people, who I swear derive no greater pleasure out of life than hiding outside a fast food joint until closing time and then filing in before the hapless employees are able to lock the doors.

You run into the slimiest people after eleven p.m., as was certainly the case that evening. More pissed off than frightened by the boorish latecomers, I was, in fact, just itchin' for one of them to start something (my hatred for humanity having reached something of a peak around midsummer of that year). But they were plainly more interested in getting fed than in anything else, which was fine by me. And I must say, throughout it all never did my veneer of polite subservience waver.

Mr. Renwald, clutching the battered old briefcase that over the years had become like a second child to him (very often it was filled with the day's take, you understand), was the first to leave and therefore the first to spot the damage. His earsplitting cry of "What the fuck?" while startling Roxy and I, did not unduly distress us – we had become more or less conditioned to Renwald's childish outbursts by this time. Rupert, deaf as a stone, heard nothing.

For once in his life, however, Renwald was understating the case. He returned inside, white as a sheet, beckoning me like an apparition from beyond. I followed him out into the parking lot, wondering what it was I'd done now, and then suddenly, overwhelmingly, I was hit with it.

My beloved Grey Ghost, the lone vehicle in our gigantic parking lot, had been tipped onto its side and laid waste to! Several of the windows had apparently been booted in, and much of the carapace was encrusted with meandering ribbons of spray paint. Whether or not this desecration had been the work of Robinson's Rowdies was a matter of conjecture at that point, but closer examination of the graffiti on the rear window left little doubt in my mind. Amid all the childish obscenities and obscure doodling were several tiny "666s" and upside down crosses.

The four of us were still circling the car in disbelief when two police cruisers pulled up, from neighboring Port Radcliff I suppose (no police station existed as yet at Robinson's Pt., probably a big part of why the Rowdies had been able to terrorize the tiny town with impunity). Apparently, Roxy had been the only one among us with sufficient presence of mind to alert them to the scene.

With the help of the two cops we were able to right the battered hulk, only to find that all four of her tires had been slashed. We also learned that the spray paint had been applied no more than three hours before. Three hours! It meant that the cocky sons of bitches had done their work while the parking lot was still full of customers! I could scarcely believe it.

Ah, but I could believe it. I knew what the vast majority of people were like now. Soulless, gutless wonders for the most part, utterly base, driven by capricious desires. What sickened me more than anything, I think, was the realization that I too would likely not have come forward.

The police left after a few minutes of awkward deliberation, aware that there was precious little follow-up work to be done. As always, the Rowdies had covered their tracks with a seemingly forensic attention to detail. I was consoled somewhat by Roxy, who stood with her arm around my shoulders throughout much of my ordeal. Indeed, the sexy blonde seemed more broken up than I, whispering words of reassurance so often and with such overwhelming tenderness you'd think I'd just lost a family member or something. We'd been friends before this, of course, but just the same her unaffected show of compassion caught me off guard.

Why the Rowdies had singled me out was anybody's guess, but I suppose it's safe to assume that I was as close to a genuine enemy as existed for them in the sleepy town of Robinson's Pt. Harvey and I *had* moved into the house where they'd once conducted satanic rites, and no less of an authority than the Head Rowdy *had* informed me on one occasion that it was consecrated ground...

I, of course, could have done without their sporadic intrusions into my life. I didn't need any more enemies – enemies surrounded me. Nevertheless, I was not about to let the Rowdies' latest offense go unchallenged, vengeful as I am by nature.

But let's forget about the damned Rowdies for the time being. They were more like cardboard characters than flesh-and-blood humans anyhow; no amount of belletristic virtuosity can alter or enhance what were, so far as I could determine, very bland (and seemingly interchangeable) personalities.

I am eager to conclude this chapter for another reason, dear reader. I am eager to relive the next one, in which the greatest five minutes of my life have been chronicled.

CHAPTER TWELVE

Prelude to the Greatest Five Minutes of My Life:

August four, 1982. Eight fifty-two p.m. Turner's Gym.

I couldn't understand it. I'd come into my latest bout comparatively well rested, and seething with white-hot rage. I was fighting very well (for me), and had surprised no one more than myself when in round three I actually displayed some agility, deftly back pedaling in the wake of the most awesome haymaker that had ever been launched in my direction. Had it connected, it surely would have killed me.

What I'm trying to say is that my opponent – the aptly named Biff Koharski – was fantastic, the type of boxer those in the game would not hesitate to label a natural. It was apparent even in this, his second fight. Without so much as a gram of fat on his rock hard body, he was a bigger 175 pounds than I was, and much stronger. Although we weren't the main attraction that evening (we were to be upstaged by a pair of fabulous lightweights a little later on), we must have provided the large crowd on hand with a thrilling spectacle, particularly in round five when we dispensed with the footwork and just stood toe-to-toe in the center of the ring, exchanging some of the best punches either of us had ever thrown. So disoriented was I by the end of the round, it was necessary for Stephan to wave me back to my corner – I would never have found it otherwise.

No sooner was I off my feet did Stephan begin slapping and kneading my delts and traps, going at it with the fury of a three hundred pound Polynesian masseuse. I tried to tell him that this was only increasing the flow of blood out of my nose, but it's difficult to speak distinctly while one's back is being pummeled. But that was Stephan for you; I had a cut above one eye, massive swelling around the other, and he felt the remedy lay in brisk massage.

A chorus of jeers and catcalls erupted from the crowd, and I knew without even lifting my head that our sad excuse for a "Round Girl" had clambered through the ropes. Her task: to announce the upcoming round number to that faction of the audience that was just a little dimmer than the rest. She was a real horse and deserved to get booed out of the ring, but I felt sorry for her just the same.

The ref stopped by my corner, and we had a brief but pleasant chat about the number of fingers he was holding up, what day of the week it was, and so on. For a moment I feared he would stop the match due to the facial injuries I had incurred, but I was fighting in a very tough and remote neck of the woods, where few wimps existed among the officials.

"Water," I squawked, after he had left. "Stephan, water…"

"Sorry."

"D-I-I-N-G-G!!"

I could feel it as I got back up. That surge of negative energy, welling up from some black place within me, electrifying my every capillary. It's what had been missing. I'd been fighting well, but – how to word this – in being as captivated as the chap in the stands with the young buck before me, I'd been fighting as Carl Fellows rather than as an agent of the evil restaurant in which I worked.

But I'm happy to report that all this changed with the advent of the sixth and final round. It was not Biff Koharski I was seeing anymore when I glanced across the ring, but Cheryl Marks, that pathetic employee of ours, and someone who could not have defeated me with an anti tank gun. I met "her" in the center of the ring, and the incredible fight continued.

Although from out of town, Koharski's good looks and flamboyant style had made him the crowd favorite, which made the idea of tearing him down all the more attractive to me. I always did operate better as a dark horse. I found "Cheryl's" head to be an inviting target, with its jut jaw and annoying bob haircut; jab after jab crashed through "her" carefully assembled defense. A looping right to the head should have obliterated any trace of pluck Koharski had remaining, but to my utter chagrin it only served to trigger his best flurry of the fight.

And so, by the middle of the round we found ourselves back where we had started (and where most evenly matched combatants, especially the sluggers, end up sooner or later): in the center of the ring, nailing each other with everything we had. He had the heavier punch, and although I had what's known in the sport as a "good beard," the shots I was taking to my flabby midsection were killing me. I knew he was capable of knocking me out, and thus had little choice but to resort to the same deceptive strategy I'd adopted in my previous fight.

With a mere twenty seconds left in the bout, the two of us were gasping for air like a pair of landlocked guppies, clinching every time we had the chance. For all the brilliance he had exhibited that day, my opponent had not paced himself very well, and was taking full advantage of my "lethargy" by curtailing his own assault. Of course, I was playing possum, and with less than ten seconds remaining in the fight I went absolutely berserk, shellacking the flabbergasted Koharski with every punch known to mankind. Had I opened up just a few seconds sooner, I am sure I could have at least knocked him down.

At the sound of the bell we threw our arms around each other, and I found strength enough to hoist him in the air. Yet at no time did I consider him the victor of the fight. The opinion that carried weight in this instance, of course, was that of the referee, and when all was said and done it was Koharski's arm he raised high in triumph. I'd stood up to some pretty stiff clouts that evening, but none so devastating as that decision. It took the wind right out of my sails, as they say.

The Greatest Five Minutes of My Life:

Immediately after my fight I found myself alone in the dressing room, trying to come to grips with the reality of my first defeat while absently peeling yards of tape from my hands. Stephan, after his initial declaration that "we wuz robbed," had gone to join his cronies in the stands.

The door creaked open, prompting me to sit bolt upright on the bench. My curiosity was definitely aroused, as all I could see of my tentative guest were eight-or-so exquisitely formed fingers. A lovely head appeared in due course, followed by an equally lovely body, and my jaw dropped practically to the floor in disbelief. Radiance!

"Are you decent?" she asked playfully, smiling her perfect smile. I could only stare at her as she sat down beside me on the bench, resplendent in her powder blue attire, her heavenly scent affecting me like a narcotic.

"You should have won," she said soberly, and at once I was sorry I hadn't. I was sorry, too, for what had to have been my atrocious appearance at that moment. Running a hand through my hair did little to improve matters, as most of my fingers were still swathed in tape.

Radiance stood up, and at first I feared she was going to leave. But she drifted only as far as the opposite side of the locker room, apparently in search of something. "So you knew I was fighting today, Radiance?" I croaked, having at last regained a degree of phonetic aptitude.

"I didn't know you fought, period!" she called out, extracting a roll of paper towels from someone's maroon colored haversack. "Allie and I just came down to watch the boxing 'cause we had nothing better to do tonight."

She returned to my side with a handful of the paper towels, slipped an arm around my shoulders for support, and began dabbing at my bloodied face.

"Does it hurt much?" she inquired softly.

But once again I was incapable of speech. She had begun to apply a moistened finger to my wounds – moistened with her *own saliva* – and the thought of our bodily fluids commingling had momentarily stunned me.

If I was stunned by that, I was blown away by what she did next. By this time evidence of a great fight in progress out in the ring area was rocking the foundations of the little gym, and the noise seemed to be beckoning Radiance like some impatient authority figure. "I'd better get back to Allie," she said, and with her arm still about my shoulders kissed me tenderly on the cheek. She kissed me on the cheek! She kissed me on the cheek!

"Thank you," I gulped. It was all I could think of to say.

After she'd gone, but with the click of her boots still resounding off the walls, I slithered ecstatically onto the locker room floor. For a time I just lay there, staring up at the grimy ceiling. To me it was as magnificent as the Sistine Chapel's, while the rest of the tiny room could have been some chamber in Buckingham Palace.

Everything was beautiful at that moment in time – Stephan's indifference to me, the Rowdies' preoccupation with me, Harv's desertion of me, Renwald's condemnation of me...I won't go so far as to declare Allie beautiful, but the fact that she had not tagged along with Radiance on this occasion most assuredly was.

So what if I lost a fight? I thought. *Who cares? With Radiance in my corner I'll not fail to win the next billion, including the one for the light-heavy crown!*

The Best Five Minutes of My Life – Aftermath:

For a guy who'd so recently been the recipient of innumerable punches to the belly and head, I got cleaned up and dressed right quick. I seemed to have energy to burn; it had to have been the kiss. Rather than leave immediately, I wandered out to the ring area where two fights were in progress. I peered a little embarrassedly into the crowd, scanning the various rows for Allie's figure, that I might uncover Radiance's in the bargain. It appeared, however, that both girls had left the building.

I decided to do the same.

Having your crush respond favorably to you can evoke more pleasurable sensations than outright sex. Whistling a little passage from Bizet's

"Seguidille" I skipped home like a small child, pitching my duffle bag high into the air, compulsively stroking that area of my left cheek with Radiance's lipprints upon it.

The most beautiful girl in the world had just kissed me! Even Harvey I'd never seen with such a girl. Too bad the little bastard hadn't stuck his head in the locker room in time to see her plant the kiss. I recall what Harv said to me once, not long after we'd met: "I figure you must have been a Casanova or a Don Juan in a previous life."

"Oh yeah?" I'd responded, impressed.

"Because you ain't gettin' nothin' in this life! You're being punished!"

I'd show him. Someday I'd appear on his doorstep with Radiance on my arm, and the look of incredulity on his face would more than compensate for all the gibes he'd made at my expense over the years.

A week-and-a-half later the unthinkable happened. After several fortifying pulls on a forty-ouncer of straight rye, I phoned Radiance at work and asked her out. She accepted.

CHAPTER THIRTEEN

A traveling circus had set up upon a vast meadow not far from St. Tarcisius' (the church that had fallen prey to the Rowdies and was just beginning to struggle back to its feet). Had the impresario known about Timothy's Take-Out, I doubt he'd have allowed his company to touch down within ten miles of Robinson's Pt. One circus in town is enough!

It is where I took Radiance on our first date. While mercifully dissimilar to that funfair debacle the previous year, the outing was not without its "repercussions."

The date began wonderfully, classically. Radiance met me at work on the afternoon of August fourteen, and from there we strolled casually back to Allie's cottage, where, if you recall, Radiance had a room. This walk was actually the highlight of the date, and ranks right up there with the locker room kiss as one of the highlights of my life. What red-blooded guy wouldn't have given his eyeteeth to be in my place that hot afternoon, walking hand-in-hand with gorgeous Radiance down the dirt road leading to her place?

You know, I call it a walk, but Radiance does not walk – she *sashays*. Let me describe to you how she was dressed: white cotton top, coyly unbuttoned, tied in such a way that her scrumptious midriff was exposed. Brand spanking new pair of Levis, indecently tight, and rolled halfway up her silken calves. Save for one delicate anklet her feet were bare, and the sight of those tootsies turned me on as much as anything.

I don't know who reached for whose hand first. I only know that we held each other's tight for much of the walk, and that it was sheer, unadulterated rapture. Conversation had become a trifle strained at one point, but I'd prepared for just such a calamity.

Earlier in the day Renwald had given me a list of some six hundred "catch phrases" to pore over, the absolute best of which it was his intention to display on our signpost. When our lapse in conversation started to get uncomfortable, I extracted the ten-page list from my shirt and handed it to Radiance. To my relief, she scanned the list with what appeared to be great interest.

The majority of these sayings were hackneyed and stilted. "Thrill to our burgers" was retarded enough, but by the three-hundredth-or-so saying the author had clearly begun to go a little batty. Thereafter we encountered such golden maxims as "Hit your aunt on the head with a hammer," and "In your pants."

Whipping out that list had been a masterstroke, as it kept Radiance on the verge of peeing herself for the remainder of our walk. I was laughing too, albeit for a somewhat different reason. (Margaret the supervisor had been about to place an obscene message up on the signpost the night we caught her sabotaging my Clean Up.)

I might as well have said goodnight to Radiance on the doorstep of Allie's cottage, because the date was a shambles from then on. For one thing, I was so nervous and sick to my stomach that I had to prop myself heavily against their living room wall while Radiance went off to freshen up. Both Allie and her look-alike papa were home, which no doubt contributed to my anxiety. Remember, each of them outweighed me by some hundred-and-fifty pounds! Whatever the case, I was about as animated as a sentinel the entire time I was there. Recalling the nights Toby Jr. and I had stolen these peoples' garbage and had taken drunken pisses on their property did little to soothe my frazzled nerves, especially since Allie's father appeared to be eyeing me suspiciously.

Ironically, it was Radiance herself who really kissed off our date, when she asked, in all innocence, "Carl, is it okay if Allie tags along? She wants so badly to go to the circus."

Because I could not refuse my Radiance anything, and I did want in the worst way to get out of that cottage, I answered in the affirmative. It was one of the worst blunders I've ever made. What could have been a true night of nights was ruined, throttled to within an inch of its existence by a hulking, belching, jealous mound of goop by name of Allie Sanborne, or Sanford, or whatever her last name was. I say "jealous" because she resembled nothing that evening so much as a vast, unassailable partition lodged petulantly between Radiance and myself.

The circus was a refreshingly unpretentious little production, and hardly to blame for the crummy time we all had. The "date" did have its moments – it was obvious that Allie outweighed the resident fat lady by at least fifty pounds, a strange "carny" type I'd seen at Timothy's bragging of his lofty status within the troupe was spotted following an elephant around with a shovel, and I won Radiance a teddy bear when miraculously I hit a target at the firing range – but in reality this circus was geared mostly toward children.

I was much relieved (though more than a little concerned) when reports of a missing lion forced an abrupt conclusion to the show.

Radiance and Allie were wise to have brought jackets, as the relatively warm summer day had become a positively frigid summer night. I, as usual, was clad only in shorts and a favorite short-sleeved shirt (which, after fifteen years of faithful service, was not exactly weather resistant anymore.) The two girls did draw close to me and link their arms in mine, which I thought was cute, and we warbled an extended version of "The Monkees Theme" as we headed home.

With a cheeriness that must have seemed forced I bade them goodnight on their doorstep, graciously declining Radiance's offer to come in and warm up. I had my reasons for acting so discourteously – among other things, I'd completely forgotten where I'd pitched my tent, and wanted to begin searching for it before I was overcome by fatigue.

I recall tramping for hours, in absolute darkness, without so much as approaching the secluded locale of my camp. I eventually passed out on a mossy little knoll, and did not awaken until dawn, at which point I again took up the search. I finally stumbled upon the tent a few hours later – in time to change my clothes and head back into work!

I reached Timothy's with minutes to spare, albeit in a slightly disheveled state.

This day was a memorable one, for it kicked off one of the all-time wackiest weeks of my life. My shift began in typical fashion – which is to say, like shit – with both employees and customers on their worst behavior. I'd always suspected that Toby Jr. hated Allie's guts, and my suspicions were confirmed when at one point Toby blew up at her, just outside the storeroom. I'm still not certain what triggered the blast, but never in my life have I been witness to such scathing verbal abuse, and all on the part of Toby Jr. Not once did Allie attempt to defend herself, even when referred to as "you fat fuck," and "dickless" (which struck me as rather a curious way of addressing a girl).

And the customers! Even had they been good humored and compliant this day they would have sickened me to death. How demeaning and frustrating it was taking the orders of these simple creatures, who as I believe I've mentioned before would gaze up at our menu board with the most tortured expressions on their faces, as if the very act of scanning through the items was causing them intense physical and psychological trauma. Ladies humongous beyond belief – two or three times the width of Allie and half as tall – clad in their ubiquitous green stretch pants, would waddle to the counter and unceremoniously drape their monstrous boobs over it (giving whole new meaning to the phrase, "take a load off").

May I take a moment to address those of the female persuasion who insist upon wearing their hair abnormally short? It's ugly, ladies – ugly, frumpy, and disturbingly mannish, and this is true of whichever outrageously expensive style you choose to cultivate if it ain't at least shoulder length. Speaking as one who loves to drool over you, I believe short hair works only for those women whose faces are exceptionally beautiful. Even then, how much more beautiful would their faces appear framed by long and lustrous hair? Roxy's locks were positively riveting, falling almost to the small of her back, her bangs curling slightly inward like the tines of a hay rake.

Allie's reaction to Toby's cruel outburst was to mentally torture me at every opportunity.

"Radiance is still with her boyfriend, you know," she'd mention casually.

"We're only friends, Allie," I'd counter, in a tone of voice every bit as matter-of-fact.

Inside, however, I was a quaking mess – particularly upon learning of the dreaded "Cuddle Nights." According to Allie, it was a term Radiance had coined the previous winter, and it roughly translated into, "Nights Spent with My Fervent Gentleman Caller." Exactly what had transpired between Radiance and her boyfriend on these occasions, Allie, reveling in my anguish, refused to divulge.

But I took comfort in what I believed was Radiance's unimpeachable virtue. She was a goddess, or at the very least my personal gift from God.

Oh yeah, and she was in love with me.

Toby and Allie left shortly after eleven, sticking me, as usual, with a ton of cleaning work. Having just spent some nine hours on The Front (our colloquialism for working the counter), I wasn't sure I was up for it. For one thing, I'd been reduced to staggering around the store like a Cyclops due to a problematic left contact lens. Also, something resembling pneumonia had infiltrated my body, the result, no doubt, of my having made like a woodland creature the night before.

Please understand that my god at the time was a cruel god. The delight He took in our suffering was secondary only to the satisfaction He derived from our capacity to overcome such suffering. Though I professed to be Christian, my god at the time had more in common with Conan's "Crom" than the loving deity of the New Testament. I shook my fist at Him and set to work, secure in the knowledge that I was at my best only when all of life seemed stacked against me. My ace in the hole, of course, was Radiance, the very thought of whom might have seen me through anything.

With Clean Up all but completed, I gathered together those garbage bags that appeared at least three-quarters full (sometimes you can hop right into the receptacle and stomp the bag's contents down to nothing), and then proceeded to haul the entire mess in the general direction of the massive, pink dumpster out back.

I was surprised to find it chilly outside. You could have fried an egg on our countertops but a few feet away. Cursing Toby for having left the side door of the dumpster wide open (but at the same time kinda grateful), I jettisoned the garbage. Heading back indoors, my thoughts were of the moonlight; how even a sliver of it could play havoc with existing shapes, transforming the most colorless and mundane of them into fantastically weird new images, the stuff of our worst nightmares on occasion.

I stopped up short, reflecting specifically on what I thought I'd seen as I'd pitched the trash into the dumpster. Although the thought of doing so embarrassed me, I just had to return for a second look.

I reopened the dumpster door, and peered into the darkness. Before I could so much as adjust my eyes I was startled by a kind of guttural, coughing growl. Too astonished to be frightened, I craned my already hyper-extended neck, popping both head and shoulders into the dumpster in an effort to locate what I was now convinced was a bona fide African Lion!

At some point during the proceedings I decided to get more light on the subject, and hefted open the two weighty panels comprising the lid of the structure. Returning once more to the side door, I found what I was looking for at last.

There he was, sprawled languidly atop a hillock of festering refuse. A very young male lion, not much bigger than a golden retriever and certainly no bigger than Jeremy. Against my better judgment I stepped into the dumpster and cautiously approached the beast, oblivious to the towering mounds of malodorous gunk on either side of me and the puddles of slop beneath my feet. It was undoubtedly a boneheaded thing to do, yet the lion made no move to attack me. As a matter of fact, he scarcely made any movement at all, except to feebly twitch his tail as I drew closer.

No one had to tell me that this was the cat that had escaped from the circus. And it was not difficult to understand why he'd chosen to leave. His exposed flank was a mass of raw, open sores, looking as if it had recently been dissected. If there was any fur on that side of his body, it was either concealed by these gaping wounds or buried beneath scabs of older ones. The thin, elongated nature of the wounds suggested that they might have been inflicted by a trainer's whip.

The sight practically moved me to tears. I've always been a fanatical animal lover, believing them to be incapable of sin and therefore more deserving of life than we ourselves are. The love and compassion I no longer felt for my fellow man I now lavished on creatures like Shindig, Jeremy, and "Baby Boy" – the name I'd chosen right then and there to bestow upon the overgrown tabby before me.

I cradled Baby Boy in my arms, and carried him into the kitchen of the restaurant, where I was pretty sure an old first aid kit was buried in one of the cupboards. The cat could not have been more obliging. In due course I located the kit, cleansed Baby's wounds, and bound him in gauze. I cooked him up a mess of Timothy Burgers (they worked for me when I was hurtin'), and in the process forgot how utterly dog-tired I was myself.

From his makeshift bed on the kitchen table the cub-who-was-not-quite-a-cub-anymore bolted down his burgers, while I stood nearby, just out of range of those big teeth. I was at a complete loss as to what to do with my ravenous protégée, although I knew what I *wasn't* gonna do.

I would rather have formally adopted him than returned him to that circus.

The roof! Perhaps I could stick him on the roof, if only temporarily, until I find a good zoo or something. Naw, that idiot Toby's up there all the time, smoking his dope! And I don't particularly want anyone knowing about this – with the possible exception of Radiance, if there's a chance she might be impressed...

The roof idea I dismissed as quickly as it had come to me, though not after suppressing a hysterical giggle at the thought of Toby climbing onto the roof for a good toke, only to be attacked by a wildcat. But it led indirectly to a much greater idea. Up on the roof was stored the one thing I'd ever created that was remotely capable of serving its purpose: my Huck Finn-inspired raft. Why not paddle the lion out to "Isolation Isle," the rocky outcrop that seemed – at least from my perspective, having never been out there – tailor made for him?

My dear friends, that is precisely what I did.

It was no easy task, let me tell you. The wooden raft was cumbersome, and all but impossible to tote down the street with one hand. The crude leash I'd fashioned for Baby Boy kept slipping off his neck, and several times that morning I had to drop everything and chase after him – thank God it was four a.m.

Things were no better out on the lake. The cat was clearly petrified, and it was when he began lashing out at me that I realized that the "Androcles and the Lion" fable we'd been living up to that point was over. And there was no escaping the little bastard on that raft.

It got pretty hectic, all right. At one point I was fully prepared to leap overboard and leave Baby Boy in command of the vessel. Fortunately for me, Baby happened upon the small lean-to I had fashioned at one end of the raft. He remained inside of it, with just his bum peeking out, until we reached Isolation Isle.

It was an arduous voyage, to say the least. Isolation Isle was almost a mile out, and I was propelling an eight-foot raft with the three-foot plastic paddle from Harvey's dingy. On top of that, I had made, in the darkness, a grievous miscalculation with regards to the "island's" position, and was thus obliged to spend another hour or so bobbing up and down the coast before finally colliding into it.

It more closely resembled some deceased Scotchman's cairn than any islet, but appeared at the same time to be the perfect anonymous hideaway – too far out for swimmers to reach, and too dangerous for even small craft to approach (safeguarded as it was by numerous, barely-submerged rock formations.) Baby Boy took to it immediately, and went off exploring with typical youthful inquisitiveness. I, on the other hand, had barely the strength for a precursory examination; upon successfully conducting one I hopped back into my little skiff and shoved off. I tossed Baby Boy one of Jeremy's old chew toys and then rededicated myself to the tiny oar, paddling with almost comical ferocity back to the mainland, which I was surprised to find bathed in early morning sunlight.

The secret of Baby Boy I kept very much to myself. He remained on Isolation Isle for five nights and four days, and the sea air seemed to do him good. I visited him a couple of times a day, and a couple of times a day he attempted to maim me. His conduct improved somewhat upon learning that with each visit came food.

Lots and lots of food. All those hamburger patties were plenty tough on the pocketbook – reason enough, or so I kept telling myself, to surrender up the big cat before the week was out. But no way would I return him to that circus. By Wednesday I was ready to act upon one of my more outlandish schemes, the inception of which could be traced to the first time Baby Boy clawed me and drew blood.

As I had Thursday and the greater part of Friday off from work, come

Wednesday night Baby Boy and I were rolling down the highway like Bonnie and Clyde. Our destination: Montreal, Quebec!

Large enough to support several zoos, and safely out of range of that hick traveling circus, Montreal seemed as good a city as any for my *felis leo*. Predictably, my scheme's weakest link was the old Grey Ghost. I'd fitted her with new tires, tuned up her engine, and had invested what few pennies I had remaining in a brand new paint job, but whether or not she'd be able to travel hundreds of miles nonstop was anybody's guess. I gambled, and, astonishingly, I won.

Looking back on the experience now, I can't believe how stupid I was. I had made no attempt to conceal Baby Boy – indeed, he rode shotgun all the way – and yet, no one had a thing to say about it, not even as we crossed the Ontario/Quebec border.

I was certain that there would be some sort of large-scale wildlife facility in either Montreal or Quebec City, and of course I was right. Just outside Montreal there was a magnificent one, and the zookeeper-in-residence had no reservations about accepting Baby into the fold, after an appropriate period of quarantine. I'd told the guy, in my stilted high school French, that I'd simply found the cat by the wayside that morning. It was all the explanation he needed, evidently.

A long trip back to Robinson's Pt. awaited me, but I was jubilant. At a time when virtually every species of animal on the planet was either enslaved, in torment, or on the brink of extinction, it felt good to have actually enriched a life.

One harrowing sidelight to this vignette: While traipsing about Isolation Isle with Baby Boy I'd uncovered traces of what had likely been, at some point, a full-blown demonic consortium. Objects I found purportedly of great value to practitioners of Satanism included the charred skull of a ram, and remnants of about a dozen black candles. Several rocks on the island's leeward side were similarly dark and sooty, indicative of some sort of ceremony involving fire. But the general impression I got was that the ceremony had been performed long before, and on one occasion only.

The very thought of demonic activity on the island had only strengthened my conviction to attend more properly to the long-term requirements of Baby Boy. It goes without saying that I believed what I'd found to be "Rowdy residue," and I recall poking about for hours in my effort to uncover one especially damning clue that might point towards the gang's lair. But, alas – t'was not to be.

CHAPTER FOURTEEN

Labor Day was fast approaching, though not nearly fast enough for me. That final week of August was hell, and August twenty-nine in particular will live in infamy as the day that even crusty little Margaret crumbled – an event I never thought I'd live to see.

After twice drawing a customer the wrong kind of pop that afternoon, she'd returned to the soda fountain in tears, and had proceeded to draw one large orange pop after another until the counter was full of large orange pops. Although her pitiful sniffling was tough to endure, none of us could find it in our hearts to console her because we hated her so much.

Working at Timothy's in August was like emulating Sisyphus in Hades. Just when you thought you'd finally "cleaned house," another tidal wave of humanity would come crashing in, more destructive than its predecessor. Many times, I realize, I have referred to Timothy's Take-Out as hell – here you have a literal analogy.

In a sense I was sorry to see summer pass, for it meant bidding Radiance a fond adieu also. I had wanted so desperately to ask her to the local end-of-summer beach bash, but was ashamed of my social backwardness in general and my inability to dance in particular. I probably could have faked my way through a couple of slow dances, but no one, not even Radiance, was ever gonna get me up for a fast one. To me, the absolute gayest sight in the world was – and continues to be – that of a grown man on the dance floor, shaking his tush.

When Labor Day Weekend finally did roll around I was more dead than alive, and I'll bet this had as much to do with my having shelved my outside interests temporarily as it did my physical condition. Without my dreams to sustain me, I'd become a zombie. If I happened to be "flying low," I didn't care. If I happened to be dribbling snot, I didn't care. I sought only to survive.

Labor Day itself was busy to a nauseating extreme, as though the general public was making a last-ditch attempt to drive me certifiably insane. They came close to succeeding. "Gotta get up early for school tomorrow, kiddies," I cackled repeatedly, to children, senior citizens, cups, napkins, straws...

And then it was closing time, eleven in the glorious Post Meridiem, the moment I'd been awaiting with baited breath since early April. The last few customers had snatched their food and beat it on home. It was Carl Fellows' moment of triumph.

My exhilaration was contagious, and had infected my two "running mates," Toby Jr. and Roxy. We were all instigators, that evening, of an event that has since come to be known as "The Great Water Fight." Staff members had playfully doused each other with water before, but never on such a grand scale as this. We're talking buckets here, folks. And what the water did for Roxy's torso, I can't begin to tell you.

What damage the store sustained was not evident until the next day. Renwald was waiting for me with news of a malfunctioning cash register and important documents rendered illegible by "some kinda liquid." My remorse was such that I offered to pay for all repairs; while this succeeded in appeasing Renwald, it set me back considerably.

September, in direct contrast to August (and July, and June) is a fabulous month to spend in a resort town. The weather is still okay, and you pretty much have the place to yourself. My hours at the restaurant had been once again reduced to forty a week, allowing me plenty of time to indulge in a favorite hobby – drifting out to sea on my raft. No longer did I compose music out there, for no longer did I harbor any illusions of becoming the next John Lennon or Johann Sebastian Bach. That, and I had recently plunged head over heels into another get-rich-quick scheme: cartooning.

While I'd never been entirely comfortable composing music, drawing cartoons was a different story. I felt I had a genuine flair for it. After all, I had a wild imagination, rudimentary drawing talent, and approached the whole business of making people laugh with a deadly seriousness. And talk about ambition – I had yet to create an original character, and already saw myself as competing for Charles Shultz's prestigious crown.

I still found time for fun. At least once a week Toby and I would hit the local and outlying strip clubs. We'd we hit the "meat markets" with considerably less frequency, as there would likely be normal women in attendance, and neither Toby nor I were capable of interacting with normal women.

Even so, it could be a fascinating experience to hang out with Toby in the latter establishments. He might not have had Harvey's ability to attract women to the table, but there would be entire evenings spent in the grip of hysterical, drunken laughter. A few of these evenings I number among the finest of my (admittedly dreary) life. One drawback to them – whereas ol' Harv was rude and insulting in my company exclusively, Toby Jr. was rude and insulting to *everyone*, and it made some of the more sensitive barflies want to kill him.

Some of the strangest bands played through Robinson's Pt., and many times their names alone (The Private Parts, Bloody Diarrhea, etc.) would be enough to lure Toby and I into the meat markets we deplored so much.

At the risk of contradicting myself, I was beginning to find nightclubs in general to be abhorrent. Whether singles' bars, strip joints, or unholy unions of the two, their dingy environments were detrimental to my being in a way I cannot satisfactorily explain.

Life at Timothy's, meanwhile, was just a bore. Delightfully boring, but a bore nonetheless. To counter the tedium I would assign myself and others the most absurd chores you could imagine, such as rearranging the hundreds of tiny catsup and relish packets (I was after that aesthetic look), and scraping gum from the undersides of countertops (the least prestigious task of them all?). I'd also developed into quite a voracious doodler, to the extent that – for the duration of the off-season, at least – none of Renwald's invoices or order forms was safe.

Autumn alighted upon Robinson's Pt. as unobtrusively as the most delicate butterfly. The leaves began to take on indescribably beautiful colors, and the lake seemed to sparkle as never before. But along with the majesty came the plummetting temperatures, and I realized I was courting serious illness by continuing to sleep outside. One of the strangest business deals in history was subsequently struck, allowing me to bunk inside of Timothy's Take-Out virtually free of charge!

All Mr. Renwald asked in return was that I embark on a series of "spy missions" throughout the county. I'm referring to the act of skulking into various restaurants, and scribbling down in a covert fashion how much everything costs. I proceeded to do this for him, accumulating data from close to fifty stores. I fear I may have done my job only too well, as it is my instinct even today to whip out pen and paper upon entering a diner or fast food joint.

Though I now had a roof over my head, Timothy's as a place to crash was no real improvement over my pup tent. For one thing, I resented the hell out of being awakened in the morning by the likes of Renwald, Margaret, and David. Also, the store was as bone numbingly cold in the winter as it was hot in the summer – more of a glorified wind shelter than a domicile in which to roast my tootsies.

Right off the bat, there was one big problem with this arrangement, and it had to do with my ever lovin' parents. It seemed they were absolutely bent on spending the afternoon of October two at "my place." As far as they knew, I was still living in the old beach house, as I continued to use 632 Lakeshore Rd. as a return address whenever I sent them mail.

It was obvious that I needed, on the afternoon of October two, a cottage, any cottage, to pass off as my "new abode." I thought of contacting Allie – who had, of course, long since returned to her home in Mississauga – but quickly dismissed the idea. Nothing was worth getting in touch with her again. Besides, her parents would never have gone for it.

Margaret, I did not even consider, for similar reasons. Not only did she despise everything about me, but also she was married to a cop, and they lived closer to Port Radcliff than Robinson's Pt.

I needed someone who lived alone, and was good-natured enough to go along with the idea. Rupert still lived by himself, amazingly, but by no stretch of anyone's imagination was he good-natured. And I knew my parents would have been suspicious, upon entering a cottage adorned in Early Old Fart. I was sure that Roxy lived on her own, though I had no idea where, and was too embarrassed to include her in all of this, anyhow. Stephan I had not seen since losing the fight to Biff Koharski, and I would rather have died than asked Mr. Renwald.

So that narrowed it down to one person. As he seemed like the ideal candidate I don't know why I hadn't thought of him first. Of course I'm referring to David Gardner.

The Superhero!

He might have been my very last choice, but he was an inspired choice nonetheless. Not only was he my age and of single status, but his cottage was right on the beach, and tasteful enough to set even the minds of my ultra-conservative parents at ease. He seemed reluctant to lend me his digs at first, but I knew (shrewd judge of character that I am) that I would have little trouble wearing this affable fellow down.

For a day that ended so disastrously, October two started out well enough. I really got to know the Superhero that morning, as together we replaced his vast array of effects with what few of my own I still carried around. He struck me as being a lonely man – perhaps not desperately so, but it did seem as though he were in need of a little conversation. The words came easier for him once he let slip his cumbrous cloak of reserve, and were very soon tumbling from his mouth in a torrent. Permit me to dispel at this time a few

175

of the many rumors surrounding this odd young fellow.

The Superhero was not gay, just very shy. He was not, as far as I could ascertain, an undercover spy or CIA affiliate. He confessed that he was still a virgin, which for reasons unbeknownst to me did not come as much of a shock.

Although I'd pretty much given up on the fairer sex myself, a few hours with the Superhero had *me* feeling like a ladies' man. I thought my track record with the chicks was dismal – this good looking chappie, this "All Canadian Boy," had never been on an actual date, having had apparently come to grips (no pun intended) with a lifetime of compulsive masturbation.

"Hell, Superher – uh, *Dave*," I exclaimed. "I'm practically a virgin myself. Well, as close to being one as you can get without technically being one... And Toby? Don't tell him I told you this, but by his own admission he's only been laid once, and had to pay for the privilege."

That seemed to cheer him up some.

I discovered later, while stowing a few of his family portraits, that we shared a deep love of classical music. Much of the time we were supposedly to have been switching and hiding various personal items, we spent listening raptly to selections from each other's extensive music collections. I introduced him to the evocative tone poetry of Debussy and Ravel, while he re-introduced me to the sprightly operettas of Strauss Jr., Lehar, and Offenbach. I was to pay for this dalliance, and soon.

As this was the first time that conversation between David and I had ever transcended vague pleasantries, I feel our dismal efforts to transform the cottage were justifiable, if not particularly intelligent. After all, was not the mighty Superhero – this creature who seemed to have been bred by Renwald for the express purpose of working at Timothy's – revealing his humanity this day?

Not only was he a human being, he was a decent human being. His utter devotion to his job might have been a trifle perverse, but I believe we all have something of the latent caped crusader within – it was certainly true in my case. Unlike Harvey, Toby, and virtually everyone else I can think of, the Superhero did not utter profanities on a regular basis, nor did he fracture the English language. The heart of a true intellectual beat inside of him, although he was on the surface a very simple man, whose only real indulgence was an absurd collection of moist towelette packets. He had hundreds of them. "After a year or so, they expand and explode," he said sheepishly.

By three in the afternoon, David was gone; milling about in his stead were

Mom, Pop, and Shindig. The three seemed quite impressed with my "new pad," though Shindig had to have known the truth. To get my folks the hell out of there, I suggested a walk on the beach.

We had a lovely stroll, stopping to dine at the one truly respectable eatery in town: The Beachcomber. It was when we got back to the cottage, as my parents were readying to leave, that disaster struck. Bear with me, as the mere recollection of it is painful.

Understandably enough (as it *was* a long drive home), my mother decided to pop into the washroom before departing. No sooner had Dad and I plopped back down upon the sofa did she wander dazedly back out to us, clutching a vial with several large, colorful pills inside. "I-I found this in your medicine cabinet, Carl," she stammered, setting the unmarked, semi-transparent container down upon the Superhero's coffee table.

Well! As young and strong as I was at the time, I can honestly say that that moment was the closest I'd ever come to fainting dead away. For what seemed like an eternity my mom just stood there in front of us, staring in horror at what she'd found. Monumentally taken aback, I was incapable even of turning my head to see how my father was coping. At length I was able to sputter the classic, "They aren't mine, Ma," and it had about all the effect on her I figured it would.

My folks slipped away without saying anything further, leaving Shindig with me despite my obvious unwillingness to take him. And though the dog was primed for a session of rough-and-tumble, it was not upon him I pounced but the container of pills. My worst suspicions were confirmed almost immediately – the pills were amphetamines.

The Superhero was on speed.

Recreational drugs. How contemptuously I leer at those who feel the need to enliven their pitiful existences with recreational drugs. How derisively I laugh at those who lack the intestinal fortitude to get along any other way. To this day I remain utterly incapable of discerning the worth of substances whose meagre benefits are so short-term. Needless to say my respect for the Superhero plummeted immeasurably upon the discovery of the amphetamines, and though I never stopped needling him (in a friendly way) to kick the pathetic things, he's probably popping them as I write this.

I could bear it no longer. So ashamed was I of having my folks believe that I was some crazed junkie, I called home within days of the incident and confessed everything. Relieved at my being clean, I suppose, my mom and dad took the news of my having to live at Timothy's pretty calmly.

My living arrangements were made bearable by the presence of Shindig in my life. The charismatic canine had won over everybody, including Mr. Renwald and Jeremy. I'd anticipated a storm of opposition, particularly with regard to keeping him in the restaurant, but Renwald turned out to be amazingly co-operative. (Was this the same man who routinely threatened Toby's mutt with castration?) Renwald had witnessed Shindig and Jeremy's classic first encounter, and had been as astounded as anyone, I think, that it had not ended in one of their deaths.

I won't soon forget it, either. I was discussing some trifling bit of business with Renwald in his tiny excuse for an office, Shindig at my feet, when all at once Jeremy appeared at the doorway. I did not think to latch onto Shindig's collar, and the two dogs made a beeline for each other. Renwald and I braced for the canine equivalent of World War III, but no violence was forthcoming; the supposed adversaries were more interested in exploring each other's bodily orifices. And when big, surly Jeremy lifted up a paw as if in a playful overture to my pooch, we thought we were in some parallel universe. After all, not only was our Jeremy notoriously ill tempered, he was big enough to have Shindig for lunch! And Shindig himself was a Staff, which translates roughly into "being totally without fear." It was a volatile combination to say the least, theoretically speaking, yet the two were already behaving like the best of pals. Even the flint-hearted Toby was impressed.

November 1982. Sleeping in the store was fast losing its appeal, not that it'd had an iota of appeal to begin with. For a guy who values his privacy above all else, I was seeing precious little of it, despite the fact that we were closing up as early as seven-thirty some nights.

If unwelcome human presence was difficult to bear, intrusions of the small, beady-eyed and furry kind were something else again. Renwald will deny this a hundred times over, but Timothy's in the winter months was something of a haven for *Rattus Norviegus*. And the audacious, abhorrent little fiends were not above scampering across one's reclining figure late in the night. They'd been bad the previous winter, Lord knows, but at least I'd not been required to share bed and breakfast with them.

It was I, the great animal rights advocate, who suggested to Toby that he bring in his .22 calibre shotgun one night and blow away as many of the rodents as he could. Toby agreed wholeheartedly, and by mid-November was dropping in perhaps every other night! For all his efforts, I think he managed to bag three, before the entire colony packed up and left of their own volition.

What had attracted the rats to Timothy's in the first place was beyond me.

If their fundamental objective was to get their tiny butts in out of the cold, they could hardly have made a poorer choice in prospective lodgings.

Close to the end of the month, Renwald's cherished "Golden Hamburger" – an ugly, ludicrous trophy of which he was tremendously fond – vanished. A grateful distributor had presented him with the award years before, and it was truly an eyesore of major proportions. Everyone on staff hated it.

But Renwald was beside himself, which made me all the more determined to recover the monstrosity (and be the one to stand, however temporarily, in his good stead). If someone had indeed stolen it, as Renwald was intimating in not-so-subtle a fashion, the culprit was likely among the staff, for the trophy had been where no customer could have reached it unless they'd had the wing span of a small aircraft.

Not that I'd believed for a second that anyone had taken it home with them. Composed mostly of cheap wood, it could not have been worth very much. But in turning the store literally upside down I had uncovered no trace of the thing. Without any "leads" as such, my suspicions centered naturally around Renwald's own son, irrefutably the most evil and unscrupulous individual on staff.

Poor Tobes! It was always upon his head that accusations of theft were being levied, whether of food, cash, or hamburger trophies. Admittedly, he had done much over the years to warrant such distrust, but this hardly alleviated my remorse upon deciding to monitor his behavior for a couple of days. I accepted a long-standing invitation to hang out with him at his cottage for the better part of an afternoon, thinking that he might have stashed the trophy in his bedroom. After all, was there a more desolate, isolated place on the face of the earth?

Turns out we did spend much of the day in his room, and I had the opportunity to search it from top to bottom. Alas, no trophy. But what a time we had! It was the first of several days spent similarly. For the duration of my stay, we just lay on the floor, listening to tapes.

Toby, of course, was no David "Superhero" Gardner, and in no facet of their lives was the disparity more apparent than in their respective musical tastes. Toby listened exclusively to heavy metal, a genre I could and did appreciate, although so much of it was sophomoric garbage. But a good power chord is a good power chord, and the melodies seemed all the sweeter when couched between them.

The fun really started when I popped in a "demo" of mine from my songwriting days. I did it just for a laugh, having long recognized my music for the shit that it was. Toby thought I'd slipped in one of his AC/DC tapes, and was therefore caught completely off guard as my feeble guitar scratching began to trickle out of his speakers. And when my equally anemic singing voice issued forth, forget it!! All I heard for the next three hours was,

"AH, HAW HAW HAW HAW! AH, HAW HAW HAW HAW HAW!!"

I don't think I laughed so much in the ensuing five years as I did that afternoon. My efforts at composing had indeed been execrable. The one recording I had thought held promise (a piece titled "Why Don't You Phone?") I'd loused up by sneezing right into the mike, halfway through the take. My patented Mickey Mouse falsetto, which I'd been forced to employ more often than I would have liked, was too a source of great amusement.

I should like to describe the Renwald abode in terms you can understand, although it may prove difficult.

It was a pigsty.

Wow, that was easier than I thought.

Massive, crumbling posters dominated the walls of Toby's bedroom, and several of their images shall haunt me unto the grave. One poster depicted a well-known rock singer clutching his scrotum (in an apparent effort to screech in an higher register, a technique I would have done well to emulate), and another had preserved for posterity Toby's biggest crush – a furious, heiling Adolph Hitler.

It was Toby, ironically, who eventually found the "Golden Hamburger" award. While tossing trash into the big pink dumpster one day, he'd become drawn to the spectacle of his overgrown pooch scratching furiously at a lustrous object half-buried in a snow bank. The dog had apparently gone and done what all of us had wanted to do for a very long time – that is, he'd snatched the trophy from its roost, taken it out back, buried it in the snow, and pissed on it!

Toby, "friend" that he was, accused my dog of having run off with it, conveniently overlooking the fact that Shinny could not have reached the thing in a million years of trying. (Meanwhile, it would have been nothing for Jeremy to have simply walked over and clamped it between his enormous jaws.) If Toby's old man was anything, however, he was sharp as a tack, and neither Shindig nor I ever received a reprimand. The trophy, more tarnished than ever because of the piss, was returned to its original spot of honor, and a baleful eye was cast upon Jeremy forever after.

Christmas 1982 came and went, with no "Rowdy" incidents to report. On Christmas Eve, inside the small chapel that was St. Tarcicius', I understand that Father Hutchison held an all-night vigil of a most unorthodox sort, arming himself with a baseball bat, and going so far as to "booby trap" the chapel's front doors.

While I myself had seen nothing of the Rowdies for months, I was determined not to let them fade from memory. As far as I was concerned, they had grievously overstepped their bounds the night they worked over the ol' Grey Ghost. If there was one thing in the world I knew how to do and do well, it was carry a grudge – I wasn't gonna fall for that "out of sight, out of mind" shit again.

I admit I feared them. I feared them paying a visit to Timothy's when I wasn't there. Try to envision doddering old Rupert attempting to hold nine hulking Rowdies at bay. I'm blanching as we speak.

Alas, there was not a trace of the Rowdies that winter.

Living in the restaurant continued to be a pain in the ass, and Toby and I were still getting fall-down drunk once or twice a week. (Not that the latter activity was something I cared for anymore. I pretty well had to get drunk; I found the atmosphere of the nightclubs that oppressive.)

In fact, the closest I came to actually missing a shift at Timothy's can be attributed to precisely this type of overindulgence, dating from precisely this period of intemperance. Rye whisky was my drink back then, and one evening Toby and I consumed a "forty ouncer" of the stuff, virtually straight.

The after effects were cataclysmic. I awoke the following morning feeling as much like a turd as it is possible to feel (while still retaining those qualities that make us uniquely human), and gamely prepared for work. Alas, I appeared to be suffering through the acute stages of alcohol poisoning, and could barely stand upright without becoming engulfed in nausea. There's just no escaping those dreadful spins, is there, even when lying flat on one's stomach. Which is basically how I spent the duration of my shift, to Margaret's disgust. Flat on my stomach on the kitchen floor, with only the soothing tiles to offset the inferno in my head. Thank God we weren't overly busy that day.

March 1983. The days of rapturous cross-country skiing and wandering the deserted streets were pretty much over, for a season or two. On mild, sunny days we were almost busy at Timothy's, and once more I was astonished at the seeming correlation between climactic conditions and junk food consumption.

I'd won two more fights that winter, each by knockout. As my opponents had been absolute crumb bums, I was inclined to see these fights as gigantic steps *backward* in my boxing "career." Similarly, I was getting nowhere with my comics. I had accumulated a veritable rogue's gallery of colorful characters, but was having difficulty restricting their hijinks to three or four panels. My forte appeared to be twenty-five page mini epics!

It is only fitting, I suppose, that I conclude this chapter with a word about Radiance. I was holding this fifteen-year-old girl to her word that she would return to us in May. I NEEDED her to come back. For as hard as I'd tried over the winter to cram my life full of activity and purpose, my longing for her had only intensified. It didn't help that I was also contending with a distressing premonition, one that had arisen seemingly out of nowhere, and that I could shake no more successfully than the obsessive pining.

I felt the two of us would not cross paths again.

CHAPTER FIFTEEN

Well, by April we were back into it. I've said it before and it bears repeating: Nowhere were the effects of global overpopulation more in evidence than at Timothy's Take-Out during tourist season. I'll bet that if Renwald had charted his yearly grosses at any given time, they would more or less have pursued this configuration:

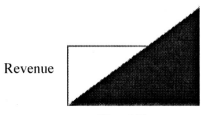

Revenue

Fiscal Year

On the day of the annual Spring Meeting, Radiance was nowhere to be seen. (Of all the damn predictions I'd made over the centuries, *this* would have to be the accurate one!) According to Allie, who was all too "present and accounted for," Radiance had found a better paying job back home. Simple as that.

Lucinda (of the chainsaw voice and the excessive body hair) was returning for another year, as was Cheryl, and I reacted to this with a singular thought: *Bully!* No attempt was made to replace Radiance, which was only right as far as I was concerned. The girl was irreplaceable.

Naturally, I was torn apart; true to form, I carried on. I was ashamed of my sensitive heart, and how it was being stomped to pieces by Radiance. I wanted nothing more than to become a machine. Cold. Plodding. Relentless. *Imperivous.*

Everything was fucked. Shindig was back with my parents, cartooning was proving an exercise in futility, and so for that matter was boxing.

Something had to give.

In early June, after very little deliberation, really, I officially "retired" from boxing, with a record of 8-1-1. A damn good record for one who'd taken the sport up on a lark, wouldn't you say? I continued to weight train, of course, as a means of counteracting my colossal junk food intake, and also to provide a visual deterrent to unruly customers.

If I failed to fully realize the "visual deterrent" objective, it was because most of the obnoxious troublemakers at Timothy's were female. Either they were in the throes of menopause, or were of a distinct subspecies, such as biker chicks or stevedore chicks. Whether you were King Kong or Milquetoast seemed not to make a difference to these women, who, for reasons known only to themselves, were inclined to ball out anyone and everyone as they would a small child.

Mr. Renwald was also given to embarrassing me in public, but it was his uncouth manner that offended more than his whining. He had but one emotion, it seemed – excitability – and wore it on his sleeve. Mr. Renwald remains the one person I know with temerity enough to curse God with one breath, and plead for His intervention with the next.

Timothy's Take-Out, so often a source of improvisational comedy at its finest, prospered over the summer of '83, no doubt about it. But at what cost? Renwald had among his staff a man who popped illegally obtained stimulants as if they were jujubes, an alcoholic teenager whose only goal in life, it seemed – apart from one day embarking on a psychopathic killing spree – was to spend each and every day off "getting incapacitated," and a supervisor who had clearly served one repugnant customer too many. Add to this list a hypersensitive manager who had just about reached the end of his tether.

I was back to roaming the countryside, squatting unobtrusively on property both public and private. Not that I was especially fond of the lifestyle, I just enjoyed seeing money that would otherwise have gone into rent accumulate in my savings account. The fact that I'd abandoned cartooning and boxing did allow me more time for sleep, but it had also robbed me of any real sense of purpose.

The sleep I was gaining was hardly quality stuff.

But I'd been right to drop the aforementioned activities, and songwriting too. Being a successful cartoonist would never have fulfilled me. Likewise with composing music – unless single-handedly resurrecting the classical idiom had been within my means. And would witnessing his tough outer husk capture the light heavyweight boxing crown truly have satisfied the "inner" Carl? I reckon not, although both Carls would have appreciated the money.

Perhaps this impassioned, soul-searching garble is just my way of stating the obvious – that I was a man without any discernable talents. My music was redeemable only for its comedic value. My cartoons, by contrast, were totally devoid of comedic value, and decidedly amateurish. As far as boxing was concerned, not only could I barely see what I was hitting (not that it mattered much against the sluggards I'd been fighting), between the physical drubbing I received from sparring and the emotional drubbing I received at work, well…I was getting too much drubbing! Those who knew of my involvement in the fight game were honoring my request to keep it from Renwald, though evidence of it was literally stamped on my face much of the time. Everyone at Timothy's came to know of the recurrent "styes" that occasionally inflated my eyelids to grotesque proportions, and the bloody noses that were liable to start up when I least expected them to (a condition that sometimes startled customers). And then there were my "severely chapped lips," which no amount of lubricant could hope to assuage.

One souvenir of my boxing exploits I retain to this day, and it's a damned embarrassing one. Like the mythical Rudolph, I find it difficult at times to conceal the bright red color of my nose, and I defy any man of medicine to remedy the situation. It's not a chronic condition in the sense that my schnoz is red all the time; it just sort of "flares up" every now and again, to my absolute chagrin.

In the end, my decision to quit boxing came down to vanity. Stephan wanted me to drop another twenty-odd pounds of my "hard-earned heft," and I was not inclined to do so. That's all there was to it, really.

Having straggled off the proverbial high road to glory, I was in no shape to approach another ghastly summer at Timothy's. I needed re-routing, or a map, or something!

July 1983. Timothy's was both busy and hot. Staff members resorted to taking their breaks in the walk-in cooler. Food that fell to the floor was unhesitatingly scooped up and sent out anyway. I found it exceedingly difficult to wander out among customers and clean picnic tables, as I looked like such a fag in my orange uniform. I had difficulty, as well, yelping the number "seven," for some reason; I found it necessary to have someone else belt out any order number that had in it a seven.

Coupons. Coupons offering Timothy Burgers "two for one," were flooding in by the bushel, and with them these unbelievable assholes who actually got pissed when told they could not use them for hot dogs or milkshakes. You'd think people would be grateful to receive two-for-one burger offers, but this appeared not to have been the case at Robinson's Pt.

Napkins. To discourage customers from taking such outrageous liberties with our complimentary napkins, we resorted to hiding them from view. In fact, if there's one question that will still be reverberating in my head after death, it'll be, "Do you have any serviettes?" Hearing this question repeated ad nauseaum annoyed me to the extent that I tended to dole out scads more napkins per order than even the greediest customer would have thought to take.

My one recurring thought that summer: *This is what hell must be like.*

No longer did I fantasize about my beloved Radiance, preoccupied as I was with imagining all of our customers as belonging to some vast, actively demonstrating union. I would invariably represent organized crime in these reveries, or some other institution that specialized in dispersing, by any means possible, unruly picketers.

At the heart of this enormously satisfying fantasy was Jeremy, the sole member of my "Crowd Control Unit." I'd fit him with an immense, custom-designed spiked collar, and then send him, jaws a-quavering, into the very core of the assemblage. What a fearful sight he'd be, slashing his way to where the quaking union organizer stood, oblivious to the bottles, rocks, and clubs of the demonstrators, his bloody saliva dangling in ribbons from his gaping mouth.

On a lighter note…

(Well, hardly…)

I must inform you of a certain robbery that occurred on the evening of July sixteen, and was duly noted in the July seventeen edition of *The Huronia*, page three:

> Tomlin's Grocery, located just outside Port Radcliff on Highway 6, was held up last night by four men, one reportedly brandishing a bowie knife two feet in length. Owner Earnest Tomlin, 63, alone in the store at the time, was not harmed. The thieves fled the scene with eighty-five dollars in cash, a bushel of blueberries, and

several loaves of French bread. Anyone
with information conceivably of value to
authorities, please contact the Port Radcliff
Police Dept.

Feeling every inch the harborer of information "conceivably of value to authorities" (how could I *not* have implicated the Rowdies in this affair?), I dropped in on both the Port Radcliff police and old Ernie Tomlin. Surprisingly – or, perhaps, not surprisingly – neither could have cared less about what I had to say, and I remember all too vividly the bitter hike back to my tent that afternoon.

If I'm ever gonna bring these devil worshiping sons of bitches to their knees, I thought, fuming, *I'm gonna have to do it myself.*

CHAPTER SIXTEEN

Sunday, July twenty, 1983, was a day I wish had never existed. Because it is so pivotal a day in what remains of the tale, however, I shall force myself to meticulously recount its events.

The previous day, while also hideous, had at least started out promisingly; they'd been calling for rain and I was scheduled to work from two to close. As was so often the case, however, the weather bureau was out by a country mile in its prediction, and we were as busy as hell all night. Why, oh why, was our revenue on any given day so heavily influenced by high and low pressure systems? Do people suddenly lose their appetite when the temperature dips a few degrees, or when rain begins to fall? Perhaps there is something about the primal, cleansing nature of a good rain that inspires people to seek out more nutritious places to eat.

Our food appeared to suit them well enough the evening of July nineteen – although you'd never have guessed it had you been the one handing it out. Fucking rude, selfish, self-righteous sons of bitches these people were, lower than vermin, their purpose here on earth anyone's guess. Uncouth defectives of both sexes would often frightfully abuse their kiddies before my very eyes, boxing their ears or smacking their asses if they so much as spoke out of turn. Even worse to endure, from the perspective of one attempting to take their order, was when the brood was in control of things. Frustrating with a capital "F!"

Anyway, these wretched families would often order our "Fun Meals," and in doing so truly made for a horrible spectacle, fumbling with our silly hats, fiddling with our silly party favors, while so obviously hating each others' guts. Had the spectacle not occurred with such frequency, I might actually have found it amusing.

It was close to five on Sunday morning when finally I crashed into my pup tent, dead tired and utterly content to pass out where I'd fallen. I couldn't have been asleep more than an hour (although very much caught up in a strange dream wherein I'd been recruited by the Hare Krishnas and subsequently discharged because I hated the food so much) when I awoke with sharp, searing abdominal pains.

What I'd originally perceived, through my sleep-induced haze, to be some kind of reaction to that starchy slop the Hare Krishnas had been feeding me, was in reality a simpler, more straightforward kind of pain to trace. And trace it I did – to directly outside of the tent, where there were quite obviously people on either side, willfully and methodically kicking at me with steel-toed boots! I crashed out of my tent with fully as much conviction as I'd earlier crashed into it, only to find myself the guest of honor at an apparent Rowdy convention.

Because I'd set up camp in the bowels of a deep ravine, my only hope of evading my foes lay in my negotiating of one of the ravine's ridiculously steep flanks. And the Rowdies were just not in a mood to let this happen. It was within the confines of that blasted ravine that we danced our dance, beneath a full and bloodless moon, and I had more than a little difficulty keeping time.

I led – or, more correctly, misled. Regressing back to childhood days, I adopted a super scary kung-fu stance in the hope of bluffing my way to freedom.

The ten-or-so Rowdies were not impressed. One barely distinguishable from the other, they moved to encircle me, ever silent, slick as spit. You cannot imagine what it was like being the hub of that steadily encroaching circle; keep in mind that these fellas all topped six feet, and for all their preppyness were more fearful to gaze upon at close range than the hairy, hog-fat bikers who so often rode through town.

I attribute the fact that I'm still walking around on the planet to our dear Lord, who in terms of sheer beneficence outdid even Himself that day. The best that could be said of my own paltry efforts is that I went down swinging; in my enfeebled condition I was hardly a match for one Rowdy let alone the entire cast. Melodramatic as it may sound, the glint off an inverted crucifix was the last thing my eyes beheld before a vast nothingness engulfed them.

Although I vaguely recall creeping along the forest floor like some kind of reptile (they tell me a trucker spotted me lying on the shoulder of Highway 6 and drove me into town), my first concrete recollection of anything following the one-sided slugfest was of Roxy standing over me, her eyes the size of dinner plates, her hands seemingly adhered to her mouth at the fingers.

"Hi, gorgeous!" I said, happy to have awoken to such a vision. We were obviously in some sort of medical clinic, and it dawned on me that this was the first time I had ever seen Roxy outside the environs of Timothy's Take-Out, save for a couple of "Annual Summer Games."

"Oh, Carl…" Roxy murmured touchingly. It seemed as though she wanted to caress my shoulder but was afraid I'd shatter into a thousand pieces.

Caress me! Caress me! My mind shrieked.

To tell you the truth, I felt remarkably well. I had obviously been pumped up with morphine or some other painkiller, which made putting sentences together difficult.

"How you know I here, Rox?"

She chose not to respond to that one, and I contented myself with reaching for a few strands of her hair and running them through my fingers. Then I decided to sit up. To my delight, I found I was able to do so with scarcely a hint of pain. The suddenness of my movements startled Roxy, and she drew back.

"What time it is?" I inquired of her.

"Two-thirty in the afternoon."

"Sunday?"

"Sunday."

There ya go. I'd probably even make it back into work.

Just then, a fellow I took to be a physician came waltzing imperiously into the room, ogled Roxy for a second, and then turned to address me, seemingly astounded that I was in any condition to be addressed at all.

"Frankly, young man, I thought you'd be out cold for another day or so. Well, you'll be relieved to know that, as far as I can determine, you've sustained no internal damage."

"Where I am?"

"I'm Dr. Cochrane, and you're in my examining room. Sorry I couldn't provide you with anything more comfortable than this prehistoric cot of ours. It's that time of year again, and this place is just crammed to bursting with victims of poison ivy and sun—"

"Quite alright, doctor, quite alright. As you can see, I'm fine." I sprang out of bed as if to prove my point.

"We'll have none of that, my friend. In fact, I strongly advise you to check into Owen Sound General for twenty-four hours. You may have a concussion. The nurse will be in presently, with the necessary forms for you to fill out."

"I'm sorry, doctor. I've gotta be at work in a few hours—"

190

"Want me to work for you, Carl?" Roxy interjected.

I turned for a moment to look at her. To the best of my knowledge, no one from Timothy's had ever offered to take on another's shift. The type of self-sacrifice Roxy was demonstrating – in even asking the question – was unprecedented. Yet here before me stood this tough, sexy looking chick, clad from head to toe in black denim, offering up her first day off in practically a fortnight. For me, of all people. I could not let her do it.

His brusque professional advice and desultory show of concern notwithstanding, the good doctor was only too happy to plunk a new patient down upon his "prehistoric cot." I assured him I would drop by Owen Sound General the following morning for observation, and, with a still-vehement Roxy protesting my every step forward, left the building.

It just so happened that Doc Coch's clinic was right beside the animal hospital where I'd taken Shindig once, and I wondered how much in the way of medicine was exchanged between the two practices. Since both were within crawling distance of the beach, I asked Roxy to take a little walk with me, and was elated when she said yes.

We must have appeared out of place that broiling July day, Roxy strolling along the shore in full "street" attire, I a mass of bruises (including a split lip and two black eyes), and crippled to the extent that I was barely able to pick my way through the jumble of sun cultists. When Rox caught sight of an unoccupied pier she yanked me onto it, with such force I could only assume she was still pissed at my having left the clinic early.

Upon reaching the pier's edge, we engaged in the time-honored ritual of removing our shoes and socks, rolling up our pant legs, and submerging our feet and calves in the lake. A therapeutic ritual if ever there was one – although not, on this occasion, for Roxy. Within seconds of dunking her lovely tootsies, she burst into tears! What little heart I still possessed went out to her, though I would very shortly have reason to snatch it back.

"I've done wrong, Carl, so wrong," Roxy choked, "and I want so much for you to f-forgive me..."

Hesitatingly, I put an arm around her convulsing shoulders. "What are you talking about, Roxy?"

"Oh, don't you understand?" she cried, and with a motion of her hand swept her long blonde hair from the left side of her head.

In the lobe of her left ear, centimetres below an exquisite pearl earring, was a tiny, inverted crucifix.

CHAPTER SEVENTEEN

What can I say? If Lake Huron had floodgates, they were wide, wide open that afternoon. Roxy divulged virtually everything she knew about her malefic brethren, which was not inconsiderable, as she had been the ringleader's girlfriend – the gang moll, if you will – for over two years. Not really a satanist herself, she had more or less accepted the whole devil worshiping business as a "quirk" of her boyfriend. And get this: the guy's name was *Kyle*. It was he who'd encouraged Roxy to come work for us, mostly to keep tabs on my comings and goings.

Despite Roxy's being indirectly responsible for attacks made on me, my car, my belongings, etc., I could not for the life of me direct my anger toward one so obviously repentant. Besides, being on the receiving end of her fevered confession was rapidly transforming me into the premiere Rowdy authority under the sun. Among other things, I learned that three of the Rowdies were triplets (which went a long way in explaining why I thought the bunch of 'em all looked alike.) And while I myself would never in a million years have glorified the assholes by referring to them as "The Sect," that, according to Roxy, was how they addressed themselves. Most incredibly, they made their home some distance north of Robinson's Pt. – in a *cave.*

From the pier, Roxy accompanied me back to what was left of my campsite. The Rowdies had made off with my gas barbeque, which – fortunately for me, I suppose – was about the only object of value I'd possessed at the time. Everything else was still around, albeit scattered far and wide.

After a few minutes of convincingly playing the helpless-to-do-anything bystander, Roxy left, presumably for the Rowdies' cave. Had I not been expected at work momentarily, I would definitely have tailed her. My mind was reeling as I set about dissembling what little of the campsite the Rowdies had not dissembled for me, and although I now had at my disposal literal volumes of information about the Rowdies and their sordid activities, my sympathy for Roxy took precedence.

Her allegiance was so obviously torn. Very much in love with this Kyle character, she had nonetheless vowed, with me as her witness, to terminate the relationship as soon as she was able. Still mourning the loss of Radiance, I fully appreciated the arduous nature of the task before her. It hurt me to see Roxy hurting, for as you've probably gathered by now I was exceedingly fond of the girl. At work she was my "little toadstool"; we would chide each other mercilessly about the amount of time we had remaining in our respective shifts, our performance on the job, etc. Naturally, I was neither thrilled nor flattered upon learning it had been her mission to win my trust, but the knowledge did little to change how I felt about her. Perhaps that's what true caring is all about.

Let's fast-forward a bit, shall we? Because Sunday at work was just more of the same old torture, compounded somewhat by my having completely run out of fantasies in which to escape. (Summer Sundays, interludes of leisurely indifference and carefree indulgence for so many, were, as far as I was concerned, accursed.)

Monday, by contrast, was about as heavy-handedly momentous a workday as I can remember having, and it all started with Roxy failing to show for her six-thirty-to-close shift. Had this faux pas been perpetrated by any of the other gnats in our employ I would hardly have raised an eyebrow, but it was just not like Roxy to play truant. She may not have been an "iron horse," but she'd always taken care to telephone us in the event of a dilemma. Until now, that is.

Something was clearly wrong.

Rupert and I did what we could to stem the onslaught of hungry customers that evening, but it was inevitable that one-and-one-half employees were going to run into difficulty against such a sustained mob scene. To be fair, several of the customers were sympathetic to our plight, a few downright creative – engaging in the most imaginative parlor games while waiting for their orders. Even so, it was one tired and happy fry cook who locked the doors on 'em at close.

Happy is right! I had forty-eight hours of doing "sweet diddly nothing" to look forward to, and could just visualize all that free time floating toward me, beckoning me with outstretched arms. Any obligations would have to wait a couple of days.

Roxy thwarted my hedonistic designs; I received word Tuesday morning that she had once again had failed to show up for work. I took her paltry ten a.m. to one-thirty p.m. shift that day, proceeding thereafter to the Renwald residence, where Toby Jr. was waiting with a typically oafish "plan of attack."

Knowing full well that the cops could not officially declare Roxy missing until sometime that evening, Toby proposed "rounding up a posse" and storming the Rowdies' cave.

It sounded good to me.

CHAPTER EIGHTEEN

Now Roxy had not told me in so many words where the cave lay, but I did have a vague idea. During the course of one particularly extensive countryside ramble I had stumbled across a yawning crack at the foot of a small mountain. Although well concealed by overgrowths of briar and thistle, it had seemed to me the very entrance to Hades. I was drawn to it only by what I'd perceived as evidence of human habitation: a few lengths of baler twine hanging from a nearby oak tree (which might or might not have been used to suspend caches), and a few lumps of commercial charcoal scattered upon the ground, as though they'd dribbled from somebody's grocery bag.

The problem with Toby's plan was not in pinpointing the cave's location, but rather in putting together a posse at such short notice. It was our desire to amass a literal battalion of burly cutthroats, but Toby could recommend no one, and the only names I could come up with were David "Superhero" Gardner and Stephan Filliman. Some battalion!

"What about Margaret's hubby?" Toby suggested, inadvertently following me as I paced about. "He's a cop, after all."

"Yeah, but even if he does happen to be off-duty, Margaret wouldn't let him out of her sight for long enough. She keeps him on a pretty short leash, you know."

"Oh, they're into that, are they? What about Allie?"

"What about her, Tobes?" I inquired, rhetorically. "You wanna bring a girl to a rumble?"

"She's a monster, Carl!"

"I'll call her."

I dialed up Allie, and was delighted when she agreed to the pretense of a "doubledate" with Toby, his imaginary girlfriend, and myself. Obviously I did not intend to have her fight. But at least now we had some size on our side.

Then, like a veritable bolt out of the blue, it happened. Mr. Renwald, who'd been listening to Toby and I thus far in abject disbelief, snatched up his jingling phone on the third or fourth jingle, only to stagger back as though broadsided when the caller introduced herself as *my mother*. (Not as freakish a coincidence as it might seem, for I'd earlier instructed my folks to leave all urgent messages with the Renwalds. Not that I'd bothered to inform the Renwalds of this...)

Apparently, Mommie and Daddie had not four hours earlier loaded up their "Chevy Impaler" (the nickname was mine, a reference to a dislodged strip of metal siding that jutted menacingly from the car's passenger side) with supplies and set out for a week's sun and fun (!!) in Kirkland Lake. Mom was calling from her cousin's home in Kingcardine, where they had stopped for a bit of a breather.

"I'm so glad I reached you, darling," declared the reassuring voice at the other end of the line. (I cannot help but favorably compare my mother – a most beautiful woman – to the dumpy, boorish *things* who routinely haunt establishments like Timothy's. We're talking night and day.) "Allen should be there any minute, with Shindig."

I hung up the phone, scarcely believing my good fortune. Allen was coming! If any one person could have conceivably influenced the outcome of a gang fight, it was this dude.

Allen is my cousin, and I've had sort of a love-hate relationship with him all of my life. It's a damn shame that such a colorful character could not have been introduced earlier in the tale. He's the kind of fellow who might have saddled Harvey with an inferiority complex, and I'd grown up worshiping the ground he walked on. Although two years younger than myself he had always been the better athlete, the better student, the better everything, and with each passing year he seemed less a human being than some divine paragon of perfection. Whereas in all my years of weight training I'd succeeded only in making my body look lumpish and grotesque, it was as though Allen had been born into his matchless physique and handsome, square jawed face. His hair was blond and very long, and he was always deeply tanned, even in winter.

I think that my decision to get into songwriting was influenced a great deal by Allen's obvious mastery of the discipline. Notwithstanding the fact that he was still unpublished, music flowed from his brain with a positively Mozartian facility. A relative newcomer to the guitar, he'd picked it up in almost no time at all, something that aggravates the shit out of me (as I've been plunking away for ages and still haven't gotten the better of the instrument!).

Toby and I raced over to Timothy's to await Allen's coming, Allie's as well, mindful of the colossal thundercloud forming over our heads. From the restaurant I phoned Stephan, who was only too willing to lend his time and effort to the cause.

Allen was the first to show up, deftly maneuvering his cherry-red corvette into the bustling parking lot. The passenger door swung open and out hopped Shindig – as though he had popped the latch himself! Toby and I must barely have been visible to the dog from where we were sitting, but he loped toward us straightaway, as if guided by radar.

"We gotta go back and get Jeremy, man! We gotta!" Toby cried, as my dog bounded first into my arms and then into his. I agreed wholeheartedly.

The other door of the 'vette swung open, and I got uneasily to my feet. Allen emerged slowly, removed his reflective sunglasses, and slouched exaggeratedly against the side of his vehicle. He was plainly contemptuous of the lesser beings about him as they scampered in and out of the restaurant. Eventually his cold blue eyes locked onto my green ones, and I lurched forward as though I were his marionette. Toby, a bit intimidated, I think, hung back with Shindig.

Dodging various incoming and outgoing vehicles with none of Shinny's intuitive grace, I made my way oafishly across the lot, approaching Allen (who was now inspecting his front bumper for unsightly insect remains) with more than a little apprehension.

"Hi, Allen," I murmured impassively to the six-foot figure before me.

He cocked his head at the sound of my voice, smiled down at me a smile that was at once picture perfect and unbearably cruel to look upon, and said, "So I hear you're a boxer now. I could hammer you into the ground in two rounds."

My gaze dropped, from the perfect face to the perfectly developed arms that were literally popping out of the pinkish tank top he wore. And I was reminded of Allen's not-quite-so-perfect side.

The guy was a supreme egotist, so outrageously conceited he seemed at times to exist by himself in a Don Quixote-type fantasy world. Outwardly every woman's dream man, he has, to my knowledge, never hung onto a chick for more than two weeks. Not that this bothered him at all; Allen was even more of a Don Juan than Harvey, lacking any sort of a conscience, and quite incapable of falling in love.

As I could have predicted, my steroid-enhanced cousin was more than willing to fight anybody. His only concern was with the storm clouds above, or, more specifically, what the inevitable cloudburst was going to do to his hair.

I briefed him of the situation at hand, and introduced him to the deathly somber Toby Jr. A few minutes of uncomfortable silence later, both Stephan and Allie joined us. Allen looked from the two of them to me in utter disbelief, as if to say, "Who the f*#k are these geeks!" He was particularly stunned at the sight of Stephan, whose hair had to have been twice as long as I'd remembered, although every last strand still stood at attention. Allie, for her part, stood gawking at Allen as though he were a national treasure, and if she was befuddled as to the nature of our "double date" she voiced no objection.

From Timothy's, the five of us trooped over to the Renwald residence, Shindig trotting alongside Toby Jr. (to whom he appeared to have taken a shine). And when Allen caught his first glimpse of Jeremy as the latter came galloping down the walk, he was prompted to exclaim, "The thing's a bloody horse!"

This in turn prompted the only spurt of honest-to-goodness creative thinking I have ever heard out of Stephan.

"Horse? Uh, guys...Why don't we use horses? Y'know, attack on horseback? If nothing else, it'll get us there in about half the time."

"Just what is going on here?" demanded Allie.

"Allie," I said, excitedly. "You are about to have the time of your life!"

Droplets of rain were beginning to fall, but none of us were about to turn back, not even Allie. This was high adventure. Of course I was a tad apprehensive – about both the impending mixer with the Rowdies, and the possibility that Roxy might already be beyond saving – but there was something about the five of us marching purposefully toward an ultimate confrontation, the two dogs out in front straining against the double lead Toby was doing his utmost to hang onto...It was cool.

Our next stop was the Superhero's cottage, and though I could clearly see the guy through his front window, he refused, initially, to so much as respond to my knocks. Plastering my face against the window until its features were no longer recognizable seemed to do the trick, and in short order the front door swung open. I had instructed the others to wait down the road a ways, not being entirely sure how the timid Superhero would react to such a flamboyant bunch.

Once inside, I gave him the rundown, and he reacted predictably. Which is to say, positively. One mention of a "damsel in distress," and he was in like flint.

It was now time to act upon Stephan's idea. By the time we'd reached the front gate of Werner's combination dairy farm and livery stable, I was pretty much sold on the notion that everyone present could ride a horse. The rain continued to sprinkle down, but as it had more or less leveled off in terms of intensity I was certain there would be no problem in borrowing a few horses.

We got our horses, all right – big, heavy, draft animals, unaccustomed to being ridden for more than ten minutes at a stretch. You see, so backward a community was Robinson's Pt., farmers in surrounding areas would routinely resort to the use of Clydesdales and Belgiums when their tractors broke down, so much so that guys like old Werner were able to make a tolerably good living from the leasing out of such creatures. But not only were these horses frustratingly slow to ride, they did not respond well to some pretty basic commands.

Fortunately, everyone turned out to be decent equestrians – except, that is, for the originator of the scheme. It was so typical of Stephan. He could barely ride at all, and when at one point we urged our horses into a spirited canter, his nag took off in an entirely different direction! All I saw when I looked over my shoulder was this yellow-and-brown blur, on an apparent collision course with a six-foot tall, electrified, barbwire fence. I think I'll take back what I said earlier about draft horses being slow. The rest of us drew up our steeds, and turned to watch the outcome. Either the crazed animal was going to career right into the fence and gore its hapless rider, or it was going to leap the fence altogether, tossing and killing the Brillow Headed One.

None of us expected it to come to a full stop with millimeters to spare, but that's what happened. Stephan, hanging on for dear life, was not thrown, and both horse and rider – their excessive verve, verve no longer – returned meekly to the squadron. Allen, easily the best rider among us, traded mounts with my old boxing crony, and we were on our way once more.

Every detail of this epic sortie is etched in my memory. I recall the ominous rustling of the oak and poplar leaves as we rode past them. I recall Allen's flat-out majestic appearance – while doing what he could to subjugate his unmanageable stallion, he resembled a knight from a bygone age. Allie's poignant refrains of, "please tell me what's going on!" might have been uttered yesterday, so clearly do they resonate in my head. Above all, I recall the near-euphoria that had gripped us all, particularly the canines, who had little trouble keeping up with the horses and appeared to be enjoying themselves as never before.

Although very much "in bondage" at the time – my heart still held captive by the lost Radiance, my body all but shackled to the counter of that damned restaurant – I too was experiencing a pronounced lightness of being, a kind of whimsy difficult to describe. "You mean, we're just gonna waltz in, beat the shit outa these dudes, grab Rox, and head back home heroes?" Toby, riding alongside of me, inquired incredulously at one point.

"Well, I certainly intend giving it the old college try!" I shot back.

"You'd better do better than that," Allen interjected, having apparently taken me literally.

Locating the so-called "Rowdy Cave" took some doing. After dazedly circling the mountain several times in search of its mouth, I produced from my saddlebag a pair of Roxy's work pants, which I allowed our dogs to examine. Highly trained bloodhounds, of course, these idiot beasts were not – upon taking Roxy's trousers into their mouths they immediately engaged in a spirited though inconclusive game of tug-of-war, which ended only after the garment had been torn to pieces. Here we'd come to save Roxy, but so far she was only out a good pair of pants!

We found ourselves, eventually, in an area that did seem awfully familiar, and from it I was able to guide everyone to the mouth of the cave. We did not dismount immediately, but rather backtracked a few hundred feet into the woods, tethering our horses there so that their neighs and whinnies would not alert the Rowdies to our presence. On our way back to the cave I confessed our true motives to Allie, who was not amused. She chose to remain with us only because she had no idea where she was.

Allie was selected to stand sentry with the dogs; the rest of us slithered through the tangle of briar at the cave's entrance. (Small wonder I'd not been able to locate the cave, with all that prickly shit blocking it out!) Descending through the almost horizontal slit was a terrifying experience, for it evoked such a sensation of finality – as though we'd never see daylight again.

If the gloomy expanse into which we'd tumbled was any indication, this cave was immense. Between the mouth and the floor was one hell of a drop, and Stephan would probably have broken his back at one point were it not for the overstuffed knapsack strapped to him.

From his unique perspective – lying crumpled on the cave floor – Stephan made an important discovery. "Ahhh! Ahhh!" he whined, pointing upward.

To the immediate right of the narrow, backlit aperture we'd just squeezed through hung a rope ladder, fully extended. For us, it was irrefutable evidence that the place was inhabited. While I assisted Stephan to his feet, David lit the three enormous tallow candles we'd brought along, and the five of us made our way out of the cave's vast "foyer" and into a tight, dank tunnel. Having taken a cue from the legendary Theseus, I was nervously unraveling a ball of string as we went along.

The tunnel soon widened into a substantial chamber, albeit nowhere near the size of that first one. Here, however, lay additional proof that we were on the right track, as the chamber was crammed with packing crates of all sizes, a few of them open. We dove into one foolishly labeled, "Weaponry," and were relieved to discover only a plethora of knives, blackjacks, and clubs – no guns. We appropriated some of the stuff, and exited through what appeared to be another tunnel.

I found it odd that we hadn't as yet encountered a Rowdy sentinel. It occurred to me that "Kyle" might not have been the invincible commander I'd made him out to be, and the thought did much to boost my confidence.

Emanating from the second chamber was indeed a second tunnel. By nature acclivous, it was a good deal longer than the first, and appeared to wind directly into the heart of the mountain. To the disgust of our comrades, Toby and I – acting on an idiotic idea we'd come up with that morning – commenced plucking various sightless insects of the walls of the tunnel and depositing them into designated compartments of our knapsacks. We'd netted perhaps thirty apiece before we found ourselves standing with the others upon a ledge, a ledge suspended over a very deep and narrow subterranean gorge.

Some twenty feet ahead, through the darkness, we could make out what had to have been the sheer inner face of the mountain, rising up God-knows-how-many feet above us. In the pit of the gorge, an estimated forty feet below, we found what we'd been looking for at last: a veritable motherlode of Rowdies, and their lone female victim, in fetters.

Our vantage point on the ledge was like a box seat at the theatre, in that Stephan, David, Toby, Allen, and myself had a bird's eye-view of what was taking place. The proliferation of candles in the gorge didn't exactly hamper visibility, either. Our biggest problem was nailed by Stephan in seven words: "How the hell do we get down?"

"There ain't no ladder that I can see," Toby added, peering recklessly over the ledge.

"Could you picture us climbing down into that, even if there were?" I asked sharply, pointing at the billing and cooing Rowdies below. (They had by this time formed a rough circle around their luckless victim, who may or may not have been Roxy.)

Our only recourse was to backtrack into the tunnel a ways, something my cousin had already figured out. His ensuing shriek of discovery had all of us backtracking, if only to shut him the hell up. But his outburst had been justified – a battered packing crate lid was found to be concealing the entrance of yet another tunnel, this one literally plunging like an elevator shaft. The plucky Toby Jr. immediately attempted to dart into it, and I was obliged to grab a substantial amount of his greasy hair.

"Fools rush in, Tobes...Don't you think 'Plan A' would be a better alternative at this juncture?"

"Yeah, you're right," he admitted. "Got carried away with the moment. What's Plan A, again?"

"Plan A" consisted of stripping Stephan down to the long red undies he had donned that afternoon at my insistence, and then whisking him off to greet the Rowdies at the height of one of their Devil invocation rituals. With his outrageous pompadour and tall, scrawny build, he was arguably the most demonic-looking fellow among us, which was, in essence, to be his task that day. We needed him to crash a Rowdy ceremony as Beelzebub incarnate, and terrify the shit heels into, if not submission, then at least a state of abject confusion.

Leaving Stephan to "prepare" for his big role, I returned to the ledge and peered down into the abyss. The girl was still okay, except for the fact that she was now bound like Ixion to the side of an enormous stone. Kyle was discussing something with an underling, although it played like a silent movie from where I was standing. He appeared to be wearing the same black robe that Harvey had found in the cellar of our beach house! My overwhelming impression of the scene: Kyle had not taken the news of his and Roxy's break up well.

I hurried back to the others, taking care to cup the wavering flame of my candle as I scuttled along. Despite the grim nature of the task ahead, I had to laugh when first I saw Stephan, "The Evil One," sweating bullets in his long, red undies, fearfully awaiting the collective high sign that would send him careening down the secret tunnel and into the lion's den beyond. His long johns were of the "back door" variety, and even had little feet!

"This is retarded," snorted Allen.

"Someone's gotta come down the tunnel with me," Stephan stammered. "I ain't goin' alone – I need some backup, man!"

"We'll be right behind you, Steph!" I assured him. "Don't sweat it."

Allen was correct in branding Plan A "retarded." It was doomed from the outset. For one thing, our descent through the secret tunnel was flat-out perilous, as specific sections of the admittedly impressive natural formation were like chutes. First in line and in stocking feet, our "Beelzebub" found it the roughest going.

We tried to look beyond Plan A's faults. As if to justify our hasty and sloppy preparations, we assured ourselves that Stephan's freakish countenance alone would be enough to break up the party. We made much of the cave's straightforward layout, and how Stephan would be in no danger of losing his bearings, conveniently ignoring the fact that I'd long since unraveled my ball of string.

As we had anticipated, this third tunnel led directly to the base of the subterranean gulch. Rowdyville! Stephan and I, the first two of our party to successfully "touch down," were hard-pressed indeed to peer out of the constrictive tunnel and not betray our presence. For the time being, our cronies behind us were kept literally in the dark.

They didn't miss much. An apocalyptic vision of Hell is all.

"Plan A," as we called it, was pretty much dead on arrival. As a matter of fact, just looking at Stephan was enough to convince me of its ineptness. Conditions seemed to favor our "Plan B" a good deal more.

How to explain Plan B...

From the outset, we'd been aware of immensely powerful downdrafts in the cave, and how they coursed through tunnels and hollows alike. Only after the collapse of Plan A did we begin to consider these winds as being potentially advantageous. The matter was foremost in our minds as we set about divesting our knapsacks of their premiere commodity: hay, courtesy of Werner's Livery Stable. We had pilfered tons of the stuff (although "pilfered" might be too strong a word, as I'd left old Werner ten bucks for his trouble), and while Allen and David spread it along the floor of the secret tunnel, Toby and I crept warily back to "Rowdyville."

Glancing out into the gorge from as close to the tunnel's threshold as we dared, we counted nine plainclothes Rowdies – and one black-robed Kyle. Although the ceremony in progress seemed unsophisticated, the aforementioned nine gave every indication of being totally in their mentor's sway. There was something about Kyle – a charisma not unlike Allen's, perhaps – that took insidious hold of the psyche and refused to let go.

And, as much as I wanted to deny it, it *was* Roxy lashed to that boulder. I thought her so incredibly brave for not crying out, until I noticed the strip of sackcloth someone had stuffed into her mouth. Her tears told the real story, and seeing them spill from her eyes made me want to do grievous harm to someone.

"If I had a chick tied down like that, I'd be on her like suction," Toby whispered.

(I suppressed the urge to smack his fat face in.)

It's too bad we could not have unleashed some sort of demon into the Rowdies' midst at that point, for Kyle was doing everything but standing on his head in an effort to conjure one up. After each of his entreaties would come a pregnant pause, and how dearly I wanted to toss Stephan into one of them, red undies and all.

The Rowdies' ability or inability to call forth a demon was the least of my concerns. Either way, the ceremony was going to culminate in some form of abuse to Roxy, and that's what I had to focus on.

In theory, "Plan B" went something like this: light the hay ablaze, hide someplace inconspicuous, wrap wet towels around our heads, save chick while Rowdies are at nearby Pine Creek (collecting water to douse the flames), confront Rowdies while they are still outside, run 'em down on horseback.

Well! Billowing clouds of smoke did issue forth from the correct end of the tunnel, and the Rowdies might even have interpreted it as a sign from Satan – had not Toby and I been caught *in front of* the bloody conflagration, with them! Apparently, our asshole cohorts had torched the hay without so much as bothering to take attendance. As it was now literally the frying pan or the fire for Toby and I, we opted for the fire. Linking arms, we tore straight through the hellish inferno, a most remarkable feat in retrospect (our route having been a precipitous one upward). No Rowdies dared follow us – to our knowledge.

We located the rest of our party in that segment of the second tunnel ending in a precarious ledge. Delirious with excitement, neither Toby nor I thought to berate them for what they had done. In fact, the five of us remained dead silent for the most part, savoring the relatively smoke-free conditions while breathlessly attempting to monitor the Rowdies' progress. No mean feat was the latter, considering we hadn't the foggiest idea where they were. After five-or-so minutes had elapsed, David and I crept onto the ledge.

Nothing much could be seen through the smoke, but it looked as though the Rowdies had fled. It was our cue to plunge down the third tunnel again, with wet towels plastered across our breathing passages and canteens in hand. We doused what little remained of the fire with water from our canteens, and pressed on.

The pit was not entirely devoid of Rowdies. Perhaps anticipating a rescue attempt, Kyle had left a couple of guys behind to stand guard over Roxy. It was a stupid, stupid mistake on his part.

Weakened by smoke inhalation, both Rowdies were quickly overpowered. One was knocked senseless, the other – a big, fat one I distinctly recalled seeing before – took up, entirely against his will, Roxanne's position on the large stone.

Evidently, cousin Allen had missed all the excitement. He'd been with us in "Tunnel Three," but that was the last anyone could recall seeing of him. Either he'd been nabbed by the Rowdies, or had simply gone his own maverick way, as usual.

Escorting the semi-conscious Roxy up that third passage was far from easy, but remains one of my fondest memories of the day. With my arm gingerly about her shoulders, my sweaty fingers kneading the bare flesh of her upper arm, I wondered if it was indeed not love I felt for the girl. I guiltily conceded that we'd probably done more to harm her with our smoke than the Rowdies had with their nastiest psychological terror tactic. Though she had yet to speak, Rox was sufficiently cognizant to take periodic sips from my canteen, and to stare comprehendingly into my eyes.

Stick with me, folks. Things move pretty quickly from here on in.

Backtracking through the sparse network of tunnels and chambers, we found virtually everybody we'd been looking for in the cave's extensive "Grand Hall." We kept just inside the mouth of that first tunnel, peering out of it with the utmost caution. Our eyes were greeted with an incredible spectacle.

Two Rowdies were lying prostrate on the cave floor, while another five were alternating their apprehensive gazes between their fallen comrades and the ceiling above. Those of us in the tunnel could not help but follow their collective gaze, and were staggered to behold Allen some thirty feet overhead, clinging to the rock like an overgrown bat. How the crazy bastard got up there remains a mystery, although his motive was immediately obvious.

With no more than a pickaxe and sturdy boots to hold him in place, he was hacking furiously at the stalactites with a large, gold-handled chisel I had seen around the restaurant. The stalactites made for formidable projectiles, falling from such a distance, and the Rowdies' comical attempts to take cover only encouraged Allen to start *hurling* them! (And make no mistake – this former minor-league pitcher could hurl.) I looked again at the two Rowdies lying motionless, half-expecting to find dozens of the rock icicles protruding from their backs.

"We gotta lure these sons of bitches outside," I whispered, more to myself than anyone else. The rope ladder was still fully extended, prompting David – the cautious one among us, you'd have thought – to suggest we make an all-or-nothing break for it. It was an idea that met with the wholehearted approval of Toby Jr. and Stephan, and to which I eventually agreed, after securing Roxanne's vote.

Rox and I were the first to creep out of the tunnel. We kept to our right as it was veiled in shadow, inching along the colossal northern flank of the cave. I clung tightly to the girl, not so much to cop a cheap feel as to conceal the conspicuous whiteness of her tank top. Turning about with the intention of waving the others forward, I was startled to find them directly behind us (although, in retrospect, I don't know why this would have startled me, when such flagrant disobedience among our ranks characterized the entire venture).

I coaxed Roxy – without question our most precious cargo – up the ladder first, but made a point of sticking close behind her. So far, so good. We'd practically made it out of the damned cave when there arose a chorus of angry voices from beneath us. It appeared that the remainder of our little party had been detected; peering down at them, it was not difficult to see why.

In regards to pure imbecility, Stephan outstrips most anyone else I can think of. At some point – for some inexplicable reason known only to himself – he'd thrown his yellow sweatshirt back on, an article of clothing so bright it was capable of illuminating anything within five feet of it. He might as well have strapped a couple of floodlights to his torso for all the camouflage the shirt afforded.

What insanity! I was hanging upside down from the mouth of the cave, alternately screaming encouragement and flinging epithets at Stephan, David, and Toby. The three cretins were tearing up the ladder about as fast as they dared with five-odd Rowdies at the foot of it, tossing it about.

"For Chrissakes, Toby, douse that candle! You're a sitting duck down there! You got plenty of light as it is! Douse that candle!!"

And then there was Allie, who upon seeing Roxy emerge dazedly from the cave decided to break cover herself, if only to escort the would-be cult victim to a more agreeable location.

Our three comrades did make it up the ladder, but with at least five Rowdies in hot pursuit. There was little time to react, and it did not help matters much when Stephan and his stupid knapsack became wedged in the cave's cleft.

I managed to free the panic-stricken Stephan, only to find Roxy gone. (I'd not seen big Allie come for her.) Oblivious to both the cries of my companions and the procession of Rowdies ascending the ladder, I wandered off, calling her name. But then I happened to glimpse Allie's unmistakable form atop a nearby hillock, amidst some boulders there, motioning as if to say she had Roxy behind one of them. I gave her a grateful nod, and then returned as fast as my feet would carry me to the foot of the mountain.

It was a scene out of a Tom and Jerry cartoon. The Superhero stood just to the right of the cave mouth, waving a two-by-four in the air, which, judging by the way two of the Rowdies were dancing about and clutching their noggins, he'd already put to some pretty good use. Tobes was on the left, set to fling fistfuls of insects into the face of the next Rowdy to see daylight. Stephan flitted back and forth between Moe and Curly – er…David and Toby, booting one of the Rowdies who looked to be recovering squarely in the balls.

So effective was this three-man unit of dispatcher-persons, I pretty much just stood and watched as they worked their magic upon the next three Rowdies to pop through the hole, including Kyle (who'd since removed his black robe and was now wearing nothing more than a jockstrap!)

"To the horses!" I cried, when it appeared our work was done. The four of us raced across the scrub to the forest beyond.

I remember tripping over a protruding root at one point, and flying headlong through the air. Although a trivial incident in itself, I recall how time seemed to freeze temporarily, how I was able to reflect upon the whole outlandish adventure I had orchestrated – and marvel at it's grandiose fabric – before tumbling back to earth.

Brimming over with self-confidence, Toby, David, and I thundered back to the scene of our earlier triumph on our huge horses. Stephan, who was having trouble subduing even the gentle steed Allen had given him, rode haltingly over to Allie and Roxy, with Allie's mount in tow. According to our ever-changing plan, Allie was to ride with Roxy to the nearest phone booth (wherever the hell that might have been) and summon the Port Radcliff authorities, as Roxy was now officially a missing person. Stephan was expected to rejoin the fracas in front of the cave, and inflict whatever damage he could upon the Rowdy forces without toppling off his horse.

This particular component of the plan was enacted remarkably true to form, though we did shuffle the cast of characters somewhat. It was Stephan, for example, who rode off with Roxy in search of a telephone, while Allie returned to us with every intention, believe it or not, of seeing action on the front.

And see action she most certainly did. A surprisingly adroit horsewoman, she was instrumental in holding several of the now fully recovered Rowdies at bay, while the rest of us darted in and out, thrashing and thwacking at them with their own weapons. We just wanted to hold the bastards till the cops arrived, although when that was supposed to have been was anybody's guess. The speed of their arrival depended solely on Stephan's ability to relay accurate directions.

Thanks to Allie we had effectively pinned the five Rowdies against the side of the mountain. But so big and powerful were they, and so clumsy and awkward our mounts, we had difficulty administering any sort of "death blow" to them. Hours of light drizzle had turned the ground to gelatinous muck, further impeding the limited maneuverability of our horses. Despite our best efforts Kyle managed to crash through our ranks, and before any of us could reach him he'd scuttled back into the cave.

If it was safety and refuge he was expecting to find in there, he was in for a surprise. Who should be on his way up the rope ladder at that moment but Allen, the one fella big enough and tough enough to stand toe-to-toe with the Rowdy king. Those of us on the outside, while some distance from the mouth of the cave, could distinctly hear his squawks of annoyance.

"And where the fuck do you think you're going? Get back up there!"

A few minutes of muffled grunting ensued – Kyle was probably attempting to shake Allen off the ladder – followed by a series of agonized bellows, decidedly Kyle's. Allen had apparently taken the pickaxe to his legs, which I imagine shifted the Satanist into reverse real quick.

Out of the cave they tumbled! Kyle, clad only in his jockstrap, immediately made a break for it, with Allen hot on his heels. From atop my huge Clydesdale I decided to join the chase, not so much to run Kyle down as to witness firsthand the inevitable showdown between these two superbeings.

I urged my horse past them both with the intention of cutting off Kyle's escape route. The tactic worked – Kyle became completely preoccupied with trying to "fake out" my overgrown steed, to the extent that he forgot his pursuer even existed.

Allen deftly tripped Kyle up from behind, and the cult leader fell heavily to the ground. I'm unsure as to exactly what occurred next, for an excruciatingly loud thunderclap at that moment prompted my horse to rear back on its hind legs. When I finally regained control of the terrified animal, the two adversaries were circling each other slowly, Allen looking positively Conanesque, Kyle intimidating even in his jockstrap. Although Kyle was the taller and heavier man, I never doubted that Allen, the physical embodiment of every hero I'd ever adored, would wipe up the ground with him.

And so it was. Watching my cousin lay into Kyle brought back memories of all the lickings I'd received at his hand over the years. For such a small-town rube he was truly a great street fighter, and at no time did he require the assistance of my horse or myself. He had abandoned his pickaxe while pursuing Kyle, but still had his outsized chisel, and attained incontestable subjugation by holding the implement defiantly to the Satanist's throat.

Allen escorted our "P.O.W." back to the foot of the mountain, while I trailed a few paces behind on my horse. I'd been skeptical (to say the least) of the rest of our party's ability to contain six full-blooded Rowdies for any appreciable length of time, and was not quite sure what to expect upon our return. My fears, however, proved groundless. Allie, Toby, and David had formed a tight little semi-circle with their draft animals, effectively hemming the Satanists in against a particularly steep portion of the mountainside, and all of our comrades were "armed" – David wielding the two-by-four that Stephan had earlier wielded with such efficiency, and Toby Jr. his bagful of bugs (though he motioned frantically at me as I rode into view to give him my own). Allie, for her part, had recovered Allen's pickaxe, and I think that of all the memorable images I retain of that day, the image of Allie brandishing the pickaxe like a meat cleaver, ready to bring it down upon the head of the first Rowdy who so much as blinked, will stick in my head the longest.

Still, it was obvious we couldn't hold 'em forever. Even the sight of their vanquished leader seemed not to discourage these eerily silent creatures. They appeared cold, calculating, and ready for anything.

I happened to notice Jeremy and Shindig gallivanting about; while dismounting I attempted to summon both to my side. Only Shindig responded, and reluctantly at that. The other one was off in his own little world, running down imaginary groundhogs, or restaurant patrons.

With Shindig, I attempted a little experiment. Dropping down to his level, I caressed him roughly for a few seconds, and then gestured between the legs of Allie's horse, crying,

"Sic 'im! Sic 'im!"

Sure enough, Shindig flew toward the unfortunate Rowdy at whom I was pointing (one of the triplets) as though shot out of a cannon, immediately seizing hold of his leg, clamping down on it with jaws capable of administering 1200 psi of crushing force.

"Aarggh!!" the Rowdy shrieked.

"Let go, Shinny!" I ordered brusquely, struggling to contain my glee.

"Anyone steps outa line, they get more of the same!" I intoned.

Norris, unable to contain himself a moment longer, rasped out a menacing, "Eat shit and die!"

"Drink puke and live!" Toby Jr. countered, without missing a beat. As if to punctuate it he farted, the very sound of which made our eyes well up.

But it was David "Superhero" Gardner who irretrievably sealed the Rowdies' doom. Acting upon his instruction, Allie and Allen (the latter upon my horse now) rode rings around the six clustered Rowdies, literally, binding them up in an almost strangulatory way with the twenty-foot rope ladder.

There was little else to do now but wait patiently for Stephan, Roxy, and the authorities. We were not overly concerned about the four Rowdies still inside the cave – conscious or unconscious, they were more or less trapped in there without the ladder.

And so, for a good three-and-a-half hours we pretty much just sat in the downpour like anuses, until eventually six raincoat-clad constables came crashing out of the forest, led by the jibbering idiot Stephan.

An additional hour and a half was then spent setting the cops straight about what happened, erasing whatever traces of Stephan's inimitable "logic" remained in their heads. Not that any of us minded the delay, except, perhaps, the trussed-up Rowdies. It had been, after all, a wildly successful endeavor, and we'd brought it off in much the same fashion that I'm convinced Hercules, Theseus, or Conan would have. None from our party had sustained so much as a superficial injury, unless you choose to include Roxy (and even she was in pretty fair shape, as the clinic doctor would later confirm).

Now that I think of it, one on our side had come to grief – Stephan's horse. It seems the bonehead had at some point *misplaced* it! I'll bet Steph is still doing old Werner's chores for him, just as the horse is likely still out in the wilderness somewhere, running feral.

Epilogue

In a sense, everything that has occurred since the dramatic recovery of Roxy has been one long, sustained anticlimax. Kyle was tried and convicted, as were some of the other more prominent members of "The Sect" (which, frankly speaking, surprised the crap outa me). I'll not bore you by reiterating the minutes of the trial, but the fact is witnesses for the prosecution seemed to come out of the woodwork, several with testimonies as outlandish as my own.

Evidently, the Rowdies were more notorious than any of us had realized. Like any self-respecting drove of pigs they had chosen not to soil their immediate surroundings, which went a long way in explaining why their burglaries within the vicinity had been so sporadic (and, for that matter, successful). They'd been much more of a problem in the tiny community of Lion's Head, for example, than they'd ever been at home. In any event, the evidence against them was damning to the extent that Kyle and a few of the rest were put away for a good long time. With the brains of the outfit contained in such a manner, the other Rowdies scattered, and largely disappeared.

Shortly thereafter, I quit work – I just couldn't take it anymore. You might be wondering if there was a specific point in time that I decided to throw in the towel, a "straw that broke the camel's back," as they say. Not really. But when I began to receive merciless and altogether unwarranted tongue-lashings from the likes of Allie and Lucinda, I knew in my heart it was time to move on. I had too much respect for myself, you know? I'd been everything from mooned by jealous boyfriends, to coerced into taking imaginary food orders from children's teddy bears. I'd been beaten down to the point that I couldn't even be rude anymore. My only thought was to escape, to put the utmost distance between these faggot nothings and myself.

The "Greenhouse Effect" may also have influenced my departure to a degree. The fact that winters and springs were getting perceptibly milder meant one thing to me back in 1983 – that Timothy's Take-Out was only going to ride its black ink to dizzier and dizzier heights. Good news for the owner, perhaps, but not for his commander-in-chief.

My decision to quit Timothy's was among the better decisions I have made in my life. Astonishingly, I managed to find new work within a week – at the fertilizer plant on the outskirts of town, where I remain employed to this day. My job there is a simple one, and quite boring, but I'm thrilled to be working a straight forty hour week, and in a customer-free environment. There was a labor dispute recently, and I have to tell you – my sympathies were entirely with the management.

I never saw Toby Jr. or the mighty Superhero again. I'm inclined these days to view the two as exaggerated extensions of myself, what I might very well morph into if I'm not careful. I'd had a bit of a falling-out with Toby, shortly before I left Timothy's.

The guy was just too evil. He was constantly battling his compulsions to trample small animals and mow down people while behind the wheel of my car. He loved Hitler, and considered him one of the world's great humanitarians for ridding our congested planet of millions of people. While the worst things I'd ever done up to that point included being drunk and disorderly, and attempting to sneak an additional item through the express aisle of McCoy's Supermarket, Tobes was into hard drugs, carried an assortment of unlicensed firearms upon his person, and routinely set elaborate booby traps for girls he knew he could never have.

Still, I would miss him. For a while there, we were the staunchest of buddies, united in our all-consuming hatred of society and of the innumerable geeks society has spawned. A favorite expression of his I shall retain in my head unto the grave: "It don't mean dildo piss. That don't mean dildo piss, pal!"

Nothing much blossomed between Roxy and me, despite the fact that I had rescued her sorry ass. Neither of us was particularly interested in the other, not that way, and I suppose it's only natural that such a twosome would drift apart before long. I ran into her a few years back at McCoy's, and we had tons of fun reminiscing about her spectacular break-up with Kyle. She also mentioned that Toby Jr. had taken up boxing, and I was positively delighted to hear it, although I had to ask her repeatedly if she was serious.

Did I mention that I've dwelt in the same lodgings now for several years? Well, I'm mentioning it now. Not long after the Rowdy corps fragmented I took up residence in their cave, and have been there ever since. It's absolutely perfect for me – cheap, tranquil, back-to-nature, and far removed from the geeks and assholes of this world. What I save in rent I either hoard or invest in literature.

I rarely venture deeper than the first two chambers, however. Not only do the bowels of the cave abound with rats, crabs, and roaches; there hangs in the gloom of the anterior chambers an aura of menace you can reach out and squeeze, perhaps not surprisingly in light of the cave's previous occupants.

And I am reasonably certain that the Rowdies had a significant lice problem, for I acquired one myself upon moving in.

The simple life suits me to a tee, as I'm inclined to regard "technological growth" as evidence only of our pathetic frailties and limitations. Over the years I've been engaged in running feuds with key grinders, cassette tape manufacturers, convenience store operators, automotive engineers…I'll take the perfection of a forest, dog, or meadow any old time.

Life in the great outdoors is conducive to working out hard, which is probably why I tore my right bicep a couple of years back. The devastating injury forced me to a crossroads: Either I would spare myself the psychological trauma of seeing my right bicep atrophy by committing suicide, or I would begin to focus more on the cardiovascular aspect of fitness, a realm I'd previously relegated to pussies and wimps. I chose the latter path, obviously, and feel no shame in reporting my weight today as a lean, mean, 138 pounds. Though I've grown my hair long, I struggle to remain clean-shaven, and am now a mirror image of Conan the Barbarian.

Well, minus the muscle.

And what of Allen, you ask? On the day of Roxy's rescue, while waiting for the cops to arrive, I had the satisfaction of going five rounds with him there in the scrub – and living to tell of it. Although he won every round effortlessly, not once was he able to knock me down, despite his penchant for low blows and kidney punches. I was a mess at the end of this bare-knuckle fistfight, but I was also quite jubilant, as if it had been my victory and not his.

My cousin is much the same these days as he was back then – still living at home, still single, still working at the quarry, and still unable to make anything of his enormous potential.

Unless someone as perfect as Radiance happens along, I will likely remain single for life. I prefer the ghost of Radiance to the warm, soft body of anyone else. I honestly thought I saw her a few years back, in Toronto. I was doing a little Christmas shopping (Christmas being one of the few occasions I venture forth into polite society anymore), and could have sworn I saw her riding a department store escalator. I nearly killed myself leaping from my escalator to hers, only to eventually lose her amongst the hordes of shoppers.

Was Radiance an actual person, or an angelic entity from another dimension? The debate rages on in my mind.

I'm still pretty militant when it comes to bad music; at the factory I'm force-fed all manner of contemporary shit. Are people deaf? Has the creative wellspring truly dried to dust? For all their technical wizardry, today's musicians seem incapable even of rendering a "golden oldie" respectably. It's so, so sad.

I don't think I've so much as spoken to a teen-aged girl since leaving Timothy's, or perhaps I've been conditioned to disregard everything that comes out of their mouths. Years of working alongside them, and trying to relate to them as customers, have led me to a startling realization: They really *are* only good for one thing.

To that handful of beautiful people I encountered at Timothy's, I can say only this: I love you, it was a pleasure doing business with you, and I wish we could all live together in a commune someplace. I doubt that overcrowding would be a problem.

I despise materialistic people, have grown to despise capitalism, but at the same time consider myself lucky to be living in a great country like Canada. At times I carry on like a large "C" conservative, ranting about the merits of corporal punishment, the evil of same sex unions, etc.

Well, that about does it. To the outside world I must seem a failure: poor, friendless, reclusive…Yet I'm so very happy now, and at peace. I was like Saint-Exupery's Little Prince during those Timothy's years, wandering wide-eyed through unfamiliar territory, encountering during the course of my misadventures a succession of weirdos trapped either by circumstance or their own devices. Unlike the magnanimous Prince, however, I hadn't much to offer my weirdos.

My folks have in effect given me Shindig, and I would be hard pressed to find a more loyal and enthusiastic sidekick. He's truly all I need in terms of companionship. Other unexpected blessings: I tend to sleep better now that I am a clock punching "nine-to-fiver," and no longer do I have any reason to fear the summer.

It was not all pain and suffering during the Timothy's years. When I do look back to that period, I prefer to remember the good times, namely the locker room kiss, and the walk with Radiance back to her cottage on the occasion of our one and only "date." It blows my mind that these memories can still elicit gooseflesh.

Timothy's Take-Out did not break me. My life's objective is still to achieve success beyond my wildest dreams – and a new preoccupation of mine is sure to take me there.

Perhaps I'll tell you about it sometime.

THE END?

Appetite for words

Paul Barker's first novel, Timothy's Take-Out, was released Oct. 9 by its publisher, Baltimore-based Publish America. The Guelph author calls the 215-page book "a humorous tale about a shy, reclusive loner who takes a job at one of the busiest, noisiest, most repulsive fast food joints on the face of the earth: Timothy's Take-Out."

TRIBUNE PHOTO
BY DOUG HALLETT

Printed in the United States
21567LVS00004B/70-111

9 781413 731644